Praise for *New York Times* bestselling author B.J. Daniels

"You won't be able to put it down."
—*New York Times* bestselling author Jodi Thomas on *Heartbreaker*

"Daniels is a perennial favorite on the romantic suspense front, and I might go as far as to label her the cowboy whisperer."
—*BookPage* on *Luck of the Draw*

"Daniels keeps readers baffled with a taut plot and ample red herrings, expertly weaving in the threads of the next story in the series as she introduces a strong group of primary and secondary characters."
—*Publishers Weekly* on *Stroke of Luck*

"Daniels again turns in a taut, well-plotted, and suspenseful tale with plenty of red herrings. Readers will be in from the start and engaged until the end."
—*Library Journal* on *Stroke of Luck*

"Readers who like their romance spiced with mystery can't go wrong with *Stroke of Luck* by B.J. Daniels."
—*BookPage*

"Daniels is an expert at combining layered characters, quirky small towns, steamy chemistry and added suspense."
—*RT Book Reviews* on *Hero's Return*

"B.J. Daniels has made *Cowboy's Legacy* quite a nail-biting, page-turner of a story. Guaranteed to keep you on your toes."
—*Fresh Fiction*

Also by *New York Times* **bestselling author**
B.J. Daniels

Look for B.J. Daniels's next novel
Forever Again
available soon from HQN.

For additional books by B.J. Daniels,
visit her website, www.BJDaniels.com.

B.J. DANIELS

NEW YORK TIMES BESTSELLING AUTHOR

OUT *of the* STORM

HQN

ISBN-13: 978-1-335-41852-4

Recycling programs
for this product may
not exist in your area.

Out of the Storm

Copyright © 2020 by Barbara Heinlein

This edition published by arrangement with Harlequin Books S.A.

For questions and comments about the quality of this book,
please contact us at CustomerService@Harlequin.com.

HQN
22 Adelaide St. West, 40th Floor
Toronto, Ontario M5H 4E3, Canada
www.Harlequin.com

Printed in Spain

This book was inspired by the stories
I heard about my uncle Ted Johnson, who was
killed in the Texas City disaster. I've heard a lot
of different versions of what happened. (Johnsons
tend to make a story better whenever possible
without any regard for the truth.) My mother was
pregnant with me at the time of my uncle's death.
Maybe that's why I've always wanted to write
this story—but with a happier ending.

I dedicate this book to Uncle Ted
(wish I'd gotten to meet you)
and all of the Johnsons who'd given me
story fodder for years. I suspect my Johnson genes
are the reason I write fiction.

OUT *of the* STORM

CHAPTER ONE

THE GOLD WEDDING band came off more easily than she thought it would. It had worn thin over the years and so had she. But still it left an indentation in her flesh, a reminder of so many things, including the promise she'd made all those years ago. She quickly slipped it back on.

"Kate?"

She looked up, blinking at the handsome young man on one knee in front of her. She was thirty-nine, a whole year away from forty. She had the rest of her life in front of her.

"What's going on, Kate?"

She swallowed and met his blue gaze. He was so different from Danny. Collin was younger, incredibly handsome, and he was alive and offering her a very different future. For almost twenty years, she'd been a widow, a single mother of two daughters and alone. She looked down at the ring he was holding out in the small velvet box. The diamond was big and beautiful.

She'd never had anything like it. When she and Danny had gotten married, they'd been teenagers and hadn't even been able to afford rings. He'd had to borrow the money from her father to buy them.

"I thought you were ready for this," Collin said as he

brushed a lock of sunshine-golden hair back from his face. The disappointment in that face brought her out of her thoughts of the past. Danny was gone. Their daughters were now raised and on their own. It was time to think about the future.

She looked down at the wedding band on her ring finger, unable not to think of the day Danny had put it there. They'd been so young, so naive, so much in love. The ring had symbolized that amazing love all these years. She'd vowed never to take it off. For years, she'd held on to his memory like a life raft, needing what it meant to her to keep her head above water during the hard times and feeling safe during the lonely nights. But she knew it was time to let go. Danny wasn't coming back.

Over the years, she'd dated, but no one felt right. Until Collin. She met his blue gaze and felt herself smile. Slowly, she slipped the ring off again, closing her fist around it.

Holding out her left hand, she let Collin slip the beautiful diamond engagement ring onto her finger. It felt heavy and a little loose.

"It's official," he said, grinning. "We're *engaged*. And none too soon." He laughed to take away some of the sting from his words as if he hadn't meant to complain. She'd been putting him off for months. While she'd loved being with him, the thought of marriage had brought back thoughts of Danny. She and Collin had both wondered if she would ever agree to marry him.

Rising from his one knee, he pulled her up off the couch and into his arms. "We need to celebrate, and I have just the thing." He drew back to meet her gaze. "No, I'm not going to tell you what it is. It's a surprise. But you need to go pack because we are leaving first thing in the morning."

"*Leaving?*" Kate looked at him in alarm. All of this was suddenly happening too fast. She felt as if she was on the washer's spin cycle. "Wait—"

He put a finger to her lips. "No more waiting, Kate. It's time you trusted me. I'm going to be your husband."

She met his eyes again. She could feel the weight of the ring on her finger. This man was going to be her *husband*. She couldn't speak around the lump that had formed in her throat, so she merely nodded. Collin hugged her even more tightly before releasing her.

"Go pack. Bring warm clothes. Leave everything to me. I'll pick you up at six in the morning. It's going to be fun, Kate. You'll see. The adventure is about to begin."

It wasn't the first time he'd asked her to marry him. A few months ago, he'd tried only to see that she couldn't take off her wedding band. Any other man would have headed for the door right then. But not Collin.

He'd given her a sad smile and said, "I think they're playing our song." Except there hadn't been any music playing in the living room of her house, and yet he'd pulled her up from the couch and into his arms.

"I'm sorry," she'd said as he drew her closer and began to move slowly to the nonexistent music.

"It's all right," he'd whispered next to her ear. "You will take it off when you're ready to wear the engagement ring I'm going to put on that lovely finger." He had leaned back to look into her eyes, and she'd felt her heart swell with love for this man who had come into her life so unexpectedly.

She'd almost given up, believing that she couldn't love again after Danny. For years after his death, her life had been full with raising their two girls alone and working to support the three of them. But now Danielle was almost through with college and Mia had a successful career as a graphic artist. Both had their own apartments. It seemed as if suddenly Kate had found herself with too much time on her hands, living alone in a home too large for just her.

After some disastrous dates, Kate had told herself that she didn't need a man, which was true—at least financially. She'd found she had a talent for writing. As a ghost writer, she'd made a name for herself writing other people's stories. She'd never had to touch the money she'd gotten from the death benefit the oil company had paid on Daniel. Invested all these years, it had multiplied again and again. One day she'd awoken to find herself a wealthy woman who wasn't even middle-aged—if the statistics were true.

And then she'd met Collin. She'd told herself that she was still young enough to start over. She'd gotten married at seventeen to the love of her life, had her first baby and her second in a two-and-a-half-year span. Daniel had been all of eighteen. By the time she'd given birth to Danielle, he'd been working two jobs to make ends meet. Then the refinery where he worked in Houston had exploded one day, and he and hundreds of others had been...gone.

There had been such confusion after the explosion. Stories of people wandering around, not knowing who they were. Because so many were incinerated in the explosion, it had been impossible to identify the remains. That morning, Danny had gone to work and hadn't come back.

In her heart, she wanted to believe that he had walked away that day with an injury that had left him not knowing who he was. That's why he hadn't come back to her. For a while she'd expected him to show up one day on her doorstep. But he'd never come back.

Her oldest daughter, Mia, had never minced words. "Daddy is gone. You have to accept that. You have to move on." Her daughters had been happy and maybe a little relieved for her when Kate had told them that she'd met someone.

"Collin's younger, but just by three years," Kate had said, feeling giddy and youthful, something she hadn't felt in years.

"*Three years?* That's nothing," Mia had scoffed.

"So, tell us about him," Danielle had said, curling up on the couch and looking at her expectantly. Danielle was the romantic in the family.

Kate hadn't known where to begin. "His name is Collin. He has his own company. He owns numerous small businesses. He's…enterprising."

Mia had rolled her eyes. "Really, Mother?"

Danielle had laughed. "It doesn't matter exactly what he does. Does he make you happy?"

"He makes me laugh," she'd said and had found herself smiling.

"Good for you, Mom. You deserve this." Her youngest had taken her hand. "I just want you to be happy. You deserve to enjoy the rest of your life."

Mia had chimed in. "Just be…careful."

When the girls had met Collin, she could tell that they'd both been surprised. "He's so handsome," Danielle had said with a kind of awe. "Not that we didn't expect he would be," she'd added quickly. Even Mia seemed to grudgingly like him. And he had fallen for them as well.

So, now here she was, moving on, she thought as she went upstairs and, taking the well-worn wedding band from the hollow of her palm, placed it gently in her jewelry box. It looked so insignificant and yet just the sight of it made her heart ache for what had been lost.

"Goodbye, my love," she whispered and closed the jewelry box. Danny would have wanted her to move on years ago. It had taken Collin coming into her life. She felt a bubble of excitement. She could hear him downstairs on the phone. It sounded as if he was making arrangements for their trip before he left for his apartment in the city.

She felt herself smiling again. Collin loved her. And she loved him. Not like she had loved Daniel. But she'd only been a girl when she'd met Danny and fallen in love. She was now a mature woman, and yet she still felt giddy at the thought of what their future held. It was definitely time.

Whatever the surprise, it required warm clothing? She could only imagine, she thought with a smile as she went to the closet to pull out her suitcase and begin to pack.

"Good, you're packing," Collin said from her bedroom doorway. "I've got everything arranged. I'll see you in the morning." He moved to her. "This trip is going to seal the deal." He chuckled at her expression. "You're going to be crazy about me when it's over."

"Who says I'm not already crazy about you? Or maybe just crazy."

He drew her into his arms for a kiss. She felt desire warm her inside and almost wished that she'd let him move in months ago. But she'd been so used to having her own space. Still, she wouldn't have minded if he stayed tonight. She was about to suggest it.

"I have a lot to do before I pick you up in the morning," he said before she could. He kissed her again, his mouth lingering over hers. She thought for a moment that he might change his mind. Then he gave her a light swat on her behind, saying he'd better leave while he could.

As she listened to him go, she felt jubilant. Glancing down at the ring on her finger, she reminded herself that she was engaged. She couldn't quit smiling. Now the two of them were taking their first trip together. She hadn't been anywhere in so long. A trip was exactly what she needed. The timing was perfect. She didn't have another book due for a year.

She was only a little uneasy about where they were going. Collin had always been full of surprises from the moment she'd met him six months ago. He was probably right about her needing him and the adventures he promised. Had it been fate, their meeting? It certainly felt like it.

COLLIN COULDN'T BELIEVE his luck when he woke the next morning. Kate had accepted his proposal. He felt like pinching himself. He showered and packed quickly, feeling as if things were finally going to work out for him. He still had to get her to the altar, but at least they were engaged. It was the first step. He couldn't stop grinning. He didn't want to rush her, but once they got back from this trip, he would talk her into a small, private wedding—if he couldn't talk her into one on the trip itself.

The trip had come together as if destined. He'd recalled her saying that she'd never seen snow. Not real snow, the kind that puts down more than a few inches and doesn't melt in a few hours. She said she'd always wanted to make a snow angel. It was one of the few times that she'd let her guard down and actually opened up to him.

He could understand her reluctance to get involved with another man after losing her first husband the way she had. But hell's bells, it had been almost twenty years. He couldn't imagine mourning anyone for two decades.

Just as a few years ago, he had no plans to be married. *Marriage?* He'd always thought it would never be him. Until Kate.

He laughed to himself, thinking of that old adage about never finding the right woman. Kate was more than the right woman. A pretty brunette with the greenest eyes. She had it all, from the looks to the elegance to the financial independence. With her, he would have everything he ever wanted and with style.

It did bother him, though, how long it had taken her to agree to marry him. He'd never had a problem when it came to charming women. He had charisma to burn, his mother used to say, his father quickly adding, "That's about all he has going for him."

He pushed even the thought of his father away. His old man was the last person he wanted in his thoughts this morning. He was about to take off with his beautiful fiancée for the trip of a lifetime. He laughed. Well, at least it would be the trip of a lifetime for him.

Still, Kate's hesitancy from the first day they met nagged at him. Even when he'd seen that she wasn't ready for marriage, he'd hoped they would at least move in together, but Kate wasn't having that, claiming it was about her independence and space.

He worried it was more about not trusting him. But he'd told her he thought it was quaint that she wanted to wait until marriage. Ridiculous, but so Kate. The one thing he'd always been able to do was get a woman into his bed. Now he was even questioning his prowess at that, given how long it had taken with her.

Kate was different. It wasn't like she'd played hard to get. She just hadn't been ready, she'd said, and he believed her. Also, he suspected the difference in their ages bothered her more than she wanted to admit. Wait until she learned that he'd fibbed about his real age. He wasn't quite thirty-four. But what did a couple years matter? It wasn't like she was robbing the cradle.

He finished packing and thought about the surprise trip. If everything went the way he'd planned it, his future was so bright he was going to have to wear sunglasses day *and* night. He grinned. "You've got this," he whispered to himself as he went downstairs to load his suitcase into the back of his sports car. Once they were on the plane, Kate was all his.

Still, as he drove to her house, he worried she might have gotten cold feet overnight. It was that dead husband of hers. Daniel "Danny" Jackson. He'd heard all about her childhood sweetheart to the point where he'd wanted to puke. The man had apparently been a saint, worked two jobs to support her and her two babies—up until the day he was blown up and ended up in a mass grave since identifying the bodies had been impossible. Collin was no head doctor, but he suspected it was one reason she'd held on to the fantasy of her dead husband for so long. She'd never gotten to bury him.

But Danny was the past now. He was dead, and Collin was alive. That had to rate for something, he thought as he wished he didn't remember the way she'd cupped that worn-thin, gold wedding band in her hand. Hell, she'd hardly looked at the huge diamond he'd put on her finger. He couldn't help a fresh stab of irritation. He'd dropped a bundle on that rock, hoping to impress her. Instead, some cheap ring was so precious she could barely take it off.

He snuffed out his annoyance as he caught his reflection in the rearview mirror. He'd hit the jackpot on looks. Blond, blue-eyed and devilishly handsome. At least that's what his mother used to say. What woman wouldn't want him? He laughed at his insecurities as the light turned green and he continued toward Kate's house. He'd make her forget that long-dead husband.

One way or another, Kate was going to love him more than she'd ever loved that *Danny*. How could she not?

CHAPTER TWO

MONTANA? KATE LOOKED out the window to see nothing but snow. It covered everything in sight, including the narrow two-lane highway. It fell from the sky in huge flakes that hurled into the windshield. The wipers clacked frantically but were clearly inadequate.

"Collin—"

"Don't worry. I was raised in Minnesota," he said. "I was driving on snowy roads at the age of sixteen."

She looked over at him. "I never know what to believe about you," she admitted, realizing how true it was. "Some of the stories you've told me—"

"All true. I'm a man of adventure, remember?" He grinned over at her, making her heart beat a little faster. Did he really know what he was doing? He was always so cocky and self-assured. It was what had attracted her to him. He'd been so different from Danny, who'd just been a scared kid like her.

They'd flown from Houston to Denver, Colorado to Bismarck, North Dakota, where a rental SUV had been waiting for them at the airport. From there, they'd driven west, leaving the interstate to cross the state of Montana on a two-lane highway. She'd never been in such wide-open spaces or anywhere with so many miles between towns.

As they headed deeper into the snowstorm, the highway seemed to grow narrower. She couldn't remember the last car she'd seen. There'd been fewer houses, almost no sign of life the farther they went. She had no idea where they were headed or what they were going to do since it was winter and freezing outside. This seemed like an odd place for Collin to bring her on their engagement trip.

When she'd asked where they were going, all he'd said was "It's a surprise, but we are almost there."

She'd never guessed when he'd told her to pack warm clothing that they were coming to *Montana*. She should have known it would be somewhere completely out of her comfort zone. Collin and his surprises.

Even as she tried to embrace the whole experience, the snowstorm was making her nervous. She pulled out her cell phone, needing to connect to one of her daughters, to reach out and ground herself through a lifeline to the familiar and safe. This new life made her feel anxious as if she were lost and would never find her way home. Isn't that what she'd believed in her heart at first about Danny after the accident? That Danny had gotten hurt and confused, that he was out there somewhere waiting for her to find him because he couldn't find his way home?

Why was she thinking about that now? Because that's how she felt, that she might never be able to go home again. She looked down at her phone. No cell service. How was that possible? She tried again and heard Collin chuckle.

"Kate, you aren't in a place where you can get cell-phone coverage everywhere. This is the Wild West. Watch for a cell phone tower. That's your best bet."

Reluctantly, she pocketed her phone. "I didn't realize there were still places like this. I guess I've lived in Houston for too long."

"And not gotten out in the real world enough," he added. "But that is all going to change, starting with this trip. I'm glad you agreed to it."

"Me, too," she said automatically. He was probably right about her needing to expand her boundaries. She couldn't remember the last time she'd been out of Houston, let alone Texas. There was a whole country she'd never seen.

Until Collin, she hadn't realized how isolated her life had been. She'd lived in other people's stories with her work. She'd been so busy raising her girls that she hadn't been aware of her life passing by.

Collin reached over and put his hand on her knee. She covered it with her own and saw the flash of the large diamond he'd put on her finger. It still felt strange, always startling her when she caught sight of it there. She looked away, hating that the ring made her feel as if she'd broken her promise to Daniel. She felt as if she wasn't just letting go of him after all these years but that she was no longer holding on to hope. Now, untethered, her future felt uncertain.

Years ago, the refinery had paid for the families of those who'd lost their loved ones to see a therapist. Kate had gone at the insistence of her family doctor, who felt she wasn't coping well with her loss.

"You don't believe your husband is dead?" the therapist had asked her.

"Rationally, I know it must be true. It's just that he doesn't feel…gone," she'd said. She'd explained that she felt Daniel could have been injured in the explosion and was alive and living somewhere, still unaware that she and the girls existed. "There was so much confusion at the hospitals with so many patients…" She'd gone looking for Danny, believing in her heart that he was still alive, but there'd been so many wounded that the victims of the blast had been dispatched to hospitals all over East Texas. The others to the morgue. So many patients had been brought in badly burned with no idea who they were.

"You aren't the first spouse who feels this way," the therapist had told her. "You didn't get to say goodbye. Nor did you get to identify his body and bury him."

Kate had nodded through her tears, thinking of the others who'd lost their loved ones that day. So many of the victims were unidentifiable and lost in the fiery grave.

The therapist had been sympathetic and kind. "You have to decide how you want to spend the rest of your life. Isn't it possible that your hope that Danny is alive and will show up one day at your door is keeping you rooted in a fantasy?"

Kate still recognized the truth in what the therapist had said all those years ago. She didn't want to let go of Danny and not just because she still loved him with all her heart. She didn't want to let go of the fantasy of him returning because then she'd have to admit that she'd lost twenty years of her life to that dream.

"Daddy was your first love," Mia had told her after she'd confessed how she was feeling. "Of course it was intense. Come on, Mom. You're not seventeen anymore. The question is this. Do you think you could be happy with Collin?"

She glanced over now at the handsome man who had come into her life when she hadn't been looking. He'd flattered her and made her laugh and refused to give up on her, even when she'd held him at arm's length for months.

Now he was offering to open up a whole new world for her. If she let him. It could be like coming back to life after a long sleep, she told herself.

"Marry me, and I promise your life will be one adventure after another," Collin had said the first time he'd mentioned marriage.

"What makes you think I'm up to an adventure—let alone one after another?" she'd asked with a laugh. She was set in her ways, comfortable in her own skin, in the knowledge of what the next day would bring and the next.

He'd looked into her eyes. "Don't you feel it? You and I were meant to find each other. I felt it the first time I laid eyes on you. I knew. I think you knew, too."

She had looked away, embarrassed because Collin had mesmerized her from the moment he'd walked over to her in the coffee shop and sat down. A brash young man with intense blue eyes, California-surfer blond hair and a grin that had made her heart bang around in her chest in a way she'd forgotten possible.

"It's fate, Kate. The stars are all aligned. The future is out there just waiting for us. You ready for the biggest adventure of your life?"

She'd thought she was. But now she felt as though she was trapped in a snow globe and regretted leaving warm Texas soil. She felt...scared.

"Isn't the snow beautiful?" Collin said, sounding downright ecstatic.

She looked out at the expanse of white, the two-lane blacktop the only color and even that was glazed in ice. The sky was overcast and yet the fallen snow shone, appearing iridescent as night had set in. She'd always wanted to see snow but maybe not this much. Also the lack of traffic made her nervous, too. She felt as if they'd left civilization behind. No houses, no lights, nothing but snow and highway. Where were they going?

"I love winter," Collin was saying. "There is something so pure about it, the cold air, the snow a clean, white blanket that covers even the dirtiest spots."

Without warning, it began to snow harder. Ice flakes flew at the windshield. Not even the headlights could punch a hole through the smothering flurry. Kate was having a hard time seeing the highway and knew Collin must be as well. She wished he would slow down. But he'd said he was used to driving in this kind of weather. She tried to relax, closing her eyes against the dizzying, hypnotic snowstorm.

Until...her eyes flew open. "Collin?" she asked minutes later. "What is that noise?"

CHAPTER THREE

JUST MOMENTS BEFORE Collin heard the sound, he'd been trying to hide his irritation with Kate. She'd said she wanted
to see snow. What the hell did she think that was falling
from the sky? And not just a little of it. Had she forgotten
that she'd told him she'd always wanted to make a snow
angel?

Then he heard the noise coming from under the hood
at the same time she did. He swore under his breath as
the engine sputtered and died. He cursed the rental SUV
as he coasted over to the side of the road and turned on
his flashers.

"What do you think it is?" she asked, sounding worried.

Did he look clairvoyant? "Don't worry. I'll take a look
under the hood." He grabbed his coat from the back seat,
popped the vehicle's hood release and climbed out into the
storm. The wind whipped snow, blinding him as he made
his way to the front of the SUV. Lifting the hood, he looked
down at the engine, wondering what the hell he thought
he was looking for. He knew nothing about car engines.

He'd hoped to find something obvious that he could fix
himself. Unfortunately, he saw nothing that looked out of
place and he was freezing his butt off.

"Do you know what's wrong?" she asked the moment he slid back behind the wheel again.

"Not yet." He tried to start the engine. Nothing. He kept trying, hoping it would just miraculously start. He didn't need this kind of trouble for so many reasons, his fiancée's worry for one. "I'm going to have to call someone," he told Kate.

"Is it that bad?" she asked, sounding scared.

He had no idea. "I'm sure it's just something simple." He pulled out his phone. He'd seen a cell phone tower a few miles back. Fortunately, he had a couple of bars. When the call went through to a local towing garage, he breathed a sigh of relief. "Twenty minutes? Sure. Thanks." He disconnected and looked over at her. She was beautiful, he reminded himself, and soon she was going to be his wife—unless he did something stupid and messed this up like losing his temper with her.

"I'm sorry," he told her. "You'd expect a rental to be in tip-top shape."

"I was surprised when the agency gave us an older model," she said. "I thought all rental cars were new."

He didn't know what to say to that since he'd asked for this year and model on purpose. Of course she would have chosen a more expensive, newer one. He smiled even though her words were a direct hit to his ego. He reminded himself that she had no idea what was really going on. Nor did she know anything about his financial situation. He had led her believe he was as set in life as she was, but he knew that unless this trip went well and didn't cost too much, it was only a matter of time before she found out.

Feeling that he wasn't good enough was something that had shamed him since he was a boy. He hated that other people always had more than he did—even though his parents were rich by most people's standards. Just not rich enough to put him in a league where he wanted to be. It's why he'd promised himself that he was going to have enough money—no matter what he had to do to get it. So far, even that plan hadn't been successful.

He told himself that his luck was going to change, and Kate proved that. "It's fine," he said, leaning over to kiss her. "The tow truck will be here soon. There's a town up ahead, Buckhorn, the driver said. We can stay there. They'll fix the car, and we'll be on our way. This is just another adventure, right?"

She nodded and smiled, but he worried she was having second thoughts and not just about this trip. "You promised adventure. You're certainly true to your word."

"Aren't I, though?" He could see that she'd lost some of her confidence in him. Not that he suspected she'd ever had much. It was getting cold in the car. He looked out and saw nothing but falling snow and hoped he could turn this situation around. If he didn't, he could lose her, and that was the last thing he wanted. Kate was the gift he'd always thought he couldn't have. To lose her over something this stupid… He shook his head and grinned at her. "You still want to make a snow angel?"

She laughed. "Surely you aren't suggesting—"

"Not now," he said as he pulled her close to keep her warm. "But maybe before we leave Montana. Wait until Mia and Danielle see the photo I'm going to take of you."

KATE STOOD IN the middle of the motel room unable to move. She could see her breath in the frigid air. Her teeth were chattering. She hugged herself, but her thin Texas winter coat made her feel ill prepared.

Behind her, she heard Collin come in with their suit-cases but was too cold to turn around. "The tow-truck driver turns out to be the mechanic, so that's lucky. Fred said he'll take a look at the car in the morning. I'm sure it's nothing. If not, the rental car agency will see that we get another car, so don't worry."

He stepped around her to put the suitcases down on one of the sagging double beds. The clerk at the desk had called this room a *suite*. Probably, Kate thought, because it had an apartment-sized kitchen against the far wall next to a two-chaired dinette set from the fifties.

It wasn't that Kate hadn't roughed it before. The worst part was that this room, this motel, this town reminded her of the short honeymoon she and Danny had taken in East Texas. She remembered the two of them laughing as they fell onto the sagging double bed in each other's arms—not really even noticing how awful the room had been.

She tried to still her chattering teeth. She'd never been this cold. She felt as if she couldn't move, could hardly breathe. "Where are we?" she asked, having seen more Closed for the Winter signs on boarded-up buildings than operating businesses on the way into town. "Nothing looks open here."

"Shirley in the motel office said it's a little slow this time of year. But she said come summer, the place is hop-ping. The town kind of hibernates in the winter. Not to worry, though. We won't be here long."

Collin kissed her as he passed her to go over to the heater on the wall. "I'll get some heat going, but you might want to take a hot shower to warm up."

The thought of stripping down in a cold bathroom to step into even a hot shower was out of the question. She turned to look at him, her expression apparently voicing her thoughts.

"Otherwise, you can hop into bed, and we'll make our own heat," he said and grinned. "Adventure, Kate. It's begun. Embrace it. I promise it will only get better."

She laughed, and it seemed to warm her a little. Or maybe it was the slight warmth now coming from the heater on the wall as Collin stepped to her.

"Having fun yet?" he asked as he pulled her into his arms.

COLLIN FELT THAT old burning sensation in his belly. Kate had been quiet on the tow-truck ride into town. She'd gotten even quieter when she'd seen Buckhorn. Had either of them blinked, they would have missed the town. What he had seen of it was closed, boarded-up buildings with *See U in the Spring* scrawled on the sheets of plywood covering the doorways and windows. What businesses were open had so much snow piled in front of them that he wondered how they would be able to find their front doors before June.

He had glanced over at her, reading her expression as the tow-truck driver, who'd introduced himself as Fred Durham, dropped them in front of the Sleepy Pine Motel. It was one of those single-level efficiencies with seven units in a long row. A blurry, red vacancy sign could be seen through the falling snow up by the highway. Behind the motel there appeared to be a forest of pine trees, branches groaning under the weight of the snow.

"Is this the only lodging in town?" Collin had asked, thinking about the kind of hotels Kate was probably used to.

"Only one this time of year," Fred had said. "You're lucky. Looks like Shirley still has a room available." He'd thought the man was kidding. Collin could see that there were no other cars parked in front of the motel rooms. An older-model compact car was parked down by the office, but that was it.

"Often during a storm like this, the rooms fill up fast with truckers," Fred told him. There were also no trucks. In fact, there seemed to be no other traffic and hadn't been for miles.

He and Kate had climbed out of the tow truck and hurried through the snow into the too-warm office. Shirley had turned out to be a hot fortysomething with short blond hair and brown, bedroom eyes. Before Kate, Collin might have talked her into warming his bed on this cold night. She hadn't been wearing a wedding band, and by the once-over she gave him, he'd gotten the feeling she was in between husbands.

"Can you give us two keys right away?" he'd asked her. "Our car broke down, and my fiancée is cold and tired." He'd smiled at Kate as he'd handed over the spare key. "I'll be right there, baby." Belatedly, he'd remembered that Kate hated being called *baby*—especially in front of other people.

He'd paid for the room and taken his key to hurry down to the room where Kate was waiting. Any other time, he would have flirted with Shirley just for fun, but he felt as if he was already skating on thin ice with Kate right now. He hadn't wanted to keep her waiting—let alone get caught doing something that would jeopardize this trip or his plans for the future.

He'd hoped making love would put him back into Kate's good graces. He'd heard he was quite talented at it. But after a few kisses, she'd said she was tired and went into the bathroom to change for bed.

"WHO WAS *THAT*?"

Shirley Langer turned around to find her lover standing in the doorway of her apartment behind the motel office. At forty-three with two marriages and divorces behind her, she often questioned what kept her in Buckhorn besides this rundown motel. Her mother's boyfriend owned the place and had hired her to run it. It gave her a place to live and him a tax write-off. Shirley got whatever money came in as her wages minus twenty percent. This time of year, though, she could go for days without a guest.

So, basically she had a dead-end job and was sneaking around like a teenager. But when she thought about getting out of this town, she'd see Lars Olson and remember what kept her here.

"Get back in there before anyone sees you," she said, laughing. She figured in a town this size everyone probably knew about the two of them, except for Tina. A redhead with a temper, no one wanted to cross Tina Mullen. Shirley'd had nightmares about Lars's live-in girlfriend coming in the back door of the motel's apartment, catching the two of them in bed and shooting them both.

"I didn't know you were coming by tonight," she said to Lars, glad to see him. She had been bored out of her mind before her only guests had shown up. "You have to quit sneaking in my back door. You're going to get us both killed."

Lars laughed. "Put the No Vacancy sign on and get your butt in here. I saw the way you were looking at that fella."

"Shoot, you know I don't like those good-looking, strong, rich, still-single types." She leaned against the counter and felt his gaze take in the deep V of her shirt. Before turning around at the sound of his voice, she'd released a couple of buttons to expose part of her lacy bra. Lars wasn't blond or rich or really single or even all that good-looking. But he had a way about him. He made her feel desirable because he couldn't stay away from her— even though he had one hell of a lot to lose if they got caught.

"What if more good-looking guys like him come in tonight looking for a room?" she asked, still not moving.

"They'll be out of luck. You heard me, Shirley. Turn on the sign."

She grinned and reached behind her. Outside the *No* on the vacancy sign came on, barely visible through the falling snow. "Wanna tell me what you're here for?"

"I'd rather show you," he said. "Damn it, woman, quit playing hard to get. I don't have much time before I have to go home."

Just the reminder of his girlfriend waiting for him was almost enough to make her send him packing without what he'd come for. But the truth was she wanted him as much he wanted her. Also she understood Lars's situation.

He had moved in with the daughter of the town's wealthiest family. Not only that, his employer was Tina's father. Axel Mullen owned the grocery store, acted as pastor on Sundays at the small church and owned a string of cabins where you could rent horses in the summer. The Giddy-Up

Cabins were closed for the season. But Lars also plowed snow for the incorporated city, of which Axel was mayor.

If that wasn't enough, a rumor had been circulating that Tina was pregnant. Lars swore there was no way it was his. He and Tina had been on the outs for months, according to him. If she really was pregnant, Lars said, it was someone else's child. But now Axel and his wife, Vi Mullen, the local postmistress, were both pushing Lars and Tina toward marriage.

Shirley could understand the kind of pressure he was under. He wanted to move out, but the house he and Tina lived in was the only one available in Buckhorn right now. He'd have to wait until spring or have nowhere to live— not to mention he'd be out of both jobs.

As much as Lars had talked about marrying Shirley, they both knew it would mean leaving Buckhorn broke with no idea what they would live on. Their love for each other was just another complication, especially in the winter.

She brushed her short bleached blond hair back from her face and turned out the office light. Good sense told her that what she was doing was dangerous. Axel Mullen owned this town, almost literally. He and his wife could make their lives miserable. Not to mention that Tina was just unbalanced enough that she might come after them with a gun.

Shirley barely stepped through the apartment door before Lars grabbed her and kissed her hard. One hand went straight to her butt as he pulled her tight against him to show her just how serious he was. The other hand had dipped down the V at her throat to unerringly find a nipple and pinch it to a hard pulsing point.

Desire sent heat straight to her center. If she was going to die, she wanted it to be in Lars's arms. She leaned back as his mouth dropped to her throat and began that familiar trip down to that magic spot he could always find.

At times like this, she didn't care how dangerous what they were doing was.

CHAPTER FOUR

"FRED SAID HE'LL have to order the part," Collin announced as he came into the café the next morning in a flurry of snowflakes. He joined Kate opposite her in the booth where she'd been waiting for him. "I talked to the rental-car agency. They're paying for the repairs. They'd rather do that than try to get us another vehicle since they don't have an office for hundreds of miles from here. So, we just have to wait until the part comes in tomorrow—if the highways haven't closed because of the storm."

She looked at him blankly.

"What?" he asked, looking genuinely confused.

"I'm waiting for the *good* news?" Outside, the snow continued to fall in a curtain of white. When it wasn't piling up on every surface, it was blowing around to form giant sculpted drifts. The latest one was blocking most of the front window of the café. When she'd sat down, she'd felt a chill and noticed the ice on the *inside* of the window. Texas born and raised, she'd never experienced anything like this.

Through the condensed view of the window, she'd been watching a man about her age with a large shovel trying to clear the sidewalks along the short main street. She wondered why he bothered since the moment he scooped a pile of snow, it quickly piled up behind him again.

While waiting for Collin, she had sat watching the world outside the window. An older man had walked up to the man shoveling. They'd stood in the storm visiting before the man had crossed the street to disappear down a short alley. She'd noticed him fighting the wind and snow, curious about where he'd been going as the younger man went back to his shoveling.

That she'd spent so much time watching the two men told her just how bored she already was. It made her worry how long before they could leave here. She feared she was responsible for them being in Montana to start with because she'd foolishly said she'd never seen more than a skiff of snow and had always wanted to make a snow angel. Once the car was fixed, she was hoping to talk Collin into flying somewhere warm for the rest of their engagement trip.

Now as she listened to him relay the news, she realized that she didn't need him to tell her that they might be snowed in here in this tiny town somewhere in Montana for the duration. She'd heard about the storm on the news this morning and the possible road closures. Apparently people really did get snowed in here.

Collin rubbed a hand over the back of his neck for a moment. "The good news," he said as he picked up the menu lying on the table between them, "is that we aren't out there broken down somewhere on the highway, because I'm hungry. Instead, we're sitting in a warm café, and I smell bacon."

She shook her head, losing some of her irritation at finding herself in the middle of Montana in a blizzard because of some offhand comment she'd made. This morning she'd promised herself that she was going to make the best of it. "Are you always like this?"

"Like what?" he asked, still considering the menu.

"So annoyingly positive for no good reason." She laughed when she said it, taking some of the sting out of her words. It wasn't his fault they were trapped here.

He peered at her over the top of the menu and seemed glad to see that at least she was smiling. He did have beautiful blue eyes. She was glad they weren't brown like Danny's had been. "No. I can be disagreeable when things don't go my way." The way he said it, she believed him, though she'd never seen any indication of it. Look how patient he'd always been with her.

"I try to see the positive," Collin continued. "Like my beautiful fiancée, this charming little town and snow. I didn't realize how much I'd missed it." He looked out the window. "You have to admit, it's picturesque." She grunted in answer. "Come on, you said you'd never seen it. Now you have."

"Now I have." Had she really told him that? Possibly. His memory was better than hers, apparently. He often brought up things he said she'd told him that she didn't remember.

"This kind of weather can be deadly, though, if you don't dress right." Reaching down, he lifted a large bag she hadn't noticed him bring into the café because she'd been so busy watching the locals outside. "For you."

She couldn't help her surprise and delight. "Where did you…"

"There's a store in town," he said, waiting for her to open the bag. "Actually, it's a clothing store, grocery, hardware store, post office and convenience store all rolled into one."

Kate withdrew what appeared to be a long down-quilted coat in dusty rose—her favorite color. She looked up at him and felt tears burn her eyes. He was so good to her. She felt awful for complaining while he was making the best of things.

"It's gorgeous."

"And warm," he said, smiling at her. "There are gloves and a scarf in the bag, too. They kind of match. I did the best I could."

"You always do," she said, studying him. She regretted all the wasted time making up her mind about him.

"I try to make you happy."

"You do make me happy. Thank you." She hugged the coat to her as he went back to his menu. She looked out the front window, half hoping the snow had stopped. It hadn't. She had walked down here the half block from the motel. Last night she hadn't seen much of the town.

This morning she realized that there wasn't much town to see. So far she'd been to the motel and café—both within easy walking distance even in a blizzard. But now, through the whirling snow, she could see other structures. Most were boarded up for the winter, making the place look like a ghost town. But there were a few signs of life, she was glad to see.

"If you give me that flimsy Texas jacket you're wearing, I'll take it back to the motel when I go. I need to make a few business phone calls."

"Maybe I'll walk around town when we finish breakfast." She wanted to avoid the motel room as much as possible. It made her think of her honeymoon with Danny.

"You should do that," Collin said without looking at her. He was still studying the menu. "What are you going to have? I think I could eat a whole cow. Or maybe just this Rancher's Special."

She checked the menu and shook her head in disbelief. "You can't eat all of that."

Collin dropped his menu, his grin widening as he lifted an eyebrow in challenge. "Wanna bet?"

COLLIN MADE THE call as soon as he got back to the room. He figured he didn't have much time since even a walk around the town wasn't going to take Kate long. This might be the only chance he had to be alone in the motel room. He'd tried making the call earlier outside the service station, but it was too hard to hear with the gale-force wind, not to mention the icy snow pelting him.

Gerald answered on the fourth ring. "Where are you?"

"Buckhorn."

"Where the hell is that?"

Collin had checked a map on his phone earlier. "We aren't that far from the border. Got caught in this storm."

"So, you talked her into coming with you. How long before you'll make the crossing into Canada?"

He hated to tell him as he looked around the dark motel room. He couldn't wait to get out of here. Between the snow and this cramped room, he felt he couldn't breathe. "Had a little car trouble but will be there in plenty of time to take care of business."

"The storm has held things up at the other end as well. But if you miss—"

"I'm not going to miss anything. I told you. I have it covered."

"That's what you told me last time, and we all know how that turned out."

"Gerald, I'm on top of this. My fiancée and I will cross the border in plenty of time to meet up with you."

He disconnected before the man could tell him what was at stake. As if he didn't know. Everything was riding on this deal. His very life. And that of his fiancée as well if he screwed this up.

ALL BUNDLED UP in her new warm clothing, Kate left the café to walk through the town of Buckhorn. The coat, hat and mittens were wonderful. Collin had thought of everything—except snow boots. She found the general store with its eclectic mix of items for sale all packed from floor to ceiling with everything imaginable. At the back was a tiny post office. She could see a woman moving around back there, filling a small wall of mailboxes.

The snow boots felt like heaven. She had the man behind the counter put her leather ankle boots into a bag. As she left there, she saw the gas station and garage at the edge of town and nothing beyond it on that side of the street. On her side, there appeared to be a bar some distance way. At least, she'd caught glimpses of a neon bar sign through the falling snow. It surprised her that even these few places stayed open this time of year with so little business.

Crossing the highway through the falling snow, she headed down the other side of town. Most of the buildings on this side were closed for the winter. She caught glimpses of houses behind the buildings along the main drag, but she didn't see anyone. Buckhorn, Montana, was a world apart, she thought. She'd looked on her phone earlier to see where they were in this huge state and had been shocked at how far it was even to the next small town.

Now, dodging snowdrifts taller than she was, she worked her way back toward the motel. The new snow crunched beneath her boot treads as the wind blew gusts of falling snow around her. She couldn't imagine living here, especially in the winter. Spending all of her life in the Houston area, she'd become used to certain benefits of big-city living—like health care. Earlier in the store, she'd seen a number posted for anyone who needed medical attention. Apparently there was a doctor about a hundred miles away who drove over a couple times a week. For emergencies this time of year, a person was to call 9-1-1 and wait for the ambulance that also had to make that same trip.

The wind had picked up. A gust whipped stinging ice crystals into her face. She stepped into the recessed doorway of a closed business and ducked her head until the gust settled. As she started to step out again, she heard the high-pitched whine of a table saw. The sound appeared to be coming from down the alley between the buildings.

Looking in that direction, she saw what seemed to be an old carriage house. The double doors were cracked opened. A thin wedge of golden light shot out like a ray of sunshine. She caught the scent of shaved wood and breathed it in as if it was pure oxygen. Her father had owned his own carpentry business. The smell reminded her of all the times she'd held the end of a board as he ran it through the planer or filled nail holes with putty for him as a child.

At the sound of a sander starting up, she felt herself drawn down the alley. She followed the familiar scent, the sound of the sander growing louder as she approached, the wood scent growing even stronger.

The sander stopped suddenly, and she heard a man whistling. It brought back a flood of memories of her father's hands as he worked and whistled. He loved making things with his hands and took pride in each piece. She had the rocker he'd made her when she was a little girl and the cradle he'd made for Mia before she was born.

Two large wooden doors opened into the old carriage house. She stepped to the one that was partially open. It left a wide crack for Kate to peer in. At first she saw nothing. Dust motes hung in the air, captured by the overhead light. Deeper in the large shop, she could make out a male figure bent over a workbench, a sander in his hands as he flipped a switch, the sound filling the space, and he went back to work.

The picture was a familiar one that formed a knot in her chest. She missed her father. Her mother had passed when Mia and Danielle were in their teens, but she and her mother had never been close after Kate's marriage to Daniel and pregnancy. So her father's death had been all that more painful only a few years later.

The sander stopped again, making her start as the small woodshop fell silent. Behind her was the quiet cold of the snow and the low howl of the wind. Inside the shop was the promise of warmth. A woodstove crackled in the corner, emitting a warm heat that she felt on her cheeks. Probably why he'd left one of the doors slightly ajar, to release some of the heat.

She hadn't realized she'd been leaning into the room until the door swung open and she stumbled in. The man suddenly turned and froze at the sight of her standing just inside the doorway, a dark silhouette backlit by the storm.

As the wind caught the door and threw it all the way open, cold and snow blew in, illuminating the man standing there in the white of the storm light. He looked startled to see her. But nothing like she was to see him. She felt a jolt as if struck by a bolt of lightning as she took in the familiar planes of his face, a face she'd given up hope of ever seeing again.

A cry escaped her lips before she said his name. *"Danny."* Before everything went black.

CHAPTER FIVE

KATE SURFACED SLOWLY, blinking in the dim light. She became aware of the heat and someone pressing the rim of a cup to her lips. She jerked up, knocking the cup of water away. It pooled on the wood floor, the coffee mug lying in a pile of sawdust at her feet. It took her a moment to realize where she was.

She was sitting on a blanket near the woodstove in the man's workshop. He'd been so quiet she hadn't noticed his dark shape squatting next to her until he reached for the mug she'd knocked away. She flinched and crab-crawled back a few inches before memory came charging back.

He picked up the mug and quickly rose as if realizing that he was frightening her. "I'm sorry. Are you all right?" The voice was low and gravelly and...wrong.

As she struggled to her feet, he reached for her as if afraid she would fall again. But at the last minute, he seemed to realize that she didn't want him touching her. He stepped back, holding up his hands as if in surrender.

In the shaft of bright light coming from the opened carriage-house door, she looked at him hard and felt her initial shock rattle through her once again.

This man was a dead ringer for her dead husband.

Yet something was all wrong about him.

"You took a nasty fall," he said quietly as if he thought even his voice was scaring her. He sounded hoarse, that gravelly voice not Danny's. "Maybe you should give it a minute before you—"

But she was already stumbling back toward the open door, wanting to run. Emotions roiled up so close to the surface that she feared she would cry. She rushed out into the storm, her mind whirling like the snow around her.

Seeing the man had come as such a shock. The resemblance so uncanny. For that moment, she'd been so sure that she'd found Danny. Until he moved. Until he spoke. Ice crystals melted instantly on her overheated cheeks as she fled from the workshop. She pushed through the snow drifting in the alley to the main road and turned toward the motel. She had to tuck her face against the snow and wind. It wasn't until she felt her tears begin to freeze on her cheeks that she realized she was crying.

At the motel, she fumbled her key from her coat pocket, struggling to get it into the lock. Her fingers felt numb like the rest of her body. The key finally turned, the door falling open, her falling in with it.

Collin looked up from where he sat on the bed, his back to the wall, the television on some old movie involving a car chase. "Hey, I was starting to worry about you." He squinted at her as she stumbled into the room, catching herself on the edge of the spare double bed. "Are you all right?"

She didn't answer as she frantically began to shed her coat, ripping the scarf from her neck and dropping the coat at her feet—until she finally felt she could breathe again. She looked at him and began to cry in earnest.

Jumping up off the bed, he rushed to her. "Baby, what's wrong?" She could only shake her head. "You have a scrape on your forehead. There's a bump. Did you fall?" A nod. Her sobs broke from her, making her chest ache as they rose from deep inside her, one after another. She was trembling as he took her in his arms. "You're okay. You're here now with me."

KATE WOKE TO DARKNESS. She could hear Collin in the bathroom. She listened. It sounded as if he was on the phone. He had the door closed as if he didn't want to disturb her. Or didn't want her to hear his conversation.

Earlier he'd gotten her out of her wet clothing and into a hot shower before tucking her into the bed and lying with her until she fell asleep. Before her eyes closed, she remembered telling him, "I thought I saw Danny." She had felt him tense next to her and wished she could stop the words. "It looked so much like him..." She'd shuddered at the memory. "But it wasn't. It wasn't him. He wasn't Danny."

She'd rolled over and squeezed her eyes tightly, her emotions a roller-coaster ride of hope and loss, embarrassment and humiliation, defeat and bitterly aching disappointment. Finally she'd fallen asleep.

His phone call ended. He came out and looked surprised to see her awake. He also looked a little sheepish, so she knew what he'd done before she even asked.

"Were you talking to one of my girls?" she asked, hating the accusation in her voice. *Her* girls. But she reminded herself that he often would call her daughters just to chat. She knew he wanted them to like him, hoping it would convince her to marry him.

"I called Mia. I was worried about you and..." He met

her gaze, looking concerned as to how she was going to take what he was about to say. "She's worried about you, too."

Kate sighed and, shoving back the covers, threw her legs over the side of the bed to get up. She was dressed in one of her nightgowns. She reached for her robe, but Collin had already picked it up and started to help her put it on.

"I have it," she said too sharply, snatching it away from his reaching fingers. As she tied the sash angrily, she said, "I wish you hadn't called her."

He took a step back, and she was reminded of the man in the woodworking shop also stepping away from her with that same worried look. "Kate, I'm sorry. I was worried."

She glared at him, embarrassed and humiliated all over again. He'd told Mia. Mia would tell Danielle. She shook her head. "You needn't have called. I'm fine. It wasn't him."

Collin looked at her agape. "Of course it wasn't, because he's…"

"Dead," she finished for him. Tears burned her eyes. She bit her lip. Now he knew her only secret. She had hoped that he'd never find out. But now that it was out… "Mia told you about the other times, didn't she?"

He looked down at the badly worn, ugly motel-room carpet for a moment. "She thought I should know." There was accusation in *his* voice now. He thought she should have told him what he was getting into.

Kate felt her anger rise at both Mia and Collin before it dissipated as quickly as it had come over her. Of course they both thought he should know. Collin was going to be her husband. It was reasonable. If Collin was going to marry her, he should know about the other times she'd thought she'd seen Danny. She shouldn't be upset, let alone angry with any of them. They loved her. But still she hated that Collin knew. Just as she hated the look in his eyes when she met his gaze. She was pathetic. An almost middle-aged woman who still fantasized about her dead husband being alive.

"I know he's dead," she said defensively. "But there is always this split second when I see someone who reminds me of him and I think…" Kate shook her head. "Then I get a good look at the man, and of course it's not him. I'm not crazy."

"No one thinks you are," Collin said kindly as he reached for her. "We get it. We just worry, that's all. For that split second, it has to be such a…shock and then such a disappointment."

She nodded against his chest. She wasn't ready to forgive him for calling Mia, and yet she let him pull her closer. She hadn't wanted her girls to know about this. It had been years since she'd seen a man who reminded her of Danny. Her girls had been so happy about her moving on, putting the past behind her for good.

After all the tears she'd cried over Danny, she would have thought there were no more to shed. "For just that one second, it was him standing there," she said in a hoarse voice that ended with a sob. "I know it's foolish, but my heart has never accepted that he died that day. I would have known if he had. Instead, I've always had this fantasy that he's out there somewhere and that he will make his way home." She pulled back to look up at him and saw pity in those blue eyes.

"He's gone, Kate. You have to quit looking for him."

She nodded and leaned into him again, feeling the

warmth of his arms and body wrapped around her. Collin was real. The life he was offering her was real. She knew it wasn't fair to him or her girls for her to keep hanging on to what she'd lost. Right after the explosion, she'd searched every crowd, every passerby, every random crowd shot on the television news looking for Danny.

But she hadn't done that for years. Occasionally a face would catch her eye, but those occasions were rare. She'd really believed that she could move on and put Danny to rest—if not for herself, then for her daughters and her fiancé.

She felt her cheeks heat with embarrassment. A month after the explosion, she'd seen a man on a news program. He was a farmer in Nebraska. She made her father call the television station. She'd been convinced it was Danny.

Another time, she'd seen him getting off a plane and had chased him down, terrifying the man and his family. There'd been other times, too. In Houston, she'd see a man walk in front of her car, and he'd looked so much like Danny that she'd jumped out, holding up traffic to go after him. It was only when he turned that she'd seen her mistake.

Now she'd done it again—just when she'd thought that she'd accepted the loss and was ready to move on.

"When can we get out of here?" she asked, her voice breaking.

"Soon, baby. I'm going to go get us something to eat." He swept her up and carried her back to the bed, lying her down gently and planting a kiss on her forehead before leaving.

She crawled under the covers and turned on the television, but she was too distracted to watch anything. Collin had been gone long enough that she'd wondered if he'd stopped by the man's woodshop to see for himself. Collin would know what Danny looked like since there were photos at her house. Their wedding picture, snapshots when the girls were born and ones of the two of them with their baby girls.

Kate stared at the engagement ring on her finger. She'd said goodbye to Danny when she'd accepted Collin's proposal. She hadn't realized that she'd still been holding out hope even after all these years—until she'd seen the man standing in the woodshop.

But it had been just like the other times. The man wasn't Danny. He looked like what Danny might look like after twenty years had passed, but he definitely didn't sound like him or move like him. So, why had she behaved the way she had? There'd been something about him. Something about his features, something about the way he was standing there...

She felt a wave of shame and humiliation. Her daughters and Collin were right. Danny was gone. He certainly wasn't down the street in some woodshop. She closed her eyes, wanting desperately to get out of this town and put this whole episode behind her.

CHAPTER SIX

THE NEXT MORNING, Collin accompanied her to the café as if afraid of what kind of trouble she might get into if she went by herself. Last night they'd eaten the dinner he'd picked up from the café in the motel room and watched a bad movie. The whole time, she'd felt Collin stealing glances at her. She couldn't bear the thought of his pity, let alone his concern. Was he having second thoughts about marrying her?

"Have you talked to the mechanic?" she asked as they walked down the main street toward the café. She knew Collin had to be as anxious as she was to get out of this town, even before what had happened yesterday. The sidewalks and highway had been plowed, but new snow had formed more drifts they had to navigate around.

"He didn't answer. It's early. I'll have breakfast with you and then go check," he said and reached for her arm as they came to a slippery part of the sidewalk.

She wanted to pull free. To tell him that she wasn't an invalid. But she bit her tongue. The bump on her temple said otherwise—at least to Collin. Nor did she point out that he'd never liked an early breakfast and usually didn't want to eat until around lunchtime.

It was obvious what was going on. He was protecting her from herself, afraid she might foolishly visit the wood-worker again. Or maybe see someone else in town who looked like her dead husband?

Once in the warmth of the café, they shrugged out of their coats and took a booth. As she looked around, Kate felt embarrassed by the looks the other patrons gave her. She knew they were probably just interested in any strangers who'd arrived in their town. But she felt as if everyone knew what she'd done yesterday. She tried to assure herself that they couldn't know. But today they seemed even more curious about her and Collin than they had been yesterday.

Excusing herself, she went to the ladies' room. More than anything, she needed a few moments to herself. Collin had been hovering over her all morning. She took a few deep breaths and splashed cold water on her wrists. Maybe she'd lived without a husband for too long. Over the years, she'd prided herself in her ability to be self-sufficient.

Now she wondered if she was ready to lean on anyone, let alone lose her feeling of independence. She wanted a man to be her equal partner. Not someone who felt he had to take care of her.

She couldn't help those thoughts. The engagement ring seemed to hang on her ring finger. She really had to get it sized. She found herself staring at it, questioning if she was doing the right thing for not just herself but Collin, too. He hadn't known what he was getting into. But now he knew at least some of it. She really doubted he knew how much she still loved Danny and always would.

But she loved him, too. She wanted this adventurous future he was offering her. Just because she'd made this one mistake here in Buckhorn, it didn't have to define their relationship.

As she came out of the ladies' room, she saw Collin talking to a woman who appeared to be in her mid-fifties. A plaited gray braid hung along one shoulder. She wore an apron liberally dusted with what appeared to be flour. Kate caught enough of the conversation that she realized he'd been questioning the cook about the woodworker.

She felt her face flush with mortification. As if she wasn't embarrassed enough by her behavior yesterday. Worse, the way he was questioning the woman, he made it sound as if the woodworker had done something wrong.

As she approached, Collin glanced up and shut up. He gave her a guilty look as the older woman excused herself and went back into the kitchen. Kate said nothing as she passed him and headed back to their table. He joined her. She could tell that he knew she was angry. Just as she could tell that he didn't want to argue, especially here in front of half the town.

"If it's all right," he said quickly, "I'm going to run down to the garage and see what is going on. I heard on the news that a lot of the highways are closed. This storm doesn't seem to be letting up." He sounded nervous, and she realized it wasn't just because he'd overstepped a few minutes ago asking the older woman about the woodworker. He was getting as antsy as she was, being trapped in this place. More so after yesterday.

"Go. I'm fine," she said, glad to see him leave, but far from fine.

He nodded uncertainly but was smart enough to not stick around and question her further.

She didn't dare glance around to see if she was still

being watched. She knew she was. She thought about skipping breakfast altogether and going back to the motel room. As she started to reach for her coat, a young pregnant waitress she'd heard someone call Lindsey rushed up to take her order.

Kate slumped back in relief. She wasn't hungry, but eating gave her an excuse to stay. Even with people curious about her, it was better than that dark motel room.

Lindsey had just left to put her order in when Kate looked up to see the older woman Collin had been talking to earlier standing next to her table.

"Mind if I join you?" the woman asked and didn't wait for an answer as she slid into the booth. "I wanted to welcome you to Buckhorn. I'm the café owner. In the summer I also run the bakery on the edge of town." She held out her hand. "Bessie Walker." Bessie smelled of yeast, sugar and cinnamon. Her smile was welcoming, just like her bright blue eyes.

"Kate Jackson." She shook the warm smooth hand.

"I see you're engaged," Bessie said.

Kate looked down at her left hand. Seeing the ring on her finger startled her. "It was recent." She thumbed the band to straighten the diamond. "I'm not used to it yet."

"Seems to me it doesn't quite fit."

"Yes, it's a little too big. I haven't had time to have it sized."

"That, too," Bessie said and smiled. "Your fiancé…"

"Collin Matthews," Kate provided.

"He was asking about Jon," the woman said, meeting her gaze and holding it.

Was that the woodworker's name? "Jon?" she repeated.

Not *Daniel*. Not her Danny. She felt her cheeks heat. Just as she'd feared, everyone in town knew.

"Jon Harper," Bessie said. "I believe you met him yesterday. He runs a woodworking shop out of the old Aldrich carriage house. Talented man. I sell what he makes at my bakery during the summer months. That's when we get the most tourists through town."

Kate couldn't imagine enough people came through and bought his handmade wood products to keep the man fed.

"He likes to work in his shop, keep to himself." Bessie shrugged. "People in Buckhorn respect each other's... quirks."

She knew what the woman was trying to tell her. Just as she couldn't help asking, "Has he been here long?"

Bessie hesitated. "Showed up in summer about five years ago. His truck broke down. Like you, he was waiting for a part to come in. By the time it did, he had rented Mabel Aldrich's guest cabin. Mabel's husband, Frank, was a woodworker and had all the tools. Frank had died that spring, so she told Jon he could use them and the carriage house." She finished as if that was either all she knew about Jon—or all she figured Kate needed to know.

She thought of the man she'd seen in that workshop and felt a chill curl around her neck even though the café was almost too warm inside.

The waitress brought Kate's breakfast and refilled her coffee without a word, before hurrying back to the kitchen.

Bessie hesitated, as if expecting Kate would have more questions. After a moment, she rose. "It was nice to meet you, Kate. I have some cinnamon rolls in the oven. Don't leave without picking up a couple for you and your fiancé. I would imagine your car part will be in at any time. I heard Fred's been calling around trying to pick up a used part to get you on your way. Headed any place special?"

Kate had no idea. "Just wanted to see Montana in the winter."

Bessie laughed. "Well, that's a new one. Most people come in the summer." That blue gaze held hers for a moment. "You stay warm, and don't forget your cinnamon rolls. With luck, you'll be on the road by this afternoon."

Kate watched the woman walk away, feeling as if she'd been told to leave town. She'd definitely been told to leave Jon Harper alone.

THE WHOLE PLACE smelled like grease and oil and sweat as Collin walked into the garage of the old gas station. His rental SUV was in the first bay. Fred was working on a pickup on the hydraulic lift in the second bay. The clank of a wrench against metal could be heard over the drone of the newsman on the radio.

Another storm right behind this one? Is that what the man had said? Collin groaned irritably. His claustrophobia was getting worse. The sooner they got out of this town, the better. Although he had to wonder how many more dead husbands Kate might see along the way. He didn't know what to think about this latest development. But at least she'd come to her senses and realized her mistake.

He'd walked by the old carriage house in the back of the short alley. He'd been tempted to check out the wood-worker for himself. But she'd said it wasn't him. So, Collin saw no reason to wade through the alley's snow. But he couldn't help being curious. This morning while Kate was in the bathroom, he'd gone down to the motel office and quizzed Shirley. Shirley was easy on the eyes, and she seemed bored and glad for the company.

"Jon Harper? He's a strange one," she'd told him. "No one knows his story. He seldom comes out of that shop of his. Bessie and Earl Ray are the only two people in town that he's said more than a couple of words to."

"Earl Ray?" Collin had asked.

"He's our local war hero. Late sixties, gray hair, military buzz cut. You'll see him around if you're here long. He hangs out at Bessie's most days. The town gossip is that Jon either killed someone or got his heart broken, and he's hiding out here." She'd shrugged. "I think he's just a loner."

Collin had asked the café owner as well while Kate was in the ladies' room. He got pretty much the same thing from her. Not much. That's why he was still curious. Just not curious enough to visit the hermit in his workshop. He did wonder, though, what Kate had seen in the man that made her think even for a second that Jon Harper was her dead husband.

"Hello there." Fred came out from under the pickup wiping his greasy hands on a filthy rag. "I think I found that part you need. With luck it will be here tomorrow."

"Can't get it here any sooner?" Collin asked, cursing silently to himself.

"Not with this storm. The part's coming up from Wyoming, where the roads are said to be even worse. Word is that even the interstate is closed to all but emergency traffic."

This *was* an emergency, but Collin couldn't bring himself to tell the man that since it wouldn't do any good, anyway. "Tomorrow, huh? Okay, I guess I can live with that if you can fix it right away, so we can leave tomorrow afternoon. Is that possible?"

"Soon as I get that part, I'm on it." Fred gave him a toothy smile and ducked back under the pickup as a young man in his twenties came roaring up on a snowmobile, snagging Fred's attention. "My son, Tyrell," the mechanic said under his breath before looking at the clock on the wall. "You're late," he called to his son who came slouching in. Tyrell wore jeans, biker boots and a large army coat that had seen better days. His expression was one of defiance as he went into the office.

Collin could see him pouring himself a cup of coffee, his back to them.

Fred made a disgruntled sound before he headed into the office. Collin could hear the two of them arguing as he left.

"Where have you been?" Fred was asking. "You'd better not be sniffing around that woman again."

He couldn't hear the son's answer. Whatever it was, it hadn't pleased Fred.

As Collin stepped out into the snowstorm, the argument faded behind him. The storm had worsened. He could hardly see the buildings across the highway. He tucked his chin into his coat and tipped his head down and walked into the wind and blowing snow. What a miserable friggin' place, he thought. He couldn't wait until he had Buckhorn in his rearview mirror—and Jon Harper with it.

The thought of going back to that motel room threatened to bring on an anxiety attack. Even outside in the storm he felt closed in, trapped. That's when he spotted a bar sign on the edge of town that he'd somehow missed before.

It had started to snow harder as Kate finished pretending that she was eating her breakfast. She couldn't bear the thought of going back to the motel. She hadn't seen

Collin, so she assumed he was still dealing with the mechanic at the garage. If he'd gone back to the motel, he'd either be on his phone or flipping the channels impatiently on the television. The program selection was limited. She suspected that nothing could hold his interest.

Kate left the café, ducking her head to the snow and frosty breeze as she made her way down to the store. She'd always been able to lose herself in a good book. The selection wasn't much, but she picked up several, thinking one of them might keep her mind off everything.

Earlier this morning, Collin had mentioned that a couple of his associates were skiing in Canada and might meet up with them if the part came in soon. "You wouldn't mind, would you? We might have to cross the border. You brought your passport, right?"

She'd nodded. She'd never been to Canada but doubted it was much different from Montana right now. According to what she'd heard about this latest storm, it covered a wide area.

After buying the books, she had little choice but to head back to the motel room. The aroma of the two warm cinnamon rolls rose from her purse where they lay wrapped in foil, compliments of Bessie. Kate knew Collin would love them. Maybe she'd eat a little of one since she'd barely touched her breakfast.

Today, she stayed on the opposite side of the highway from Jon Harper's woodshop as she walked back. Not that she wasn't aware of the sound of a saw coming from the old carriage house. Today, he had the garage door closed, but she could see a sliver of light stealing from the crack between the two doors.

She thought about what Bessie had told her about Jon.

He'd shown up five years ago. What had she been doing five years ago? She had to think for a moment. She felt her pulse jump as she recalled Mia's graduation from college in late spring. How she'd wished that Danny had been there to see his oldest receive her college diploma. He would have been as proud of his daughter as she'd been.

For some time after the explosion took Danny from her, it had almost been like a game, wondering where he would have gone if he'd been hurt and suffering from a form of amnesia. What would he have done?

He'd always been good with his hands. He could fix anything. Make anything. She'd known that he'd have found a job and wouldn't have gone hungry. That's why she'd thought that was him in Nebraska working on a farm.

Being reminded of the mistakes she'd made over the years made her forget to watch her step. She slipped on the ice under the snow and almost fell. As she righted herself, she looked across the highway at the sliver of golden light that shone from the crack between the double carriage-house doors. She had heard the whine of a saw earlier. Now there was nothing but a cold silence. Maybe he wasn't even over there, and even if he was…

She stood in the falling snow, the wind whipping flakes around her, wondering. The more she'd tried not to think about him, the more she had. Jon Harper wasn't Danny. But it nagged at her. She couldn't understand why she'd been so sure that first instant she'd seen him standing in his shop.

The other times she'd thought she'd seen Danny, her heart had threatened to explode from her chest, she'd had trouble breathing, she'd felt the blood rush from her head even, but she'd never fainted. So, why this time? What had it been about this man? Something about his silhouette? Or had it only been the way he was standing?

It left doubt in her mind. She'd been in such a hurry to get out of that room with him, as if she'd been running scared. Not embarrassed. That was later. No, this was a different form of terror that had her racing from that woodshop and out into the storm.

Kate knew she'd have to go back. She'd have to see him again. She couldn't leave this town unless she was certain, otherwise there would always be that nagging doubt at the back of her mind.

The thought of seeing him again after yesterday and making a fool of herself made her a little sick to her stomach. Jon Harper. A snowplow went flying past in a roar on the highway, kicking up a cloud of snow. She waited until the cloud drifted away before she crossed the paved two-lane.

Her throat went dry as she neared the woodshop. She'd been so sure it was him until she'd heard the rasp of his voice. Not Danny's voice. Of that she was certain. But what bothered her was that even when he'd been hovering over her, she couldn't remember if she'd seen the color of his eyes. Danny's were brown, a warm, soft sable with dark lashes. His hair had been brown, too. Brown eyes and brown hair. Could either be more common?

There was one true belief that she'd held in both her head and her heart all these years. If she ever got to look into Danny's eyes again, she would know him without a doubt—no matter how much he had changed.

As she paused at the opening into the alley, she saw a new set of tracks. Someone else had been here. Her tracks were nearly indistinguishable from yesterday. These tracks appeared larger. The older man she'd seen yesterday? She remembered seeing him come out again before she'd finished breakfast. It had been the same man she'd seen before. She'd recognized his lumbering gait and his buffalo-plaid coat.

With her tracks from yesterday nearly gone with the storm, it was as if she'd never walked down this alley. Never seen that man. Never thought he was her long-lost dead husband.

Even the older man's tracks were now sunken shadows in the deepening snow. In a few more hours, the falling snow would erase all trace of both of their tracks. She took a step into the alley, even though the snow now came over the top of her boots.

"Kate?"

The sound of Collin's voice made her flinch. She turned, startled to see him coming toward her through the drifts that had formed on the sidewalk. He looked upset, as if he'd seen where she'd been headed. Just a few more minutes and she would have been pulling open one of the carriage house's double doors and stepping inside.

"Are you headed back to the motel?" Collin asked, clearly pretending he hadn't known what she was about to do. She couldn't blame him for not wanting to make an issue of it.

"I bought some books at the store to read," she said, also pretending that she'd only stopped here to catch her breath. She hugged herself against the cold and driving snow, disappointed and yet thinking that he'd probably just saved her from further embarrassment. "What did you hear on the car?" she asked as she joined him.

"Fred's hoping the used part comes in tomorrow. He

thinks he can get the engine fixed and we can leave by afternoon," he said as they headed in the direction of the motel.

It took all of Kate's strength not to look back at the carriage-house doors and that slice of light bleeding out. She'd thought she'd heard the creak of one of the doors opening down the alley. Was Jon Harper standing in the doorway watching them leave? If she turned, would she see his face, and would that be the end of it? Or just the beginning?

CHAPTER SEVEN

"YOU WEREN'T THINKING of going back to see that carpenter, were you?" Collin asked after they'd finished the cinnamon rolls. He'd wordlessly eaten most of the two. She'd had only a little of one before handing it over for him to finish. As good as they had smelled, she wasn't hungry, even though she'd barely eaten her breakfast.

She met his gaze as she wadded up the foil the rolls had been wrapped in and tossed them into the trash. "I have to set my mind at ease. Once I see him again—"

Collin swore and shot to his feet. "Kate, why put yourself through that? Look, you made a mistake. For a moment, something about him reminded you of your dead husband." He was pacing the small motel room now. "You're a rational woman. What would he be doing in Buckhorn, Montana, even if he was alive?"

Working with his hands—just as her father had done. But she said nothing, letting Collin pace and talk.

"Not to mention, what a coincidence it would be that we get stranded here and, lo and behold, there's your thought-to-be-dead husband."

Kate heard the truth in what he was saying. Jon Harper wasn't Danny. Yet she found herself silently arguing, why not? Why couldn't a man with no memory of the past end up here? Buckhorn was the kind of place a loner might fit right in. Bessie had said that his vehicle had broken down—just as theirs had. Why couldn't this man who was good with his hands find a way to survive here?

"I know it sounds ridiculous, but there was something about him that made me think he was Danny. I need to know what it was. I have to be sure it's not him."

"Then I'll go with you," Collin said, grabbing his coat from where he'd dropped it and shrugging it on. "Come on, let's get this over with." She didn't move except to shake her head. He stopped to look at her. "Why not?"

She couldn't explain it. "I need to see him alone."

Collin took a step back. "You're kidding, right?" He shook his head angrily. "Are you *trying* to get out of the engagement? Is that what this is about?"

"No, that's not—"

"It sure seems that way," he said as he yanked off his coat and threw it on the spare bed again. "So, go. Go see him. Go satisfy your curiosity. When the part comes in for the car tomorrow and Fred gets it fixed, we're out of here. A plow came through earlier, so at least one road must be open. But there is another storm coming behind this one. We'll have a window of opportunity. We can't miss it." He stilled, his gaze sliding to her. "Tell me this isn't going to happen again in the next town or the next."

She mugged a face at him, and his expression fell as he came over to squat down in front of her. "Baby, I love you. But you have to put Danny behind you for good. This is a new beginning for both of us. I need to know that you're in it one hundred percent with me—not some ghost."

Her heart ached at the hurt she saw in his eyes. She

cupped his handsome face in her palms. She hated that she was putting him through this. Leaning forward, she kissed him. "I'm sorry. Once I'm sure—"

His cell rang, and she withdrew her hands from his face as he rose to reach for his phone. "Yeah," he said into it and turned to her, mouthing that he'd take it outside.

Kate picked up one of the books she'd bought at the store. She opened it, read the first page and then realized she couldn't recall what it was about. Her mind was on Jon Harper.

Rising, she went to the window. Collin had walked down past the row of motel rooms to a covered area out of the wind. He was pacing as he talked, which meant it was business.

She grabbed her coat and stepped outside the room. Collin had his back to her as she turned the opposite direction to walk down the highway toward the workshop. She had to get this over with; then she could leave this town and never look back.

The snow was falling so hard and fast that when she looked behind her, she could no longer see Collin and could barely make out the motel's vacancy sign. She walked faster. She desperately wanted this over, needed this over. Once she looked into Jon Harper's eyes, she would know. She would apologize for frightening him yesterday and for acting so strangely. She would assure him that she wouldn't bother him again.

Then, she could leave this town having no doubts. No regrets.

She trudged down the short alley through the deep snow, her eyes on the carriage-house doors. Both were closed. Was there still a light coming from the narrow crack between them? What if he wasn't there?

The thought made her heart pound. She couldn't wait another minute, let alone leave town without seeing him again. If the part came in early, Collin would insist on them driving out ahead of the next storm.

She'd reached the double doors and pushed on the one that had been partially open yesterday. It gave way so quickly, that she almost fell headfirst into the workshop again. She stumbled in a few feet, caught herself and stopped.

He was standing in the opposite doorway, silhouetted against the falling snow behind him. His hands were empty and at his sides. She noticed the breadth of his shoulders. This man was so much stronger looking than Danny had been, but then again, Danny had been a boy compared to Jon Harper.

"I… I…" She swallowed. "I didn't mean to bother you again," she finally managed to say. Her voice sounded high and strange, even to her ears.

He stepped in, closing the door behind him, but not before she'd seen an old log cabin in the pines a dozen yards behind the carriage house. As the door closed, she blinked in the sudden dimness after the glare of the snow outside. Only a few bare light bulbs hung from the ceiling. The main source of light was a lamp where Jon had been working yesterday. It formed a pool of melted gold on his workbench but left the rest of the shop in varying degrees of shadow.

As he came into the shop, he picked up a hammer and a chisel before moving to where he'd been working yesterday. "You're not bothering me."

Again she heard how wrong his voice was. There was a roughness to it that hadn't been there before.

"I wanted to apologize for yesterday," she said as a cold gust blew snow in behind her, and she realized that she'd left the door ajar. She turned to close it and then, getting up her courage, stepped farther into the shop. Her heart hammered with each step, but she had to get close enough to look into his eyes. From a distance they appeared to be brown, but she had to see them up close to know for certain.

He had gone to work on the board lying on his workbench as if she wasn't there. She watched him, studying first his profile, trying to see Danny, trying not to see him. The man's hair was brown and longer than Danny had ever worn his. It curled at the nape of his neck. She fought the urge to touch it, remembering the feel of his hair in her fingers. She felt desperate for him to look at her so she could meet his gaze and finish this.

There was a wariness about him as she stepped closer. She thought about what Bessie had told her. He liked to keep to himself.

"I didn't mean to scare you yesterday," she said quietly.

He'd been easing wafer-thin pieces of wood from the board with his chisel and hammer. She saw his hands and felt a hard tug at her heart. His fingers were long and beautiful. Danny's mother always said he had the hands of a classical pianist, not a laborer. "Too bad I'm tone-deaf, huh?" he'd joked. She remembered those hands on her body, the tender way he'd touched her, the way he'd made her body sing.

"Your hands," she said and swallowed the rest of the

words as he slowly put down the chisel. She cleared her voice. "You have nice hands. Ever play the piano?"

He turned then to look at her. She was close enough that the ambient light from the lamp caught on his face, giving her the first good look she'd had of him. Her breath caught in her throat, and for a moment, she feared she would black out again.

His face was so familiar and yet different enough to force doubt into the heady excitement that had her pulse thrumming. She felt a start as she saw that a portion of his face and neck had been scarred as if burned. Her skin felt hot, her heart knocked in her chest.

Danny.

His features had changed from the boy she'd loved into those of a man.

But nothing could change his eyes. Soft sable brown.

It felt as if this shop was a time machine and she was now whizzing back through the years as she looked at her husband. After the explosion, she'd lain in bed, crying herself quietly to sleep at night so as to not disturb the babies. She would pray for just one thing. *Please God, just let me see him again.*

Her whole body was trembling now. "You…you look like someone I used to know." Her voice came out a hoarse whisper.

He said nothing, his face expressionless except for his eyes. There was confusion there as well as kindness.

She didn't know what to say, either. Clearly she was making them both uncomfortable. But in his eyes, she saw the truth. Yes, he'd changed, but those eyes, they couldn't lie. Just like his hands. Just like the feeling she'd had the moment she'd seen him… Jon Harper was Danny. Different, yes. His voice and other things about him. But she wasn't wrong this time.

"You're so much like him," she said, her words gushing out. She looked into those familiar brown eyes and felt a jolt.

While in all that warm sable brown she saw kindness, there was no recognition. None. She reminded herself that he wouldn't know her if she was right about him coming out of the explosion with no memory.

"His name was Daniel Jackson. He was my husband," she said, her voice cracking with emotion but she had to get the words out. "I was told almost twenty years ago that Danny died, but I've never believed it in my heart. You look so much like him." Her voice broke into a sob.

He shifted on his feet, his eyes also shifting away. "I'm sorry for your loss." When he did meet her gaze again, she saw pain and realized it was for her. For this stranger who was pouring her heart out to him while he had no idea who she was or who Daniel Jackson was.

"We have two beautiful daughters, Mia and Danielle." She couldn't seem to stop, although she had to look away for fear of breaking down crying. It was too painful to keep searching those eyes. Danny's eyes. And finding no recognition at all.

"Mia has a successful graphic-design business. Danielle will be graduating from college in the spring. She wants to teach elementary school. They both grew up hearing stories about their father." Kate took a few deep breaths, letting them out as she looked around the workshop before she settled her gaze on him again.

He hadn't moved. Nor had his expression changed. But there was something more now in his eyes… Something that brought tears to her own and an ache of longing to her chest. He looked in pain—all of it for her.

She swallowed the lump in her throat. "I should let you get back to your work," she said and saw his relief in the way his body seemed to relax.

Kate took a step backward. "You make beautiful things." Another step toward the door. She could almost feel the cold coming in through the crack between the two doors. Another step and she collided with the rough wood behind her.

He was still standing there, unmoving, those brown eyes on her as she opened the door. She wanted to say something that would make him remember her, remember them, but there were no words, only the unbearable ache in her chest as she stepped through, closing the doors behind her to find herself alone again, surrounded by an alien, cold, white, unforgiving landscape.

CHAPTER EIGHT

"THE PART CAME IN!" Collin looked and sounded joyous as he finished the call the next morning. "It's time to get this engagement trip going again. Tonight we sleep in the best hotel we can find. I'm talking four-star. And food! I want a big juicy Montana beef steak with a potato the size of my head. I can't wait to hit the road."

Kate had come back yesterday from Jon Harper's workshop to find Collin propped up against the wall on the bed watching some poker tournament on the television. He seemed nervous and out of sorts. He hadn't asked where she'd been, and she hadn't told him.

Instead, she'd taken off her coat and boots and climbed in the other bed with one of her books. She'd apparently fallen asleep there, because that's where she'd awakened this morning. She couldn't remember anything she'd read. Last night, he'd gone over to the café for food and been gone much longer than it should have taken. When he'd come back smelling of beer, she hadn't said anything.

They'd eaten propped up in the two beds. He'd found a movie to watch, and Kate had pretended to read until she'd turned out her light and gone to sleep. Collin hadn't joined her in the bed. She'd been relieved this morning when she'd awakened to see that he'd already showered and dressed and was on his way out.

He was in such a good mood after the call that she couldn't bring herself to broach the subject of Jon Harper with him. Collin often seemed so young, so free, so confident, something she felt she'd never been. She'd been forced to grow up fast after she lost Danny. All these years alone with her two girls, she'd felt afraid that she couldn't do it right alone. She felt that same fear now. She'd barely slept at all last night for fear of what she was going to do.

She knew how desperate Collin was to leave. And it wasn't just getting out of this awful motel room or having more choices of where to eat other than Bessie's café. Nor was it meeting up with his associates across the Canadian border. He wanted to get her out of this town and away from Jon Harper. Because like her, he was afraid of what she might do.

"Get packed," he said as he reached for his coat.

"I can't leave yet." The words felt like marbles in her mouth. During her sleepless night she'd tried to convince herself that leaving with Collin was the only thing to do. Collin loved her. He was offering her a second chance in life. Even if she was right and Jon Harper was Danny, he didn't know her. He wasn't her Danny anymore. Being around him seemed to be as hard on him as it was on her. Knowing that he was Danny and not being able to reach him was excruciating.

That wasn't even what hurt the most. She'd seen something in his eyes. He needed her to leave. Wanted her to. He'd almost been pleading with her to go and not look back. Whatever had happened to him over the years, it had made him into the recluse he'd become. She was the last thing he wanted or needed.

But how could she leave him? "I can't go yet," she said.

"*Not this again?*" Collin demanded.

She rose from the bed. Yesterday after seeing Jon, she'd been so filled with emotion, she'd felt raw, as if her flesh had been flayed with a knife. She hadn't had the strength to tell Collin what she now knew, especially knowing what his reaction would be. This morning he'd been busy on the phone with his associates, discussing the weather and how long it would be before he could get out of Buckhorn. She'd been dreading the moment when he got off the phone.

She'd known after he'd disconnected that she couldn't put it off any longer. Not that she had any idea how she was going to explain it to him or what would happen next. "I can't leave," she repeated.

He shook his head. She could see he was getting angry with her, something he'd never done. "If this is still about that carpenter…" He met her gaze, his blue eyes hard as ice chips. "That's where you went yesterday. That's why you were acting so odd last night. You said you just wanted to read your book, but I knew it wasn't about the book. You barely turned a page all evening. It's about that man you are determined is your dead husband. I thought you said you were mistaken. So, you went back, and what? What happened?"

She swallowed back the bile that rose in her throat. "I had to see him again because I hadn't gotten a good look at him."

Collin swore and raked a hand through his blond hair. His handsome face twisted in anger. "I knew you were determined to go back there, but why would you put yourself through that? Are you just a glutton for punishment?"

"I finally saw his eyes. He's Danny."

Her fiancé exploded, stomping back and forth in the small room. "Did he tell you he was your husband?"

She shook her head, looking away. "He doesn't remember me."

Collin let out a bark of a laugh as he paced. "So, he doesn't know you at all, right?" She nodded. "Then, that should be the last of it."

"How can it be? It's *him*. It's Danny. I'm sure of it. How can I desert him now after I've found him?" She was pleading with him to understand. "When I looked into his eyes—"

"Have you lost your mind?" Collin stopped pacing so quickly, his look so furious, that she couldn't go on. For a moment she thought he might grab her and shake her. He certainly looked as if he wanted to. "I'm sorry. I shouldn't have said that. I just can't deal with this right now." He snatched up his coat and stormed out into the cold.

Kate looked down at the ring on her finger, a reminder of that new life she'd actually thought she'd been looking forward to. She couldn't blame Collin. He'd put up with so much from her since they'd met. And now this?

Tears burned her eyes. Was she throwing away a chance for happiness based on…what? Jon Harper didn't know her. From the way he'd acted, he wanted nothing to do with her. Even if he was Danny…

That was it, though. He *was* Danny. She saw it in his eyes. She felt it at heart level. She'd found the first man she'd ever loved, the same man who'd stolen her heart all those years ago, the father of her children.

She reminded herself that she and Danny didn't know each other anymore. They were different people than they'd been. They'd spent all these years apart. It wasn't as if they could pick up where they'd left off. As if the fact had slipped her mind, he didn't remember her or their daughters or the life they'd shared and seemed to want to just be left alone.

She knew it made no sense. Like Collin had said, what were the chances she'd find him here? But she also believed that there were things in this world that couldn't be explained.

Maybe it was no coincidence that the rental car had broken down outside of this particular town or that she'd heard the sound of the sander and had gone down that alley to look inside the old carriage house. Hadn't she always known in her heart that he was out there somewhere? Hadn't she prayed that she would see him again?

How could she just leave? Her heart ached with the belief that she'd found him because he needed her. What had he been through the past twenty years? She thought of the burns on his neck and throat. Were his true scars much worse?

Bessie had made it sound as if she knew nothing about Jon Harper. Surely someone in this town knows more about him, she thought. She needed to know where he'd been all these years. Kate remembered seeing that man coming from Jon's workshop the other morning.

Leaving a message for Collin saying she'd gone out, she pulled on her warm clothing and headed out the door and into the Montana winter.

"You must be happy," Bessie said when Kate walked into the café minutes later, shaking snow off her hat and coat. "Heard the part came in for your car. Bet you're ready to get out of here. Not many people can take Buckhorn in the winter. Too far from the big city, too cold and too isolated. Too far from sunny Arizona," she said as she filled the coffee cup Kate had turned over when she'd sat down in the empty booth.

"Do you have a minute?" Kate asked.

The older woman looked leery but slid into the opposite side of the booth, saying, "I've got blueberry muffins in the oven. They'll be ready in a few minutes. But I can sit for a moment. Don't leave without me packing you a couple for the road."

Kate didn't know how to ask, and fortunately for her, she didn't have to. The man she'd seen coming out of Jon's shop passed in front of the café window. A moment later, he entered the café on a gust of cold air and snow.

Bessie looked up, her whole face lighting up. "Hey, Earl Ray," she called.

For a moment Kate was taken aback at the expression on the older woman's face. If that wasn't love, she had no idea what was. "Who is that?" she asked.

"Earl Ray Caulfield," she said with obvious admiration. "He's our local war hero and one of the nicest men you'd ever want to meet."

Kate glanced at Earl Ray, who had taken a seat at the counter. Like Bessie, he seemed to be in his mid- to late-sixties. He was a big man, strong-looking with a full head of salt-and-pepper hair. He looked in good shape for his age. The young pregnant waitress was pouring him some coffee and visiting with him. Kate noticed that he had a nice laugh, and it was clear that Bessie wasn't the only one enchanted with the man.

A timer went off in the kitchen. Bessie rose. "I'm sorry. Was there something you needed?"

"I just wanted to thank you for the cinnamon rolls. They were delicious."

The older woman nodded. "Glad you enjoyed them. Don't forget the blueberry muffins I'm sending with you. I hope the rest of your trip is less eventful." With that she hurried off.

Kate ordered the breakfast special when Lindsey came over. While she waited, she eavesdropped on Earl Ray's conversations with both Bessie and Lindsey and anyone else who came or left. Clearly, everyone liked him.

When her meal came, she ate, realizing that she was starved. Bessie and Earl Ray were visiting at the counter. From the difference in last names, she assumed the two weren't married. But there seemed to be some definite chemistry between them. She assumed that he wasn't married because no one asked after his wife. So, what was the story between Bessie and him? Those thoughts distracted her from thinking about Danny while she waited for Earl Ray to finish his coffee and head home.

COLLIN KNEW IT was too early for a drink, but that didn't stop him. He walked through the snow to the far end of town to the bar. The bar sign was on, and he could hear music as he pushed open the door. Brushing off snow, he shrugged out of his coat and moved to the bar to drape the snow-covered coat over a stool before taking the one next to it.

The place was empty except for the bartender, who

was apparently named Dave if you could believe the T-shirt he was wearing, and another man at the opposite end of the bar. A news show was on the small television behind the bar.

"What can I get you?" Dave asked as he came down the bar. He was a rotund man with thinning hair who Collin guessed was somewhere in his forties. Collin tried not to see himself in the man. How easily he could end up at just such a dead-end job in the middle of nowhere if things didn't improve and soon.

"A draft, whatever you have." He pulled out his wallet and threw down a twenty. His cash was running low. He'd put this trip on his credit cards, but even those were reaching their limits.

The bartender set a glass of beer on a cocktail napkin in front of him and went back down the bar to visit with his other customer. A local. Both of them, Collin thought by the looks of them. He couldn't imagine a more miserable life, trapped in this town, working at a bar, unless of course you were a carpenter in a shitty old carriage house making wooden toys and rockers for tourists.

He took a sip of his beer and looked down the bar at the men. "So, what do you do around here for fun?" he called down to them.

The man on the bar stool laughed. "Dave," he said to the bartender, "do you even remember fun?"

Dave laughed. "Well, we all know what you do for fun, Lars."

Lars chuckled and slid off his stool, bringing his drink with him, as he joined Collin. "Heard your SUV part came in. Bet you're glad to get out of here." He held out his hand. "Lars Olson. I work at the store and plow snow for my almost-father-in-law who owns almost everything in this town except for this bar, that motel you're staying in and the abandoned hotel."

"Me and the bank own the bar," Dave called down the counter. "Another two thousand seven hundred and ninety-nine payments, and it will be all mine."

"Exactly," Lars said. "I just wanted this man to know how bad things are around here for all of us. So, tell me your hard-luck story."

"What makes you think I have one?" Collin asked, bristling.

Lars laughed. "Don't take offense. I could use some cheering up since I have to go to work soon. I was hoping your story was worse than mine." Dave said something under his breath and turned up the news. It was clear that Lars had already had a few beers this morning.

Collin realized he didn't mind the company as Lars climbed onto the stool next to him. "Well, you already know about my rental car breaking down and the part finally coming in," Collin said. That meant that Lars had probably heard about Kate's obsession with the carpenter. "That's as good as my news gets. So, tell me something," he said before finishing his beer and signaling for another. "But first, wanna another one?" Lars nodded and tipped his half-empty glass in a silent salute.

When Dave brought two more beers, he reminded Lars he had to plow the streets yet today.

"Got it covered," Lars assured him and turned to Collin. "Dave's my best friend. I even work nights sometimes as a swamper, cleaning up his bar to help him out."

Dave returned to the television before Collin asked, "What do you know about Jon Harper?"

Lars considered his beer for a moment. "I understand your interest, but you have to also understand Buckhorn. We protect our own."

"You consider Jon Harper one of your own? I thought he's only been here a few years?"

Lars met his gaze. "I know you don't want to hear this, but Jon is an okay guy. Actually he's better than most of us. He's the kind of man to give you the shirt off his back if you're in need."

"I've seen his shirt. I'm not impressed."

Lars laughed. "He's contributed to this community and helped people just passing through, never wanting credit for it. In fact, some people he helped on the highway outside of town told a newspaper reporter about what he'd done for them. The reporter came to town, wanting to do a story on Jon. He wasn't having any of it. He's that kind."

"Sounds to me like he has something to hide. What do any of you really know about him?"

Lars shook his head. "If you're asking who he was before he came here, your guess is as good as mine. He doesn't talk much, *never* about himself. I get the feeling he's been through some rough times that have left him leery of people."

Collin swore under his breath. Maybe the man *was* Danny Jackson. He finished his second beer. He knew better than to have another. The car would be ready this afternoon. In the meantime, he had to make up with Kate. But all he could think about was what Lars had told him about Jon Harper. He sounded exactly like the kind of man Kate would be attracted to.

CHAPTER NINE

WHEN EARL RAY finally shoved off his stool, pulled on his coat and headed for the door, Kate tossed some money on the table and followed him out—only to collide with a solid body just outside the door.

"Sorry," the man said in a deep, sleepy-sounding voice.

She drew back to look up at his face. She'd gotten glimpses of the man coming out of the closed Crenshaw Hotel on the edge of town. He wore a stocking cap pulled low so only his dark eyes peered out. His long hair and beard were the same color as his eyes. He wore an old army coat that looked as if it might have belonged to his father—or was something he'd picked up at a thrift store. The look on his face was so serious that he gave her a start.

"Sorry," he mumbled again and held the door for her so she could exit.

She could see Earl Ray down the street and headed in that direction. She hadn't gone but a few feet, though, before she heard Bessie call after her.

Earl Ray was already half a block past the next street. Having no choice, Kate turned back.

"Are you all right?" Bessie asked. "You look...startled."

"It's nothing. That young man—"

"Finnegan?" Bessie huffed. "Says he was hired as caretaker at the Crenshaw Hotel. Looks to me more like a bum who just needed a place to stay for the winter. With the owner dead and the place boarded up for the past two years, guess we have to take his word for it. Finnegan probably isn't even his real name."

Kate shifted on her feet. Bessie seemed to realize how anxious she was to get moving. "You forgot your blueberry muffins." Bessie handed her the package. "You left so fast... Guess you're just in a hurry to get out of town. Enjoy." The woman wheeled back inside the warm café as someone called her name.

When Kate turned, there was no sign of Earl Ray.

She moved down the snowy sidewalk as quickly as she could. Glancing in whatever windows weren't boarded over as she passed, she saw no sign of the older man. He wasn't in the stores. There was no sign of him anywhere.

At the corner, she looked down the street and caught a glimpse of his red-and-black-checked coat as he turned the corner.

By the time she reached the corner, Earl Ray was entering a small house with a snowy hedge around it. She slowed to catch her breath in this silent world of falling snow. How did the residents of this town not go crazy with the snow getting deeper and deeper by the minute and the already freezing air growing colder day after day, she wondered. It felt as if the snow would never stop falling, as if it would bury the town, bury them all before winter was over.

Kate shivered as she stopped at the shoveled sidewalk that led up to Earl Ray's door. She had no idea what she was going to say. Like Jon Harper, the man inside this house didn't know her. Had no reason to trust her.

But that didn't stop her as she walked up to the door and knocked. It took him a few minutes to answer. She could hear him moving around inside moments before the door opened.

He'd gotten out of his coat and boots and now stood blinking down at her in a gray flannel, plaid shirt, jeans and stocking feet. "Hello," he said and smiled as he pushed open the storm door. "You look cold. Are you lost?"

She couldn't help but smile at this friendly face. "Do you have a minute?"

That made him laugh. "Oh my dear, I have nothing but time. Please, come in." He stepped back to let her enter the house.

The first thing she felt was heat, wonderfully warm heat that rushed to her cheeks. The house had a cozy feel to it, with overstuffed furniture, photographs lining the mantel, books on the end tables and thick rugs on the wood floor. The place had a woman's touch, and she realized she must have been wrong about Earl Ray not having a wife.

"Here, let me take that," he said. With numb fingers, she slipped out of her coat and scarf, letting him take them as she kicked off her snowy boots, leaving both the boots and the treats by the door as he ushered her in.

"How about a cup of hot coffee?" he asked. "Come into the kitchen. You can sit right by the stove and warm yourself up."

Kate did as he suggested, taking a chair next to the heater. She hadn't realized how cold she was. She felt her fingers and toes begin to sting and then ache as they warmed. She rubbed her hands as the warmth radiating from the heater began to thaw her out.

Earl Ray put a mug of steaming coffee in front of her. "I

always keep a pot going this time of year," he said conversationally as he took a chair across the small table from her. He had keen blue eyes and bushy graying eyebrows. He reminded her a little of a Santa Claus she'd liked at the mall.

"Thank you," she said, cupping the mug in her hands, letting the steam rise to her cheeks. The coffee smelled good in the inviting kitchen. "Is your wife—"

"She passed some time ago," he said. "So, what brings you out on a day like this?"

She could feel that earnest gaze on her as he took her measure. "Now that I'm here, I don't know where to begin."

He chuckled at that. "I'd suggest the beginning, unless you have a time restraint."

Collin could have the car back at the motel by now, impatiently waiting for her, probably still angry with her and getting even more so. Or maybe he would just leave. The thought came as a relief. She just hoped he didn't go down the street looking for her at Jon's shop.

Earl Ray cleared his voice. She took a sip of her coffee and met the gaze of this stranger sitting across from her. Everything she saw in his open face encouraged her to pour out her heart. She knew how much she needed to talk about this and felt both relief and gratitude. "I lost my husband almost twenty years ago." She quickly filled him in about how young and poor they'd been, about Danny's death and how she'd raised her two daughters alone. He glanced at the diamond on her ring finger. "I only recently took off my wedding band. I'd promised Danny I never would." She had to look away for a moment and gather herself again. Her ring finger still felt naked and odd— even with the heavy diamond ring on it.

"I've never believed in my heart that he died that day.

There were so many people missing after the explosion. So many bodies that couldn't be identified." She looked up at him. "The truth is I now realize that I have never stopped looking for him. A few times, I thought I saw him, but I was wrong." Earl Ray didn't seem to be wondering why she was sharing this with him, nor did he rush her along or seem anxious for the story to end.

"I know I'm going to sound off my rocker, but the other day when I met Jon Harper…" She stopped, fearing what his reaction was going to be. "I… I…felt something, and yesterday when I went back…" Earl Ray was waiting patiently. "He's different. Of course he would have changed in all these years, but when I looked into his eyes…"

"You think Jon is your husband, Danny," he said simply, matter-of-factly.

She met his kind blue eyes. "I do. I feel it." She placed her hand over her heart and fought back tears. "I know it's him."

"What about your fiancé?" Earl Ray asked.

Kate shook her head, her eyes stinging. "Collin is wonderful. I love him but…"

"Not as much as you still love your first love."

She nodded. "I can't help it."

He smiled then and picked up his coffee to take a sip. "I have the same problem, if that helps. My wife has been gone now for some years, but I can't seem to move on."

That explained what she'd seen at the café with Bessie, Kate thought. Clearly the woman was in love with him, and Earl Ray seemed genuinely fond of her. "Do you feel that if you did move on, you would be betraying her?"

He nodded. "I suspect you feel the same. But that isn't why you followed me to my house today, is it?"

"No. I saw you coming out of Jon's workshop the other day. You *know* him." Earl Ray nodded. "I need to know where he's been, how he ended up here, if what I believe in my heart could possibly be true."

"Why don't you ask him?"

"Because I'm a stranger to him. There is no recognition in his eyes at all," she said, her heart breaking as she admitted it. "I've always believed that he was hurt badly and walked away from the explosion not knowing who he was. It happened to others. Why not to Danny? But I guess I also believed that once he saw me…"

Earl Ray nodded. "You've seen the burn on his face and neck? I can understand how that might convince you that he's your husband. Don't get me wrong. There's a lot to be said about seeing the soul through the eyes." He fell silent for a moment. "It sounds to me as if you're at crossroads right now. Your fiancé is promising you a shiny new future, while Jon… Even if he is your first husband, he doesn't remember you or your past together. He might never remember. It goes without saying that he's not the same man you knew. Nor are you the same woman."

Kate heard the truth in his words. "I've said the same thing to myself, but how can I leave believing that he's Danny, believing that he needs me and just doesn't know it? Did Jon ever tell you anything about his past?"

"I'm sorry. You've met him. He's not much of a talker."

"Neither was Danny. But surely he mentioned something when he arrived here."

Earl Ray shook his head. "The man keeps his own counsel. Keeps to himself. All I know is that he arrived here early summer about five years ago. He seemed down on his luck and needing a place to light for a while. Seemed honest enough. Mabel Aldrich helped him out, the rest of us did what we could. Frankly, I'm surprised he's stayed as long as he has. There's something about him, a restlessness. I wouldn't be surprised if he moved on sooner than later, especially if he feels crowded."

She started, hearing the warning in his words. "You're suggesting that he would leave to get away from me?"

"Maybe not you, exactly. But maybe his past? I hate to even bring this up, but if we're being honest with each other here, let's say Jon *is* your husband. You said the day of the explosion that he was working two jobs and you two were just barely scraping by. He was just a kid himself with two little babies and a wife to take care of. Maybe he saw a way out and just walked away that day and has regretted it ever since. That would be a hell of a lot of guilt to live with. Not sure most men would stand under the weight of it."

It wasn't the first time that she'd considered this. She'd heard stories of several men who had done just that after the explosion. She'd just never admitted it was a possibility because it was not like Danny. But if that was what had happened, that he'd walked away on the spur of the moment and then could never come back, then she could understand it tearing him apart inside. "Thank you," she said and rose to leave.

"I'm not saying Jon did that. In fact, I highly doubt it from what I do know of him. He's an honorable man, but even honorable men make bad decisions, ones they regret for a lifetime."

She nodded, desperately fighting tears.

"I didn't mean to upset you," Earl Ray said quickly, also getting to his feet.

"No, you haven't. I've lived with all of this for almost twenty years. I have my own guilt. I know how hard he was working back then. The day he… The day of the explosion, he hadn't wanted to go to work. He'd said he wasn't feeling well, but it was payday, and we needed that check." Her voice broke. "I encouraged him to go." She touched the chain at her throat. "It wasn't until I got the call later that day about the explosion that I found his wedding ring in the bathroom by the soap dish. He'd forgotten it there."

"We all have those kind of regrets," Earl Ray said, as if seeing the two wedding bands nesting together, one worn thin, the other almost brand-new. "Can't change the past. So what are you going to do?"

"I honestly don't know," Kate said. "But I can't leave. Not yet."

He walked her to the door where she pulled on her boots. He held her coat and scarf for her and picked up her blueberry-muffin package and handed it to her. "Be sure and eat those. No one makes blueberry muffins like our Bessie."

She heard admiration in those words. She thought she also heard love for the baker. "Why is it so hard to let go?"

He shook his head. "It just is. I keep thinking that one day I'll wake up and I'll be ready." He chuckled. "At this point, I doubt I'll live that long." His gaze met hers and held it tenderly. "I don't envy the decision you have to make. If you ever need a cup of coffee and a good listener, you know the way back to my house."

CHAPTER TEN

COLLIN WAS WAITING for her back at the motel. When she'd
seen the car parked in front of their room, the engine running, her heart had dropped. She'd slowed, her emotions
battling with her usually rational mind. If she didn't go
with him, she knew that would be the end for her and Collin, a man who was promising her a future. She'd accepted
his ring, promised to marry him and had put him through
so much, and yet he was still here.

Then there was Jon. Even if he was Danny, he didn't
even know her. He might leave town just to get away from
her. The thought broke her heart. So, why would she put
herself through that? Why stay here trying to get the man
to remember her?

She still didn't know what she was going to do as she
pushed open the door into the motel room.

"Baby!" Collin cried as he rushed to her. "I was so
worried about you." He pulled her into his arms, holding
her tightly. "I'm so sorry about earlier." Drawing back to
look at her, he said, "I was an insensitive jerk. Can you
forgive me?"

She looked into this face she'd come to love. It still
bowled her over that a man like Collin could love her so

much. She felt the ring on her finger. How could she keep hurting this man because she couldn't give up the fantasy of a life again with Danny? They were on their engagement trip—his surprise for her because she'd once mentioned that she'd never seen snow.

Well, she'd seen it now, she thought as it melted into puddle on the floor at her feet—more than she could have ever imagined.

"Collin," she began. No longer able to look into his eyes and see the hurt, she stepped from his arms and turned to take off her coat and boots. This was all her fault, not his. All he'd done was love her. He certainly hadn't asked for this.

"Look, I've been thinking," he said behind her. "Of course you can't leave until you know whether or not this man could possibly be your...husband. I mean, if he is, you're still married. Not sure how that works. But anyway, there must be some way to find out, right?"

She turned slowly to look at him, knowing how hard this must be on him. "I told you. He doesn't remember me."

That stopped Collin for a moment, before he said, "Right. But then, he wouldn't if he was someone other than Daniel Jackson."

"Or if I'm right and he had a head injury from the explosion and didn't know who he was."

Collin frowned for a moment. "Okay, so you're saying he still might have amnesia and that would explain why he doesn't recognize you." She nodded. "But he's been somewhere all these years. All we have to do is find out where. If it was Texas..."

She felt tears fill her eyes as she stepped to him to hug him. "Thank you," she whispered as she looked up at him.

"I love you, Kate. I want to marry you. So, we find out where this man has been and solve this."

As she nodded, she realized that he thought this could be taken care of before their rental car ran out of gas in the motel parking lot. "It might not be that easy. I asked a couple of people. No one seems to know anything about him."

Collin stared at her, surprise and something else she couldn't quite put her finger on in his expression. "Well, wouldn't the simplest way be to ask him?"

She stepped away again. "I'm not sure he'll talk to me."

"Well, he'll talk to me. Leave it to me. I'll take care of it."

EARL RAY TAPPED at the right hand carriage-house door but didn't wait for an answer. He could hear Jon inside the shop sanding one of his latest projects.

"Jon," he said as he entered and closed the door behind him. Jon turned off the sander as Earl Ray sat down on the stool where he always sat when he came to visit. He liked sitting and watching the younger man work. The warmth of the old carriage house, the smell of the sawdust, the crackle of the fire all filled him with a peacefulness that relaxed him.

They didn't talk much, didn't need to. Earl Ray had seen the dark shadows in the man's eyes the day Jon had arrived in Buckhorn. He knew pain when he saw it. What he hadn't known was what had put it there. Something more than whatever physical pain Jon had endured, of that he was sure.

"I heard the most remarkable story earlier," Earl Ray said conversationally. Jon glanced at him before picking up a piece of fine sandpaper and beginning to hand-sand the piece of wood he was holding. "It's about this young woman. Twenty years ago or so, her husband left her and their two young daughters and never came home." After Kate had left his house, he'd gone online. It hadn't taken but a minute to find the story about the explosion all those years ago near Houston. He'd been horrified for all those who had lost their lives—and for the ones they'd left behind.

"Anyway," he was saying. "There was an explosion at one of those plants down in Houston. So many people died, some never identified. The wife never believed her husband had died that day. She thought he'd been injured and didn't know who he was and had walked away. She's been looking for him ever since."

No reaction from Jon, not that he'd really expected one. Still he sighed and continued. "She never quit loving the man all these years. Raised both daughters, seems she did okay for herself. Nor did she ever stop looking for him."

Jon had stopped sanding. He was staring down at the board now covered with a fine layer of dust.

"Any of this sound familiar to you, Jon?" No answer. "The thing is, this woman has one hell of a lot of love left in the past that she just doesn't know how to deal with. What makes it an even more tragic love story is that a new man's come into her life after all these years of waiting for the other one to return. He's offering her a second chance at happiness, but she won't take it unless her first husband is really gone."

Still no response.

Earl Ray rose, picked up his hat and gloves and headed for the door. He stopped, his back to the woodworker. "I suspect she won't leave town until she has her answer. Nor will she be able to move on emotionally." With that, he pushed open the door and headed toward the café. He'd done what he'd come to do, right or wrong.

He'd made decisions in the war that affected the lives of other men. But none were as heavy on his heart as this one. He'd interfered, something he tried very hard not to do anymore in other people's lives. He just hoped he'd made the right decision and now Jon would do the same.

By the time he reached the café, he was craving one of Bessie's blueberry muffins, and he had a feeling that she'd saved him one. Mostly he needed to see Bessie, to hear her laughter, to see her smile. She was the balm that soothed his regrets and gave him a reason to get out of bed in the morning.

Even the thought brought with it the guilt. Some days he couldn't remember his wife's face or hear the sound of her voice in his head. He felt himself slowly losing her all over again. It broke his heart, a heart that Bessie kept stitching back together, and he kept letting her, bringing with it another kind of guilt.

Yet the past still had a death grip on him.

He thought of Kate Jackson as he pushed open the café's door. He hoped she would be able to move on. It would give him hope that he could someday as well.

"Earl Ray!" Bessie cried when she saw him. Her face broke into a huge smile. "Blueberry muffins still hot from the oven."

He nodded, smiling. "You know me so well, Bessie."

KATE STARED AT Collin as she felt her heart drop at his words. *He was going to confront Jon Harper?* "No, I—I don't want you to."

"Baby, you're awfully protective of a man who is probably a complete stranger. I'm not going to beat the truth out of him. I'm just going to talk to him and try to clear this up, that's all. Unless you don't trust me to handle this."

"It's not that." She could see that he was waiting to hear what it was in that case. She had no answer for him. She *was* protective of Jon Harper because she'd seen something dark in those sable brown eyes. A pain that she attributed to the explosion, his injuries, the path his life had taken over all these years.

Earl Ray had said they'd known Jon needed help when he'd landed in Buckhorn. Some of them had reached out to him. She understood their need to do that. She wanted to help him as well. The last thing she wanted to do was hurt him even if he wasn't Danny.

But he was. So what was the point of questioning him?

"Collin, I was thinking that maybe you could go on up to the border and meet your business associates and leave me here until—"

"No, I'm not leaving you here alone," Collin said emphatically with a shake of his head. "Come on, Kate. Try to see this from my perspective. This is…"

"Crazy?"

"I wouldn't have used that particular word, but *bizarre* would work." He sighed. "Or *totally frigging off the wall.*"

She could see that he was losing his patience, and she didn't blame him. "I just need a little more time."

He shook his head and looked at the floor. "I'm going to talk to him." He held up a hand. "I'll be nice. I promise. All I'm going to do is find out where he's been the past twenty years while you were working and raising your daughters."

"Collin—"

"No, let's say you're right, and this man is your husband. Maybe he had a brain injury. Could have happened. Or maybe, Kate, he didn't. He was a teenager working two jobs and still you were barely making it. I know what that feels like. It makes a person desperate. So maybe he saw an opportunity to walk away." Earl Ray had said the same thing. "How are you going to feel about him if that's the case?" She met his gaze, her eyes brimming with tears. He swore. "Are you seriously still that much in love with him that you'd take him back even if he did walk out on you all those years ago?"

She'd once dreamed of finding him, of bringing him home. She'd known that he could have walked away. It hadn't mattered. Did it now? For so long, she'd told herself he had to be dead, otherwise he would have found his way back to her.

"I don't know how to feel about any of it," she said. "I'd given up hope of ever seeing him again."

"Well, I'm going to find out what his story is." Collin grabbed his coat and was out the door before she could stop him.

She thought about going after him but could just see the two of them busting into the woodshop, making complete fools of themselves. It was bad enough that Collin was going. She picked up a book but couldn't concentrate. Instead, she paced the small motel room, wondering what Collin was saying to Jon. More importantly, what Jon was saying. She thought about getting in the shower to warm up when the door opened and to her surprise he'd come back.

"He's not there," Collin said. "Apparently, he's taken off. I found the cabin he lives in out back. His truck is gone, and his landlady said he drove off a few minutes before

I got there. She checked his cabin. What few belongings he had were gone. He left rent money and a note thanking her. He's gone, Kate. He isn't coming back."

CHAPTER ELEVEN

JON HARPER PARKED his old pickup in the lot and limped inside the bank. He'd driven the fifty miles to the nearest town of any size through a blizzard, even though his landlady Mabel had tried to talk him out of it.

"Lordy, Jon, have you noticed the weather?" Mabel had asked. "Now's not the time to be going to the big city." Lewistown was hardly the big city. "Can I loan you whatever you need and save you the trip?"

He shook his head. "Thanks anyway, Mabel. Don't worry. I'll be careful."

She'd looked worried, but not as worried as she would be when she found his few belongings missing from the cabin she'd rented him the past five years. He'd left an envelope on the table in the cabin's kitchen with the money he owed her and a thank-you note. He figured she wouldn't find it for at least a few days, maybe more. It would take that long before she'd know that he wasn't coming back. Then the whole town would know. Including the woman staying at the motel.

At the bank counter, he asked to get into his safety-deposit box. A clerk took his key and, using the bank's key as well, pulled out his large box and handed it to him along with his key.

"Just let me know when you're finished," she said and stepped from the room.

He realized that his hands were shaking as he opened the box to see the stacks of bills he'd accumulated. Not nearly enough to disappear. He'd told himself that he needed at least one more good summer before he could move on. Now he realized that had been a lie. He'd liked Buckhorn. Even though he'd known it was dangerous, he'd stayed.

For years, he'd made a point of never staying long in any one place. But he'd made a mistake in Buckhorn. He'd been content there, and he'd let himself believe that no one was still looking for him. He'd lived on the run for so long, always looking over his shoulder, always moving on before he got too settled and people started asking too many questions.

Pulling out the duffel bag he'd brought to carry the money in, he knew this was his fault. He'd stayed too long. He'd got to believing that he was safe. In the middle of nowhere and miles from the interstate, only a few tourists wandered through in the summer. Not that he saw them. He let Bessie sell his wooden products so he never had to deal with the public.

The last thing he'd ever expected was a beautiful green-eyed woman to walk into his shop and turn his world upside down. Clearly, she had the wrong man. That man she told him about was long buried. But he knew Earl Ray was right. She wouldn't stop digging into his past and worse, he didn't know how to convince her that he wasn't the man she was looking for. But she'd certainly reminded him why he needed to keep moving.

He thought of the look on her face when she'd opened her eyes after fainting in his workshop. He hadn't understood it at the time, but now after what Earl Ray had told him… His heart ached for her. She was chasing a ghost, whether her husband was alive or dead. The man was gone. She was never going to find him and bring him home, that much he knew. People changed. They disappeared into someone unrecognizable.

He should know. He'd been running from the past almost as long as she'd been looking for hers. His heart went out to her and the pain he'd seen mirrored in those amazing green eyes.

His first instinct was to run and get as far as possible from Buckhorn and this woman. He had nothing to offer her and wasn't sure he could convince her of the mistake she was making.

But what had made him realize he had to leave right away was what Earl Ray had told him about her having a second chance for happiness. He'd seen the big diamond on her ring finger and glimpsed the man a couple of times in town. He looked decent enough. She'd be a fool not to take hold of this new life she was being offered and not let go. He certainly didn't want to be the one to stand in her way. Once he was gone…

Jon began to stuff the money into the bag. Running was the only choice he had, he told himself. He couldn't look back. It was best for all of them, especially for her. He stopped loading the bag as he thought of what she would do when she found him gone. When she pushed open the workshop door, when she asked his landlady, when it was discovered that he'd run without a word. He imagined the look on her face, what he would have seen mirrored in her eyes.

With a curse, he slowly began to put the money back. He couldn't do this to her. Not after listening to her story about her husband and their daughters. He couldn't just disappear like her husband had—because she would keep looking for him or someone who resembled him. She would keep chasing a ghost.

Worse, she might give up her chance for happiness because of him. He didn't need that on his conscience. He had enough as it was. But staying in Buckhorn any longer had become dangerous. If he wanted go on living, then he had to convince her to move on.

He put the money back into the safety-deposit drawer and shoved the box back into its slot. He realized he'd have to hurt her, but it might be the only way to give her a little peace. There would be no peace for him, though, he knew. If anything, the woman and her questions about him would probably get him killed.

But as he drove out of town, he told himself that if this had to end, then let it end in Buckhorn.

"Kate, come on. Think about what you're saying." Collin raked his hand through his hair. Since he'd found Jon gone, they'd continued to have the same argument. She could see that he was losing his patience. She understood his frustration. Everything he said was true. Unfortunately, that didn't make any difference to how she felt.

"Why would he leave if he isn't Danny?" she demanded. That was the question that she kept asking herself.

Collin swore. "Because he didn't want you coming back

to his workshop day after day." He rubbed a hand over his face. "Baby, why would you want him even if he *is* your dead husband who left you not once but *twice*. Take the hint. He doesn't want you. He left to get away from you." He must have seen how his words landed on her and instantly stepped to her. "I'm not trying to hurt you. But Kate, we're engaged to be married. I love you. I want us to spend the rest of our lives together. I thought this trip would be the beginning of something good for us. This man can't offer you *anything*—even if he wanted to."

"Maybe he's not gone for good."

Stepping away from her, Collin let out an explosion of air. "So, what are you going to do? Sit around here and wait to see if he comes back? Is that what you want to do? You want to break up with me for a shot-in-the-dark chance that this man is your husband, let alone that he's going to miraculously remember you and want you again? Are you really going to live in that cabin out back of his workshop? Sell your house in Houston and spend winters in this town? Or are you planning to move him into your home in Houston? Maybe he could run his workshop out of your garage. Think about what you're doing, Kate."

He made it sound so ridiculous that she couldn't help but see what a fool she was being. "You're right," she said. Jon Harper had left. She had to accept that, even if he was Danny, he didn't want her or need her. He just wanted to be left alone. How much clearer could the man make it?

"Can we get something to eat before we leave town?" she asked, feeling weak and shaky. She felt sick at what she'd done. She'd run Jon Harper out of town. She hadn't thought about what he wanted or needed. It had been all about her. All about finding Danny and her fantasy of bringing him home. Not to mention what she'd done to her relationship with Collin.

"Then I'm ready to leave with you," she said. "I'm sorry I've put you through all of this."

The relief on Collin's face made him step to her and take her again in his arms. "We'll get something to go at the café, and then we're out of here."

She nodded against his shoulder, wondering if she was going to be able to eat a bite. She couldn't believe Jon would leave like that unless everything Collin had said was true.

If Jon Harper was Danny, he wanted nothing to do with her. Which meant he'd recognized her the first time she'd stepped into his workshop. He didn't have amnesia. He'd never had amnesia. He'd simply walked away the day of the explosion and never looked back. He'd left her and the girls. Just as he'd left her again today. He didn't want her. Worse, he didn't want her coming after him anymore.

And if she was wrong and Jon Harper wasn't Danny? Then what she'd done was even worse because she'd run a complete stranger out of town. Worse yet, she'd wanted a complete stranger over Collin.

"Could we walk to the café?" she asked him. "I need the fresh air." She wasn't ready to get into the rented SUV. She needed to clear her head. She thought she might be sick to her stomach.

Collin stepped outside to turn off the car engine. Together they walked down to the café through the falling snow, since driving a block made no sense anyway— except for the fact that he was anxious to get going.

She breathed in the frigid air, feeling the snowflakes like feathers on her face. The deep snow pulled at her boots, making her drag through it, making her feel as if this place was trying to pull her down. She'd thought she'd been ready to move on with Collin. Now she knew that once this trip was over, so were they. A deep sadness filled her. She just wanted this trip to be over. She wanted to go home and lick her wounds. Even as she thought it, she wondered if she would ever be the same.

As she watched the snow falling silently over her, she yearned to see blue sky and sunshine, wishing they'd never come to Montana. If they hadn't, she would never have seen Danny again, her heart told her. Because no matter what a mess she'd made of their lives in this small Montana town, her heart knew that Jon Harper was Danny. Hadn't her deepest desire been to see him one more time?

Collin held the door into the café for her. He looked cross when all the patrons turned to look at them. He muttered something under his breath and practically shoved her in. She hated that she'd embarrassed him. But at the same time, she'd saved them both from making a terrible mistake. Her behavior here proved that she wasn't ready to move on. Right now, she doubted she ever would be.

They took a booth. Bessie seemed surprised to see them still in town. "I thought the part came in," she said as she brought over two glasses of water and two menus. "Is the highway closed again?"

Collin shook his head. "Thought we'd better have something to eat before we leave." Kate felt his gaze on her. She knew she must look the way she felt, miserable. This trip had been about celebrating their engagement. She'd ruined it. She'd always dreamed that when she found Danny, he would know her in just one look. He'd remember what they had had and would come back to her. She'd been such a fool.

"Can we get it to go?" Collin asked.

"Smart," Bessie said, her gaze lighting on Kate. "You look a little peaked."

Kate picked up her menu. The words blurred before her eyes.

"How about a couple of deluxe cheeseburgers, fries and two chocolate milkshakes to go," Collin said, no doubt seeing her distress. Either that or he was just anxious to leave.

Bessie took their menus and went to place their orders.

"I'm sorry," Kate whispered as she wiped at scalding tears.

"Me, too." He pulled out his phone and began to answer a text and swore under his breath.

"Bad news?" she asked.

He shook his head as he pocketed his phone. "Just another delay. Nothing to worry about. My associates won't be able to meet us until day after tomorrow. Not a problem. It will just give us more time to see more of Montana."

She nodded, having had enough, but saying nothing. She'd put him through so much and yet all she wanted to do was ask him to take her to the nearest airport so she could fly home. What was the point now of going to Canada to meet his associates? Maybe once they were on the road, she'd ask. He probably wanted to see the last of her as it was.

Bessie brought out their burgers and fries in a brown paper bag, the grease already soaking through the paper. The smell made Kate's stomach roil. The woman handed them each a milkshake in a foam cup with lids and two straws. "Have a nice trip." She seemed to hesitate, her gaze on Kate again. "Be careful." With that, she took the money Collin gave her, thanking him when he told her to keep the change, and hurried back to the kitchen.

Kate noticed the looks they got as they left the café. Why did she feel as if she was letting everyone down, not just herself but these people as well? Collin took her arm and steered her out, letting the door close behind them. Snow swirled around them in this snow-globe world of white. She felt dizzy from the whirling flakes, from the cold, from the emotions, from the unshed tears that lodged in her throat and made her chest ache. She huddled down into her scarf and the collar of her coat against the bite of the wind and air crystals that stuck to her face and eye-lashes.

"I'm getting a little sick of this stuff," Collin said as they headed back toward the motel and their waiting car. "But I promised myself that you would finally get to see snow. Still want to make a snow angel?"

"Maybe we should cut this trip short," she suggested and then saw his expression and wished she had bitten her tongue instead.

"I've already told my associates we would meet them. I can't get out of that. Do you understand? This is impor-tant. It would raise too many questions if you don't come with me. You owe me this much."

"I'm sorry, but I don't understand why it is so impor-tant that I meet these men."

He sighed and raked a hand through his hair before his gaze came back to hers. "It was supposed to be a surprise, but since you won't let this go… I commissioned a special wedding dress for you."

"You what?"

"I saw this dress in a magazine. It looked perfect for you. My associates found a place in Canada that would make the exact one in your size. That's the other reason we're going to Canada."

"Oh, Collin." It was so thoughtful and so unexpected. She felt tears burn her eyes.

"I still have to pick up the dress and pay for it even if you…don't want it. But I wish you'd at least go to Canada with me. I'm going to look like enough of a fool to my associates when I pick up the wedding dress and I have no fiancée with me. After that, I'll be happy to put you on a plane—if that's what you want."

She nodded. "Of course. I'm sorry." He was right. This was the least she could do. "I'm just cold and tired and—" The rest of her words died on her lips as she looked across the street and saw the light coming through the crack in the carriage-house doors. Over the wind spinning snow-flakes through the air, she heard the high whine of a saw.

Jon Harper had come back.

CHAPTER TWELVE

COLLIN MUST HAVE followed her gaze and then seen her expression. "I'm putting an end to this right now!" he swore, shoving the bag of burgers at her as he threw down his milkshake into the deep snow before stomping across the highway.

Caught off guard, she watched him barrel toward the light glowing in the workshop. She felt fear for what he would do in the mood he was in. But her overwhelming emotion was one of euphoria.

Danny had come back. She wanted to laugh and cry at the same time. Her heart filled to overflowing. He hadn't run out on her. He never had. He just didn't remember her. And for some reason, he couldn't leave her this time.

For a moment, she didn't move, could hardly breathe. The bag holding the burgers had been greasy. Now it was wet from the falling snow. She spotted a trash can and dumped the bag and her milkshake into it. She felt scared. Her future hadn't been this uncertain since the day of the explosion. Would it make a difference what Collin said to him? Or what the man she knew was Danny said to Collin?

She started across the highway to follow Collin but stopped as he came rushing out of the old carriage house.

He saw her standing there, her arms akimbo, and slowed. She wondered if he saw the hope in her expression. Or the fear. Or maybe worse, how excited she was that the man had come back. Jon could have kept going, but he hadn't.

Collin walked across the highway toward her. He looked defeated. She felt an ache in her heart thick with guilt and relief and regret. He'd been so good to her and look what she'd done to him. She didn't want to hurt him. But she couldn't walk away from the man she believed was her husband. There had to be a reason why she was feeling this way. Why she'd felt that jolt the moment she'd seen him standing in his workshop. She wasn't wrong this time. Maybe more painful, she was still in love with Danny. She always would be. Maybe that's why she hadn't found another man—until Collin. Her heart had always been overflowing because of Danny's love.

COMING OUT OF the café kitchen, Bessie found a small crowd huddled at the front window trying to see through the frost on the glass and the falling snow outside.

"Seriously?" she asked as she joined them and saw that Lindsey was crying.

"What?" she demanded of the pregnant young waitress.

"It's just such a touching love story," Lindsey said. "She thinks Jon Harper is her dead husband. She's been waiting for him to come back for twenty years. She'd given up hope and agreed to marry Collin Matthews. He's the blond man she's with." As if Bessie didn't know that. "But then their car breaks down on their engagement trip, and she stumbles into Jon's workshop and sees him and knows in her heart he's her husband. Only he doesn't know her because he has amnesia."

"It sounds like a soap opera," Bessie said. "And where did you hear all this?"

"Shirley, at the motel. She said they yell a lot, and one day when she was cleaning an adjoining room, she heard them arguing about it." Lindsey wiped her eyes. "It breaks my heart. What if Jon really is her lost love?"

"I wouldn't believe everything Shirley says she's heard through a motel-room wall," Bessie said, though kindly. She knew that a lot of this was Lindsey's hormones at work. "And don't go spreading this story. They're leaving town."

"I wouldn't count on that," the cook said and pointed across the street. "Jon left, but he came back." Now in her fifties, Rene Carson had been passing through sixteen years ago after being dumped by her boyfriend. She'd come into the café hoping to earn enough money to catch a bus back to California and had ended up staying instead.

"Everyone in town already knows the story," said Vi Mullen as she peeled herself off the window to return to her seat. "She's not leaving." Mabel Aldrich nodded as she hurriedly returned to her seat in the booth across from Vi.

"She better not leave," the cook said and turned back to the kitchen. "I've got ten bucks in the pool. I'm counting on her to stay."

"I've got all my pin money on her staying," Mabel said.

"Don't tell me that people are wagering on this," Bessie said with disgust. "What is wrong with you? This is their lives you're gambling on."

"Rene's right. Jon is the love of her life." Lindsey was wiping her eyes again. "How can she leave him now that she's found him? It's so sweet."

Bessie didn't see anything sweet about it as she looked

out the front window to see Kate covered with falling snow as she stared at Jon's workshop. Collin Matthews was making his way toward her. Bessie could just imagine the conversation that had taken place with Jon and Collin into the workshop.

"It's more of a human tragedy than a love story," she said to herself before turning away.

When Collin reached Kate, he must have seen the tears streaming down her face. "Let's talk at the motel," he said, taking her arm. "It's freezing out here."

She still hadn't moved. Past him she could see that he'd left the one carriage-house door open. A familiar figure stood in the doorway. The man who called himself Jon Harper. She stared at him, her heart thundering in her chest, until he stepped back and closed the door.

"He's not Danny. Do you hear me?" Collin was practically yelling over the snow and the wind that whipped the flakes around them. "He says you're wrong. He wants you to leave town. He says he can't help you, he's sorry, but he isn't the man you want or need."

She didn't argue as she let him lead her back to the motel. The cold and his words made her feel numb, her tears freezing on her face and mixing with the falling snow that clung to her. She was so cold, so tired and yet so determined. Jon had come back. No matter what he said, there was something there between them.

Collin opened the motel-room door, no doubt thankful he hadn't turned in the key yet, and stood back to let her in. Always the gentleman, she thought, the ache in her chest worse at the thought.

"What are you going to do?" he demanded, his voice sounding hoarse with emotion or the winter cold.

"I have to stay. At least for a while."

He bit his lip as if to hold back his frustration with her. "Did you hear anything I said? This is another one of your mistaken identities, can't you see that? What do you possibly hope to accomplish by staying in this town? Hanging around a man who doesn't know you, doesn't want to get to know you, a man who just wants you to leave him alone?"

She shook her head, her throat constricting with the fresh tears she was fighting to hold back. She'd always been so practical. She hadn't fallen apart when she'd heard about the explosion or when Danny didn't call or when he was listed as one of the many missing and suspected of being burned beyond all recognition. She'd had two babies to raise and no time for a nervous breakdown.

"I'm so sorry about all of this," she said, knowing how this must look. Probably everyone in town thought she'd lost her mind. "You should go on and meet your associates, take care of business. I'm sorry about the wedding dress."

"And just leave you here?" He shook his head. "What if I don't come back?"

It wasn't a threat. It was a reasonable question. "You don't have to."

"Just like that?" He let out an angry breath and walked a few steps away from her. "I had no idea you were still so in love with him."

"Neither did I."

He turned back to stare at her, the look he gave her almost sympathetic. "I don't know if I'm coming back for you."

"I'll find a way to get to an airport when the time comes."

"When the time comes?" Collin asked. "And when is that?"

She shrugged. "I don't know."

He raked a hand through the snow crystals clinging to his now-wet blond hair and looked at the floor. "I don't know what to do. I certainly don't know what to say to you."

She slipped the diamond from her finger and started to hand it to him.

"No," he said adamantly. "Please, no. I'm not leaving you here alone. I have another two days before my meeting. Don't worry. I won't get in your way. I'll give you all the space you need to figure this out, but I'm not giving up on you. Not yet. There's a storm coming, but it isn't supposed to be as bad as the last one."

Kate looked down at the ring lying in her palm. "I can't wear this right now."

"Sure, I get it. Then, just hang on to it, because if I have my way, you're going to wear it again—along with a wedding band." He headed for the door. "I'm going to see if I can get another room. I don't really think it's going to be a problem."

She watched him go, feeling her heart break as she pocketed the ring. She'd never wanted this. She couldn't believe how understanding Collin was being. It was a struggle for him, she could see that. For her as well. How could she not love this man even more than her memories of Danny?

What *was* she going to do? This was idiotic. She couldn't just stay in this motel and visit the workshop each day. Nor could she let this go on any longer than it had to. She knew what Collin had said Jon had told him. But could he say that to her face?

JON HAD BEEN expecting her. He heard the old wooden door swing open and felt a gust of cold air and snow blow in. Turning, he saw her standing there, silhouetted against the storm, and felt his heart break for her. For a moment, he thought he couldn't do this. Taking a breath, he motioned her in and watched as she closed the door behind her.

"I'm sorry to be such a problem," she said, looking nervous and unsure of herself.

He could tell that it was something new for her. This woman was confident. He remembered what Earl Ray had told him about her raising her two daughters by herself and not just supporting herself all these years, but thriving. If she'd really been on her own for twenty years, well, she'd certainly managed better than he had.

"We can talk in my cabin," he said, thinking of her nice clothes. He couldn't have her sitting on that old stool that Earl Ray seemed to like. "It's warmer and not as dusty and dirty."

He led her out the back door, telling himself that once they talked, once she saw the way he lived, that would be the end of it. But he couldn't help being curious about her. Especially why she was so convinced he was her husband, Danny. But first he had to know about her fiancé.

"That man with you. He's your fiancé?" he asked as he pushed open the cabin door and stood back to let her enter.

"We only recently became engaged," she said and stepped in. "I've been a widow for twenty years. Sorry, I think I already told you that."

"You must have married young," he said as he followed her inside, slipping past her to go into the tiny kitchen area.

"Seventeen," she said. "My husband was eighteen. We'd been in love since we were kids growing up in Houston Heights. We would have been married twenty-two years this coming summer."

He slowed but didn't turn around as he entered the small kitchen. "So you're thirty-nine. Coffee?"

"I will be. Yes, coffee, please," she said behind him.

"Have a seat. That rocker's pretty comfortable by the stove." He realized that he hadn't spoken this many words in years. His throat hurt as it always did from lack of use and from the fire he'd breathed in that had burned and scarred him inside and out.

"Did you make this?" she asked.

He turned to see her stroking the sanded-smooth back of the rocker. "Yes." He felt uncomfortable, but then again he had since the first time she walked into his workshop. She thought she knew him. The way she looked at him was with such love that it embarrassed him. Because of her misplaced adoration, he didn't like her seeing the way he lived. Even though he'd never cared before what anyone thought.

But this woman wanted him to be someone he wasn't. Someone he'd never been. Surely she could see that now. He couldn't imagine though why she could ever think he was her dead husband. A man like him hiding out in an isolated town in Montana? Couldn't she see by looking at him that he had nothing to offer—even if he'd once been her husband?

That's why he'd wanted her to see the cabin, even as much as it hurt him to show her. She needed to see the way he lived, see him with all his scars in the bright light of the winter sun coming through the window. She needed to know that he was no one's savior. Anyone woman could do better, especially this one.

She sat down in the rocker as he brought out two chipped, mismatched mugs, filled them with coffee and handed her one. "Thank you," she said, looking up at him, then quickly down into the coffee as if embarrassed.

He watched her cradle her hands around the mug, still staring down into it, and felt a strange sense of intimacy. Maybe bringing her to his cabin had been a mistake. He worried that anything he did would be a mistake as he took a seat on the only other chair in the kitchen, one he kept pulled up to the small table. He didn't need another kitchen chair because he never had company. That too she must see.

When she looked up, he met her green eyes and thought he'd never seen anything so wide and bottomless, so beautiful, so trusting, so loving. He felt sick to his soul that he couldn't tell her what she wanted to hear. He could see the shards of her broken heart in those eyes when she looked at him. His heart ached to take away that hurt, knowing it wasn't his place even if he could.

"I wanted to ask about your husband," Jon said to break the unbearable silence. Normally, he loved the quiet. When Earl Ray stopped by, they often didn't talk, both comfortable without words.

But with this woman sitting in his cabin, he felt anxious. The sooner they got this cleared up, the sooner she could get on with her life. Also the sooner everyone's focus would be off him. He just hoped it would be soon enough. "He died in an explosion?"

"A refinery in Houston."

"I'm sorry." He took a sip of his coffee. It tasted bitter, but that was nothing new. "You never got to identify his body?"

She shook her head and looked around his cabin for a moment as if she knew where he was headed with this, since that would explain why she was convinced her husband was still alive. She'd never gotten the closure she needed.

"That must have been hard for you. You have two kids you said?"

"Two girls, Mia and Danielle. Mia was one and a half, Danielle just a few months old at the time. They're both adults now. Mia has her own graphic-design business and is very successful. Danielle is finishing college at Rice University. She wants to teach elementary school."

"I'm sorry, you did tell me that." He shook his head. "How did you manage by yourself? Did your husband have insurance?"

"No insurance, but there was a settlement from the refinery. I never touched that money, though."

He stared at her, his next words coming out too sharp. "Why not?"

She looked down again. "Because I always believed that Danny wasn't dead and that when he came back, we'd have to return it. I did invest it, though."

Smart lady. "So how did you live?"

"We had to move back in with my parents for a while, but I got a job editing and ended up a ghost writer." She looked embarrassed. "Apparently I have a talent for telling other people's stories."

"You can make a living doing that?" He couldn't help

his surprise. Everything about this woman came as a surprise, however, especially the depth of her love for her husband and her faith that he had somehow survived. He wished he were that man more than she could ever know.

"It wasn't easy, but we've done fine. The girls are strong, independent young women now."

"Like their mother," he said, thinking of how much she had accomplished and how little he had. Both of them had gone through their share of pain, but she hadn't let it defeat her. He reminded himself that now she had a chance for happiness. He couldn't bear that she might miss it because of him.

"You're engaged." He noticed that she wasn't wearing her engagement ring and swore silently.

"We were. I thought I could move on. I can't."

He didn't know what to say. This was not going the way he'd hoped. "I'm sorry about that. He says he loves you and wants to marry you."

She looked away again. "Can you tell me how you got your scars?" she asked quietly.

He'd known the question was coming. It always came up eventually. "Car fire." Those were just his visible scars. They both fell silent again. "Look, I'm sorry about your husband, but I'm not him. He sounds like he was a nice guy. I know he would want you to spend that death benefit, marry this man who obviously loves you and write *yourself* a happy ending."

"You have a slight Texas accent."

He took a sip of his coffee and put the mug down on the side table next to him, trying hard not to show his frustration. "Texas road construction. The twang, though, was from being born in Arkansas." He leaned forward, elbows to his knees. "Katie—"

Surprise registered all over her reddening face. "That's what Danny used to call me."

"Sorry, I thought your boyfriend said it was Katie."

"It's Kate. Kate Jackson."

"Kate, you seem like a really nice lady. I wish I was your husband, but I'm not. I'm just a guy with few prospects who only wants to be left alone."

She nodded, her cheeks reddening even more.

"I don't want to hurt your feelings," he continued. "But you don't belong here in this town or around me. I've nothing to offer you other than a mug of coffee—instant, at that."

She put down her cup on the edge of the small kitchen table and ran her hand down the arm of the rocker. "You make beautiful furniture."

"Thanks, but that rocker is one of my rejects. That's why it's in my cabin instead of sold last summer at the bakery Bessie owns. That's how I make my living, such as it is. I never stay anywhere long. Though, I've been in Buckhorn too long. If you come back through on your trip, I won't be here. That's the way I like it."

She seemed to study the arm of the rocker. "Even your rejects are beautiful. I suspect you're too demanding of yourself."

He chuckled at that. "That's me, too demanding of myself."

Kate raised her gaze to his. "I don't believe you." He started to explain that what he'd said had been sarcasm, but she cut him off. "That's how Danny was. He wanted so much for our little family. I worried that he would kill himself to make sure that we had everything we needed. He would have sacrificed himself for us. He was that kind of man. I suspect he did sacrifice himself. If he walked away that day, it was because he foolishly believed that he was worth more dead than alive."

Jon shook his head. "I hate what you've been going through for all these years. But isn't it time to put the past behind you, to move on, to find happiness with someone who has something to offer you? Let Danny go. He's gone. You can't bring him back."

Her smile shredded his heart. "I recognized you the moment I saw you. Maybe it was the way you were standing. Or your profile. Once I saw your hands, the long fingers, I thought of what your mother used to say. She always thought you should have been a pianist instead of a laborer." He tried to stop her, but she kept talking over him. "I didn't know heart-deep, though, until I looked into your eyes. Your eyes are sable brown and there has always been such kindness in them. Your eyes can't lie. They never could. I knew you weren't dead. I gave up hope when Collin came into my life. But in my heart, I knew that when I found you, I wouldn't be able to let you go no matter what."

"Kate—"

"Do you know who you really are? If so, why didn't you come back?"

He pushed away his coffee before turning his gaze on her. It hurt to look at her. He saw so much of the injured woman inside her, so much of her shattered heart, so much of the man who'd left her to fend for herself. "I told you, I'm not him. I wish I was so I could give you the closure you need. But I don't know this Danny you talk about. *I don't know you.*"

"But I know *you*. I'm staying in town."

He groaned inwardly. This was *exactly* what he didn't want. "Please don't do that. I know how badly you want me to be this man you once loved. Even if I was him, how many years has it been?"

"Almost twenty."

"Right. Twenty years. A love like the one you've told me about can't endure. People change."

"Not your heart. I can see it in your eyes. I don't know what happened to you or why you never came back. But somewhere inside you, you *know* me." She pulled her coat around her as she rose from the rocker. Her smile was filled with sorrow and pain and, worst of all, hope.

He cursed as he watched her go out his front door into the storm. "Katie," he whispered and felt such a pain in his chest that it doubled him over.

CHAPTER THIRTEEN

COLLIN STORMED AROUND the small motel room feeling like a caged animal. He couldn't believe this was happening. It was as if he'd never known Kate at all. The moment he'd returned to the room, he'd known where she had gone. Back to that man.

It was as if she'd lost her mind, and all over some two-bit woodworker in an old carriage house in the middle of Nowhere, Montana. What the hell was wrong with her? She'd seemed so smart, so together. Was she really ready to stay in this town with some stranger rather than go with him? What could she be thinking?

That was just it. He had no idea and that scared him. He felt as if he was losing her. He scoffed. Impossible. He had more to offer her than Jon Harper—even if the man *was* her long-dead husband.

But he wasn't. Jon Harper had made that perfectly clear when Collin had stormed into his workshop. He'd sworn that he wasn't Daniel Jackson. Why would he lie? It made no sense. The man had been adamant. But had Kate believed it? Hell no.

He told himself not to panic. He'd made a call to his associates in Canada. He had at least another day, maybe a little longer. Kate had no idea why it was so important that she went to Canada with him. So as long as he played it cool… But how was he going to convince her to come with him? If he could just find some solid proof that Jon Harper wasn't her dead husband.

He stopped pacing. It shouldn't be that hard to prove. He pulled out his cell phone. He had a friend in the Houston Police Department who owed him a favor.

"Nels," he said when the man answered. "I'm in a little bind. I need to know about a man named Jon Harper. Spelled J-O-N, apparently." When he'd been in the man's workshop, he'd seen a small plaque with the name carved in it. Must be so people knew who to write the check to for one of his masterpieces.

"Do you have any idea how many Jon Harpers there are in the world?" Nels demanded. "I'm going to need more than that."

"Like what?"

"DNA, fingerprints."

"Okay," Collin said, even though he didn't have a clue how he could get either. "I'll see what I can do. But I'm going to need an ID on him ASAP. Like in the next day or two."

"You've got to be kidding," the cop said. "Listen, I know I owe you, but you have no idea what you're asking. DNA would take days, if not weeks, and fingerprints won't do any good unless he has a record."

A criminal record. That could explain a lot about the man, Collin realized. "I'll get his fingerprints. I'll overnight them. I'm betting they're in the national database." He hung up. Hadn't he thought from the first that the carpenter had something to hide? Why else stay in this town?

If Collin were right, a man like Jon Harper would have a record. Which meant his fingerprints would be on file.

The hard part was getting his prints. It meant paying the man another visit.

KATE COULDN'T GO back to the motel. She was shaken after her visit with Jon. Seeing the way he lived broke her heart. It was as if he'd been punishing himself all these years. Doing penitence for walking out on her and the girls? Or did he really not remember her on a conscious level?

Inside his cabin, she'd gotten a good look at him. The light coming in the kitchen window had been blindingly bright. She'd seen the scars on his face and throat clearly. Just as she'd seen glimpses of the face that she'd fallen in love with all those years ago. When he looked at her… His brown eyes gave him away.

So why did he keep telling her that he wasn't Danny?

Because he honestly didn't remember her? But he'd called her Katie.

She knew that wasn't proof and that Collin could be right. Even if Jon was Danny, he didn't want her. Because she was a stranger? Or because he'd wanted out all those years go? If he had wanted her, he would have come back to her.

So why didn't she move on? Why didn't she leave with Collin? Maybe it wasn't too late to make a new life for herself. What *did* she hope to accomplish by staying here even a few more days?

She stepped into the café, moving to a booth away from the doorway and cold breeze that had followed her in. Through the front window, she stared out at the falling snow, convinced it was never going to stop. She wished for Texas and the humid warmth and the familiarity of her home. The security of it. The ignorance she'd had there. Only days ago, she'd never laid eyes on Jon Harper. Never seen Danny's eyes looking back at her. Never thought she'd find herself in this quandary.

Only days ago, she'd known who she was. Now, she was second-guessing herself. Even questioning her mental stability. And yet her heart swelled at even the thought of Jon Harper. She'd felt a connection the moment she'd seen him standing in his workshop that first day. Dust motes hanging in the air around him. His strong profile etched against the glow of the lamp—and her memory.

"I thought you'd be miles down the road by now," Bessie said as she appeared at the end of the booth. All Kate could do was shake her head. "Something tells me you didn't eat the lunch you got to go. When I feel like you look, food is the only answer."

Kate had to smile. Bessie—just like everyone else here—had encouraged her to leave as soon as she could. So, it surprised her that the woman seemed to be dispensing kindness, if not sympathy, today.

"What would you suggest?" Kate asked, knowing there was no food on this earth that was going to make her feel better. But she was ready to try anything.

"I have a batch of corn bread about to come out of the oven. I think a big piece with butter and honey to go with my ham and bean soup will do the trick."

Kate tried to laugh but it came out sounding more like a sob. "Why not?"

Bessie disappeared back into the kitchen. Kate watched the snow, hypnotized by the flakes sweeping past the window as she tried to rein in her emotions. The snow had risen higher on the window. If it didn't stop soon, she would suffocate under its cold, feathery flakes.

She wondered what Collin was doing. Probably losing his mind over her. Why didn't he just give up on her and leave? Did he love her that much? She took in a deep breath and let it out, afraid she was giving up her chance for happiness.

But even as she thought it, she knew that she could never be happy with Collin—not knowing that Danny was alive. She wasn't wrong. But, she'd been wrong before and that made her doubt herself. In her heart, though…

Shaking her head, she wondered how she could have thought that marrying Collin was a good idea when clearly she'd never gotten over Danny. Not even after twenty years of being alone. There was only one man she wanted. That alone broke her heart because that man didn't want her, even if she was right and Jon was Danny.

"Here," Bessie said, handing her a napkin to wipe her eyes. She put down a bowl of ham and bean soup and a plate of corn bread on the table, then pulled a bear-shaped plastic container of honey from her apron pocket.

Bessie slid into the booth opposite her. "Eat," she ordered. "You think you can't eat a bite, I know. But you can and you will because you need to, and I'm going to sit here until you do."

Kate fought back tears as she watched Bessie butter the bread and cover a piece with thick honey.

"Take a bite of my soup and a bite of the corn bread. It isn't that old dry box mix. Corn bread needs sugar in it, no matter what some of the old timers say."

Taking a bite of each, she chewed. The soup was hot and savory, the bread sweet and salty. Her stomach rumbled, and she realized Bessie was right. She hadn't eaten much since she'd left Texas, and she couldn't keep going the way she had been. She ate obediently as Bessie talked about everything from the weather to her favorite recipe to the weather again.

To Kate's surprise, when the woman finished talking, Kate had finished the bowl of soup and the corn bread.

"Better?" Bessie asked.

She nodded, feeling more like her old self. She'd been strong for so long, capable and determined. Seeing Danny in Jon Harper had definitely thrown her for a loop, but she would get through this. She had to. "Do you think I'm delusional?"

"Probably," the older woman said with a laugh. "But aren't we all sometimes?"

She looked into Bessie's blue eyes. "I know it's him. I know it in my heart. I see it in his eyes. I just don't know what to do about it."

Bessie nodded. "Let's say he's the man you think he is. He must have his reasons for telling you he isn't. Maybe you should trust him."

Kate hadn't realized that he might be running from something other than her. Other than the explosion that had scarred him inside and out, changed his body and his voice and maybe even his will to be that person she'd known and loved?

"You think I should leave town." It really wasn't a question, but Bessie answered anyway.

"Honey, you seem to have a man who loves you, wants to marry you," she said quietly. "What about him?"

Kate shook her head. How could she marry Collin when she'd given her heart away to Danny and never gotten it back? Jon had made it clear that she was wasting her time. He'd almost convinced her that she was wrong about him. Almost.

"Not everyone gets a second chance at love," Bessie was saying. "You have one, and you're still young. You still have a lot of life ahead you. I'd be real sure before I threw that away. Maybe you should take what's being offered you and not look back." Bessie rose to take her dirty dishes to the kitchen. "Maybe you should leave Jon to be the man he is now."

WHEN COLLIN CHECKED and Kate still hadn't returned to her motel room, he walked down the highway through Buckhorn. He kept trying to curb his anger. This woman was going to be the death of him, literally. He'd been patient, waiting until she was ready to put the past behind her and marry him. This trip was to be a beginning. And now this?

Outside the café, he'd looked in to see her sitting in a booth with Bessie. He'd turned away quickly before either of them saw him. He couldn't help feeling relieved. At least Kate wasn't with Jon Harper.

Just the thought of the man made his temper boil up again. Kate was still determined to stay here until who knew when. Something had to give, because he and Kate would be crossing the Canadian border tomorrow evening before the small border crossing closed. He wasn't leaving her here. She was coming with him.

He realized there was only one way to convince Kate to go—but only if he could prove that Jon Harper wasn't her husband. He swore as he crossed the highway and shoved open the door into the workshop.

Jon turned, putting down the mug of coffee he'd been drinking. He didn't look happy to see him.

"So, what all do you make here?" Collin asked conversationally as he closed the distance between them. He picked up a board the man had been working on.

"Rockers mostly."

"Huh. In different sizes?"

Jon nodded. "I make some toys."

Collin could see that the carpenter wondered what the hell he was doing back here. "What's this you're making?" he asked as he drew Jon away from the workbench. "What do you get for something like this?"

"A couple hundred," Jon said of the full-sized rocker.

"That much, huh? How long does it take you to make one, though?"

"A month at least."

Collin swore in surprise. "Not much of an hourly wage."

"It isn't about that."

"No?" he said. "What is it about?"

"I like making things with my hands."

Collin nodded distractedly as the carpenter loaded more scrap wood into his stove. "I just wanted to let you know that Kate and I are leaving tomorrow. Together."

"That's good to hear," Jon said, finishing what he was doing and closing the woodstove door. "I hope you have a nice trip."

Sneering, Collin walked out.

IT WASN'T UNTIL the man left the workshop that Jon glanced toward the workshop bench. He'd wondered what Collin's real reason was for stopping by. Now he knew.

His mug of coffee was gone. He could see a dark spot on

the dirt floor where the coffee had been poured out when he'd turned his back. Probably when he'd put more wood in the stove. He could think of only one reason the man had taken his coffee mug—and it wasn't for a souvenir.

He leaned against his workbench, sick with the knowledge.

Worse, he'd seen something in Kate's fiancé that made his gut roil. He told himself that just because he didn't like the man didn't mean there was anything inherently wrong with him. But he couldn't help wondering if Kate really knew who she had promised to marry.

Trying to stay calm, he considered what to do. He'd pushed her toward this man, believing it was the best thing for her. Now he wasn't so sure. The man had taken his coffee cup. That meant he knew someone who could get prints or DNA off it. Once those prints went into the national database, the authorities would know exactly who he was—and worse, *where* he was.

He swore. This was a game changer. He hadn't wanted it to come to this. But wasn't something like this what he'd feared if he couldn't convince the woman she wasn't the man she was looking for? Now he was down to two options. One was to leave immediately and keep going. He would have to empty out his security box and ditch his old pickup right away. Trouble would be hot on his tail. He wasn't sure he could run far or fast enough before they caught up to him and killed him.

Running meant leaving Kate Jackson to that wiseass who'd just been in his workshop. All his instincts told him that Collin wasn't who he was pretending to be. But then neither was he, Jon reminded himself with a curse. Which meant his second option was even worse.

Once his prints hit that database and he hadn't run, he was as good as dead. Worse, he would bring his trouble to Buckhorn. But he couldn't just let Kate marry this man until he knew for sure that Collin Matthews was good enough for her.

Which meant he had to move fast.

CHAPTER FOURTEEN

YESTERDAY, AFTER HIS visit to Jon Harper's workshop, Collin had taken the mug he'd lifted from the workbench straight to the post office. The post office was almost a joke: a small wall of numbered metal boxes and a tiny window with a plate that read *Postmistress Vi Mullen*.

He'd peered in, seen no one. "Hello?" No answer. He'd heard rustling somewhere in the back behind the small bank of postal boxes. "Hello!" he'd called louder.

That's when he'd noticed the bell. It was silver and round with a small dinger on top. He had shaken his head in frustration. He'd known that she'd heard him call out to her. She'd just been waiting, determined he was going to ring her damned bell.

He'd slammed his hand down on it. The bell had practically skittered off the narrow ledge of the counter through the tiny window. He was about to hit it again, when the bell had been whisked away by a small pale hand.

The face that had appeared on the other side of the opening made him jump. A pair of ball-bearing-dark eyes had glared at him from a wizened, ghost-white, hard-angled face. Her pursed lips had only accented her wrinkles.

"Yes?" she'd snapped. Vi Mullen had appeared to be in her late fifties going on seventy.

"I need to send a package." He'd wrapped the cup in a page from a newspaper at the motel since that's all he had. "I need a box for this."

She'd considered what he held, then had shrugged and disappeared for a few moments before returning with a box. "Is it breakable?" Clearly it was. "You'll need some of this." She'd shoved a small roll of plastic Bubble Wrap through the hole. "I suppose you don't have any tape." Had he looked like he had tape? She'd shoved some of that through the opening along with a pen that had feathers taped to it. So no one pocketed it?

"Over there," she'd said, pointing to a small counter and then she'd gone again.

He'd muttered to himself as he'd taken everything over to the counter and carefully wrapped the cup in Bubble Wrap, then put it into the box. After writing the address on the box, he'd returned with everything to the arched window to ring the bell again.

She'd appeared at once and had begun to add up his bill.

"Wait, you're charging me for the roll of tape and this whole roll of Bubble Wrap?"

"The US post office doesn't supply tape or Bubble Wrap for nothing," she'd said primly.

"Well, I don't want or need the rest of it. Is your supervisor around?"

She'd smiled at that. "I'm Vi Mullen, postmistress," making it clear she was the boss. Her eyes had narrowed. "And you're that fella staying at the motel with that brunette."

He'd hated the way she denigrated his relationship with

Kate. "She's my *fiancée*. We're getting married." Her look said she'd known better.

"From Texas, I heard. Strange time to be taking a trip to Buckhorn."

"We weren't *taking a trip to Buckhorn*. Our rental car broke down." As if she didn't know that.

"Still," she'd said, eyeing his package and the address he'd written on it.

He'd remembered what Lars had told him about his live-in girlfriend's mother. *"Vi's the worst gossip in town."*

"Doesn't seem like there would be much to gossip about," Collin had noted. "Does anything ever happen in this town?"

"You'd be surprised," Dave had said and then quickly walked away. Lars had looked down into his beer and changed the subject.

"I need to overnight it," he'd told the woman, and she'd let out an irritated sigh and started to redo his bill. "Will it get there by tomorrow?"

"Should now that the highway's open," she'd said and asked if what was inside was liquid, perishable…

He hadn't caught the rest. "No," he'd told her. She'd seen that it was a cup. Was the woman just being difficult? He'd handed her the money. "I don't want the tape or the Bubble Wrap." He'd shoved it back through the opening.

She'd pursed her lips again but had taken the items back. "You paid for it."

"I did. Now you can charge the next sucker for it who walks in here."

With that done, he'd left, feeling as if a huge weight had been lifted off his shoulders. With luck, he'd find out the truth about Jon Harper. He was convinced the man was hiding here in this town because he had a criminal record. But more important was proving that Jon wasn't Daniel Jackson. Once that was done, he figured Kate would finally knock off her fantasy about rekindling with her dead husband, and they could leave.

The day had passed with him spending much of it at the bar. He was running out of money, though, and worried things would get worse before they got better. Back at the motel, he asked Kate to dinner, but she said she'd already eaten. So they'd gone to their separate rooms.

This morning he'd texted her, asking her if she wanted to meet at the café for breakfast. He'd been in a good mood after receiving confirmation this morning that Nels had received the package.

Now as he walked up to the café, he told himself that he could still make this work with Kate. Could he marry her and be happy? Happy enough, since he wouldn't have to worry about the necessities. He could depend on Kate to pay for those, while he ran his businesses behind the solid domestic front she would provide.

He just worried that what had happened here in Buckhorn could make that impossible. Even when he proved that Jon Harper wasn't Daniel Jackson—and exposed the carpenter for the man he really was—Collin didn't see her marrying him now. She didn't look at him the way she had before this trip. She'd broken the slender thread that had connected them. Not that he'd ever felt she was as crazy about him as she should have been. It made him wonder if he could ever trust her.

But he wasn't ready to throw it all away just yet.

He had a new plan. Which meant he couldn't let on what

he was thinking. He had to play the role of the understanding fiancé just a little while longer.

EARL RAY KNEW the moment he saw Jon that things had gone badly. He'd tried to warn the young man. Or at least let him know what was at stake so he could decide how he wanted to handle it.

But from the look on Jon's face, things had gotten worse. Not that Earl Ray hadn't heard about what was going on through the Buckhorn grapevine—which was very short and fast in the winter months. Kate and Collin were staying another night—but were now in separate rooms. At least that's what Shirley at the motel had said. And Kate had been visiting Jon's shop while her fiancé, Collin, had been spending more time at the bar. If that didn't spell trouble, he didn't know what did.

"Do you still have some of your old connections?" Jon asked without preamble.

Earl Ray didn't bother pretending that he didn't know what the young man was talking about. Not that he'd ever told Jon anything about what he'd done in the military. Everyone believed he was the town's local war hero. He had the medals. He just hadn't been on the front line as that kind of soldier.

"I need to know about the boyfriend," Jon said.

Earl Ray's raised a brow. "Kate Jackson's fiancé?" he asked, just to be clear.

Jon limped over to the window and looked out. He was limping worse than usual. No doubt it was the stress. Did he think he'd been followed? From his expression he was worried—and not about the woman's fiancé.

"What's happened?" Earl Ray asked, knowing it was even worse than what he'd heard on the grapevine.

Jon turned from the window. "Collin Matthews paid me a visit. He stole the coffee mug I'd been drinking from."

Earl Ray didn't need to ask what that meant. "What do you know about him?"

"Just what Shirley at the motel told me, so little more than his name. He used a credit card for the room. When he went to get the second room for himself, the card was declined, and he had to use another one. Sounds like he doesn't have as much as he pretends. I'm betting he comes from money, but I'm curious how he makes his own now."

"You sound suspicious."

"Just a feeling. One more thing. Kate Jackson. From what she said, she might be well-off or at least comfortable. I need to know if that is true." Earl Ray raised a brow, making Jon shake his head. "I'm not interested in her money."

"But you think Collin might be."

"I'm worried about her. I suspect he's marrying her for the wrong reasons. Can you find out as soon as possible? I'm not sure how much longer they're going to be in town."

Earl Ray nodded. What Jon didn't say but what he heard was that the man didn't know how long he would be in town, either. "You told her you weren't the man she was looking for?"

"I told her."

"She didn't believe you," he guessed and didn't need confirmation. He saw the answer on Jon's face. "Still thinking about leaving?"

"I did leave. I had to come back. I couldn't have her thinking I was that man she married in Texas. I was afraid she would keep looking for me."

"No, you couldn't have her believing that," Earl Ray said.

He either ignored the jab or didn't hear it. "I'm doing my best to convince her otherwise."

"I know you are. But I have to ask—"

"No, you don't," Jon said as he headed for the door. "You know me. Thanks for doing this for me. I want her to have that happy ending, so I hope this guy is on the up-and-up."

"Me, too," Earl Ray agreed. "She seems like a nice young lady who's had a lot of heartache."

"Haven't we all." Jon hesitated. "If you ever want to talk about what it takes to move on with your own life…"

He got the message. Everyone had their secrets and their weaknesses, some more than others. He stepped closer to cup Jon's shoulder with his large palm and said, "I wonder what the chances are of this woman showing up here in the middle of winter and just happening on you? Do you believe in divine intervention? How about destiny?"

"That would only be the case if I was Daniel Jackson, now wouldn't it? Otherwise, it is just one misguided, heartbroken young woman with the rest of her life in front of her—if she can break away from what's holding her in the past."

"And how are you going to help her do it?" Earl Ray asked.

He shook his head. "First I have to know if Collin Matthews is the right man for her."

"And if he's not?"

Jon swore under his breath. "Let's hope I'm wrong."

BREAKFAST WITH COLLIN was beyond uncomfortable. The entire meal was strained, even though he seemed to be his old self, laughing and joking and telling her how beautiful she looked this morning. If she hadn't seen that other Collin, she might have bought at least some of it. She wondered why he'd suggested breakfast at all, since he'd barely touched his food and neither had she. He was antsy, although he tried to hide it.

Kate watched him check his phone, something he'd been doing all through the meal. Clearly, he was expecting a call. From his *associates*, as he called them.

"I have to go," he announced to her relief. Rising, he said, "I have some business to take care of. I'll see you back at the motel." He left her at the café to finish her coffee and pay the bill.

When he'd gone, she realized that he hadn't asked her what she planned to do for the rest of her day. The days were so short here in the winter. While it had stopped snowing, it was still gray and cold out.

"Tomorrow's supposed to be pretty," Bessie told her as she refilled Kate's cup. "Sun's going to shine. Bet you're ready for that."

Kate nodded and tried to smile. She should be happy. Collin had said during breakfast that if she wasn't ready to leave by tomorrow, he would go alone. She could stay as long as she needed to, he'd said. He would check back with her after he finished his business.

So, why didn't she believe him? Because it felt too easy? Because she suspected he was trying too hard to please her? She hated that she was questioning his motives. He had every right to be angry. They were supposed to be on their *engagement* trip. And here she was in love with another man.

She glanced across the highway toward the old carriage-house woodshop. The light was on and had been since early this morning when she'd walked down here to meet Collin. She no longer asked herself what she was going to do. That was probably the same reason Collin hadn't bothered to ask. Because like her, he already knew. She was staying for as long as it took.

Finishing her coffee, she rose to pull on her coat and head across the street. She didn't know what she hoped to accomplish. She just had to be near Jon Harper. Nor did she have any idea if he would allow that to happen or if he would leave town as he'd said he probably would. So far, he'd put up with her visits and her stories about her and Danny and the girls.

She didn't think he would turn her away and tried not to make more of that than it probably was. He was a nice, kind man who felt sorry for her. Even though it hurt, it was enough for now.

JON COULD FEEL the clock ticking. Yesterday he'd seen Collin Matthews head down the street carrying something. The coffee mug. The man was walking in the direction of the post office—just as he'd known Collin would. Now it was only a matter of time before the truth came out.

But this morning all he could think about was Kate. He knew she would be stopping by his workshop. He had a rocker he wanted to finish, one he'd promised to Tina Mullen. He just wasn't sure there would be time before he had to leave.

But he couldn't leave until he heard back from Earl Ray. Once he left, Kate would go with Collin. Jon couldn't bear the thought that he would have thrown her together with the wrong man for her. Unless his suspicions about the man proved wrong.

As he'd showered and dressed for work, he'd felt an excited anticipation that upset him more than his impending death. He wanted to see Kate again, as foolish as it was. He knew he would have to leave soon—to protect her. Or maybe her fiancé would talk her into going with him before that. Either way it would leave a hole in his heart, one she'd made. One he had no choice but to keep letting her make because he couldn't send her away.

At the creak of the door opening, he turned to see her silhouetted against the light and snow. She hesitated for a moment before she stepped in and closed the door behind her. He caught the hint of her perfume and felt his pulse jump. For so long, he had lived like a hermit, staying clear of anything that could bring his downfall. He'd known the first time she'd walked into his workshop that she was dangerous, because she reminded him of what he'd missed, the lies he'd told himself about what he could live without. When he'd forced himself to go back to work after her first visit, his hands had trembled.

For so long, he had closed himself off from the world. He'd numbed himself against feeling anything other than tired at night after he'd worked in his shop all day. He hadn't wanted to feel or remember or list his regrets. He'd been content if not happy. It had been enough.

"Could I just sit here and watch you work?" she asked.

He heard her start to pull up Earl Ray's stool and said over his shoulder, "You're welcome to sit in the rocker." He didn't dare look at her. He'd brought the rocker out of his cabin this morning, telling himself he might as well let Earl Ray use it instead of that old stool.

Lying to himself had become a habit, he realized. He'd brought it out for her, hoping she would stop by. He heard her sit down, slip off her coat as if settling in and staying for a while. He felt himself begin to relax as well as she began to talk. She had a melodious voice that was easy to listen to as he worked. She talked first about the weather and how tomorrow the sun was supposed to come out. Then she talked about Texas, growing up there.

He knew that eventually she would get to Daniel Jackson, the boy next door who she'd fallen in love with as a young girl. She talked about how their parents had tried to keep them apart but how they couldn't stay away from each other, until finally they'd taken off and eloped, Kate lying about her age. How excited they were when Mia was born and then Danielle, and how Danny, as she called him, never complained about working two jobs.

"He built the girls a big dollhouse," she said, a smile in her voice as she recalled their lives together. "He had so much fun doing it. All the little details, like the shutters and the stairs and the curtains at the kitchen window. He was good with his hands. He used to whittle, too. He carved all the furniture for the dollhouse. It took him a while because he got home so late from his jobs, but even when he was exhausted after such a long day, he would sit on the porch and whittle something for the girls. It was his tireless patience that I admired the most. And his love for me and the girls." Her voice broke.

Jon said nothing as he continued to work. The workshop filled with the sound of only his hand-sanding or the crackle of the fire in the stove. A few minutes later, he turned and saw that the rocker was empty. She'd slipped out. He'd stared at the closed door, wondering if she would be back. He hated the hope that rose in his chest—and the fear—that she would. Or worse, wouldn't.

Then he reminded himself that he couldn't stay in Buckhorn much longer. And neither could she.

COLLIN HAD KNOWN it was just a matter of time before his creditors got hold of his cell phone number and started dunning him. He'd held them off for as long as he could. Things were getting ugly, and they weren't even the kind of creditors who would break your legs. He had those, too, and they were the ones that had him running scared.

He told himself that once this business deal was done, he'd be fine. But even as he thought it, he knew it wouldn't be enough money for long. He had to think long-range. That was where Kate came in. She'd been his long-range plan—until she'd seen that damned carpenter.

Seldom was he at a loss as to what to do. But Kate losing her mind over some loner had come out of left field. Like anything could have prepared him for this. Now he was putting all his hope into proving that Jon Harper wasn't her Danny boy. But what if he was wrong? What if Jon Harper's criminal record was clean? What if he really was Kate's long-lost husband?

Of course, he wasn't.

But would she even believe him when he proved Jon wasn't Danny?

He pushed open the door to the bar, glad to see it almost empty except for Lars and Dave. Sidling up to the bar, he gave Dave a nod and took a stool next to Lars.

"Still here, huh?" Lars said, smiling as he motioned to Dave that he was paying for Collin's beer.

He picked up the draft Dave placed in front of him and

tilted it and his head in thanks to the man. "Leaving soon. At least, I hope so." His friend Nels had to come through for him. It was just a matter of running the prints. He tried not to think about what he'd do if Jon Harper's prints weren't on file. He was so sure the man was hiding from something and that usually meant a criminal background.

In the meantime, he wouldn't think about Kate. He was pretty sure she was with the carpenter right now in his cruddy little workshop. Just the thought made him take a gulp of his beer.

"Rough day already?" Lars asked with a sympathetic smile.

"There a woman in your life, Lars?"

Dave laughed and then quickly turned away. Lars picked up his beer and took a drink before answering. "Trust me, I have my own female problems. Maybe not quite like yours, but damned close. So, what are you going to do about it?"

"Have another beer," Collin said with a curse. "What can I do? My fiancée has lost her mind."

Both Lars and Dave said "Women!" at the same time. Dave poured them both a glass of beer and said, "On the house," and went into the back.

"If I want to get rid of my live-in, I'd have to give up where I live, where I work. Hell, I'd have to pack up and leave town before either she or her father got a gun and came after me."

"I suspect you're exaggerating," Collin said.

"I wish. On top of that? She's pregnant," Lars said and held up his hands. "It's not mine. I swear. Needless to say, my girlfriend is furious and threatening to have my nuts cut off."

He studied the man. "All that in this small town?"

"You want to know the worst of it? I have no idea whose baby it is. Everyone in town thinks it's mine, including my girlfriend."

Collin shook his head. "You might have it worse than me. Short of killing the live-in, pregnant fiancée, I don't know what to tell you to do."

Lars chuckled. "Don't think I haven't thought of it." Dave returned with a case of beer to stock the cooler, and Collin and Lars watched the news on the television over the bar while they finished their drinks.

Collin realized he'd found peace in the bar with these men. He didn't even mind if Kate was with the carpenter. Let her spend all the time she wanted with him. Wouldn't make a lick of difference come tomorrow afternoon when she was going to get into that rental car and head to Canada with him, come hell or high water.

He'd even let her look back fondly on this town and her carpenter all she wanted. It wouldn't do her any good. By then it wouldn't matter who Jon Harper really was. Because Collin had made up his mind. He wasn't going to let the woman ruin his plans. He couldn't. Too much was riding on this.

CHAPTER FIFTEEN

NOT LONG AFTER Kate left his workshop, Jon had gotten in his pickup and driven to Lewistown. He'd stopped by the bank, taken out all his money and closed his account. Then he'd walked around town until he realized he was hungry. He'd found a café and got something to eat. All the time, he found himself watching the people around him. He knew the kind of men who would be coming after him. He told himself he'd know them on sight.

But that didn't mean he'd have enough time to react. He realized he needed to start carrying his handgun from now on.

It was dark by the time he'd headed home.

Home? He definitely had stayed too long in Buckhorn.

He wondered if Kate had come by his workshop this afternoon. He'd had to leave, needing to get ready for his final exit. But also, he didn't think he could bear any more stories about her life with her husband and children.

Anxious to hear from Earl Ray, he worried. The more he'd thought about Collin Matthews, the more he feared Kate was in trouble. He couldn't shake the feeling.

As he drove into town, he was relieved that the rental

car was still in front of the motel. They hadn't left. His cell rang. Earl Ray.

"Tell me what you found out," he said into the phone as he took the call.

"Kate Jackson *is* well-off. She's made a good living and has substantial investments."

He thought of the payoff she'd gotten from the refinery as he got out of the pickup and went inside. She'd said that she hadn't spent it. Instead had invested it, apparently wisely. "And her boyfriend?"

"Collin Matthews did come from money. He inherited a bundle. He owns a string of small businesses in Houston. A laundry, a vending-machine business, a parking lot, a half dozen car washes."

Jon went through the cabin and out the back door into his workshop. "So, he's legit?" Jon wanted to be relieved, but he felt as if he was waiting for the other shoe to drop.

"He's up to his ears in debt. Gambling. He loses. A lot."

Jon stepped to the carriage-house doors and looked out on Buckhorn. "How deep in trouble is he?"

"Deep. I wouldn't be surprised if he was involved in money laundering through the businesses. If he isn't, he will be. I'm surprised the feds haven't red-flagged him. He might be in Montana looking for a way to pay off his gambling debts and get his head above water."

"By marrying Kate."

"I'm not sure that would be quick enough," Earl Ray said. "Bessie saw a map he was looking at on his phone at breakfast. He's headed for the Canadian border."

Jon swore. "Drugs?"

"If I had to guess, I'd say fentanyl. That's the hot one right now," Earl Ray said. "With so many states legalizing marijuana, it isn't worth getting caught sneaking weed over the border anymore. It crossed my mind that he might want Kate along. Fiancée, celebrating the engagement, looks better than crossing the border alone. Less suspicious. Or he could be just on a trip and always wanted to go to Canada."

"Why go to Saskatchewan otherwise? What would be the point? It looks just like Eastern Montana, only flatter." Jon rubbed his jaw, feeling the scars, knowing that the really bad ones were deep inside him. "I really was hoping this guy was legit and that she would marry him."

"Were you?" Earl Ray asked, an edge to his tone.

"You're barking up the wrong tree, my friend. I'm not her husband."

The older man sighed. "So, what are you going to do with this information?"

He ran a hand over his face. He hadn't slept well in years. But last night the nightmares had been worse. All the explosions and fires had felt so real as if they were burning him all over again. He feared they were premonitions of something worse that was coming.

"I just wanted to make some furniture, keep my head down, put in the rest of my time," he mused, knowing that everything had changed now.

"You don't have to get involved," Earl Ray said. "You could make an anonymous call to the feds and let them pick him up at the border. Of course, if she decides to go with him, she'll be an accomplice, but she'll probably get a lighter sentence at least."

Jon let out a bitter laugh. "You think I won't make that call? I told you. I don't know this woman. None of this has anything to do with me." Earl Ray said nothing on the other end of the line, as if he knew that when Jon wasn't having nightmares about explosions and fire, he was having sweet dreams about Kate.

"Then, do the sensible thing," Earl Ray said. "Leave and don't look back. Let her make the decision to go or not go with Matthews."

He shook his head, not even registering his friend's words. "You ought to hear the way she talks about her husband. You'd think Daniel Jackson was a *saint*. Nothing like me. Hell, no man could fill her husband's shoes. Certainly not me."

"Or Collin Matthews," Earl Ray said. "But like you said, it doesn't have anything to do with you."

COLLIN HAD APPARENTLY woken in a great mood, because when he came to her door the next morning, he was all smiles. Kate figured it was because he was planning to leave today. Yesterday he'd said he would go alone if she was staying behind. She hoped he hadn't changed his mind.

"I need to run a few errands this morning," he said. "Mind having breakfast without me?"

She hoped that her relief didn't show on her face. As he started to leave, she stopped him, realizing she wouldn't be able to eat a bite without getting this over with. She wanted him to know for certain that she wasn't leaving with him.

"Collin, I'm sorry you have to go alone," she said and braced herself for his angry response. "But as I told you, I'm staying." To her surprise, he smiled.

"I know, Kate. It's all right. You can stay here as long as you want. I wish you were going with me, but it appears you have made up your mind."

She hadn't expected this and felt choked up. "Thank you." It came out on a croaked whisper. "I'm sorry."

"No reason to be sorry. Sometimes things just don't work out like we planned them." He gave her a sad smile before turning and walking out the door.

She stood, still shocked and so relieved that she wanted to sit down and cry. She'd expected a huge fight and had been dreading it. Now she just felt weak and tired. Maybe once Collin left, she would be able to sleep again.

But she knew that he was only part of the problem. How long was she going to stay in this town and keep trying to reach the man who called himself Jon Harper? Eventually she would have to go home. She would have to go back to work. She had a book to write, and she missed her daughters.

For now, though, she would stay. She began to dress in her winter wear, her decision made. She would stay as long as she could. Maybe he would never remember her. Or maybe one day she would stop by his workshop and he would be gone.

Maybe she was being a fool, she thought as she finished dressing. She probably was, because if Jon Harper wasn't Danny, then she was in love with a complete stranger. And she could not explain that even to herself. It just was. And it scared her and exhilarated her and made her happier than she'd been in a very long time as she headed for his workshop.

BESSIE CAME OUT of the café's kitchen with two orders that hadn't been picked up to find everyone again pressed up against the front window, trying to see across the street.

"What in heaven's name is going on now?" she demanded. When a bunch of locals had come in, she'd thought it was because today was Fried Pies Day.

Now she realized why business had been so good lately. The café had the best view down the street of Jon's workshop. She put down the two plates of food and looked at her waitress.

Lindsey was in tears again but quickly wiped them away as she left the crowd at the window and hurried back to the kitchen where Rene had placed another order on the pass-through.

"She's over there again," Vi Mullen said as she moved away from the window, smoothing her blouse and taking her seat again. Clarice Barber kept peering out for a moment, before reluctantly joining Vi in her booth.

Bessie didn't need to ask who they were talking about.

"She isn't going to leave town," Mabel Aldrich crowed as she slid in beside Vi. "Best get your purse ready, Vi. You're going to lose this bet. Kate and Jon. It's love. She's found her true love. I'm so happy for him."

Bessie groaned. "I'm afraid you're all going to lose on this one. Clarice, I hope you're not involved in this."

"She's the one who started it," Tyrell Durham said with a laugh.

"I've got my money on her dumping the fiancé." Fred, dressed like his son in overalls from the garage, laughed as the two of them took their seats again in a booth and Lindsey brought out their orders. "I just wish she'd make up her mind."

"You're worse than a bunch of old women," Bessie joked.

"We *are* old women," Mabel said. "Except for Fred. He's just old." They all laughed, his son the loudest.

"Kate is making the right choice. Jon's a good man. That other one… My mother taught me not to say anything if I couldn't say something nice, so I'm not going to tell you what I think of him."

"She's right," Fred said. "Kate is better off with Jon."

Bessie shook her head. "I hate to disappoint you all, but this might not be the love story of all times. I have a bad feeling about how it will end. Not only are most of you going to lose your money, but someone's going to get hurt."

"She could be right," Vi cut in and lowered her voice. "The other day Collin Matthews came in and wanted to overnight a package to Houston." She nodded, seeing that she had everyone's attention. "It was a cup wrapped badly in a page torn from a newspaper. Still smelled of the coffee that had been in it. I knew I'd seen that cup before, so I asked Clarice about it."

Clarice nodded enthusiastically. "It was the same coffee mug that I gave Jon in our Christmas gift exchange."

Vi pursed her lips. "Now, what would Collin Matthews be doing with Jon's cup, let alone sending it to Texas?"

Bessie felt a tiny electrical shock move through her. Her gaze went to Earl Ray who'd been sitting quietly at the counter taking all of this in. His eyes met hers, and she saw the same worry there.

The door opened on a gust. Collin Matthews didn't seem to notice the awkward silence that fell over the place as he came in from the cold. Everyone had quickly gone back to their coffee or meals. Collin was busy looking at his phone as he slipped into a booth. He only glanced up when Bessie put a menu and a glass of water in front of him.

"Coffee?" she asked, thinking that she wasn't getting

involved in this love triangle. Yet as she waited for him to stop texting to answer her, she felt Kate could do a hell of a lot better.

COLLIN STARTED TO place his order when his phone rang. He glanced up, surprised how many people were having breakfast this morning at the café. He saw who was calling and said, "I need to take this," and, having no choice unless he wanted the whole town to hear, got up and went outside. He hadn't been expecting a call from his friend Nels until later in the day. Thinking he had hours to kill in Buckhorn, he'd decided to get a late breakfast after the beers he'd had at the bar. Wouldn't be that long before he'd be driving. He didn't know where Kate was, but he could pretty well guess.

"Are you sitting down?" Nels asked.

It was freezing cold outside, and he was in no mood for games. "Just tell me you have something good."

"You now owe *me*, buddy," Nels said. "I ran the fingerprints the minute I got the mug. I hadn't expected anything. Most people don't have their fingerprints on file. You can't believe what came up. You were right. His name isn't Jon Harper."

Collin swore, his breath coming out in a white puff of air. "Please don't tell me that it's Daniel Jackson."

"Nope, it's Justin Brown."

"Who the hell is that?" he demanded, stomping his feet to stay warm. When he glanced toward the window into the café, he noticed that everyone in there was watching him. He turned his back on all of them. Damn voyeurs. As if he didn't know they were following his life and Kate's. What else did they have to do in this godforsaken town?

"Justin Brown is just a cop who busted some mob-like crime syndicate in Oklahoma, of all places. Most of them went to prison, but they still had contacts outside. They hired some thugs to kill him. Blew up his car. They're still looking for him."

He couldn't believe this. "You're sure?"

"That's the name that matches the fingerprints on the mug. Justin Brown. One of the most wanted lawmen in the country. There's a bounty out on him. Not even *dead or alive*. Just plain *dead*."

"How much?" Collin asked.

"Not enough to get yourself involved in this mess, I can tell you that. This could get real ugly, fast. I wouldn't want to be around when these guys catch up to him."

Collin didn't know what to think. Hadn't he known Jon Harper was hiding something? But, while he'd thought the man was on the run and hiding out here in Buckhorn, Collin had never expected this.

"Do me a favor. Find out everything you can about Justin Brown, especially what he did before he became a cop, and let me know. Thanks. You're right, I owe you, and I'll make good on that when I get back to Texas." He disconnected and considered what to do with this information. All he knew for certain was that he no longer wanted a late breakfast. He needed a good stiff drink because all it would take was one phone call, and Jon Harper would no longer be a problem. As it was, Nels could be making that call right now.

CHAPTER SIXTEEN

KATE WAS SURPRISED that Collin hadn't already left. She'd gone to breakfast by herself. Bessie had made sure that she ate, sitting down to visit with her as if they were old friends.

After that, she'd gone to see Jon. Each time she pushed open the old carriage-house door, she was half-surprised to see him. Earl Ray had warned her that he might run. But each time, she was relieved to find him hard at work. She had seen that he was finishing a rocker as if it was for a customer. Was that all that was keeping him in Buckhorn?

She'd taken her seat in the rocker she knew he'd brought out to the shop for her. It was the same one that had been in his house—the one he felt wasn't good enough to sell.

Today, she'd told him about a summer day she and Danny had spent at the beach in Galveston. As she talked she could almost feel the salty spray on her face, smell the briny scent, sense the soft sand between her toes.

Jon had given no sign that he'd been listening, but she'd known he was. At times he had stopped for a few seconds, looked away as if remembering something before he'd returned to his work.

There was so much she had wanted to tell him, but

she promised herself there would be other days. She had slipped out, leaving him to his work, hoping he knew she would be back, praying he wouldn't run away from her, and fearing her stories of a past meant nothing to him because they hadn't been his.

And yet, she couldn't help the closeness she felt to him. Her heart always beat a little faster in his presence. Whatever the connection between them she felt, it was as real as the snow and cold outside his workshop. At least it was for her. She told herself she would keep trying. She wasn't giving up. Today there had been a moment when Jon had stopped working and looked at her. Their gazes had met and held. It was as if he was trying to reach out to her from some dark place inside him.

But the moment had passed, and she'd known it was time for her to leave. Talking about the past was exhausting enough without the weight of hope she felt each time she told Jon her treasured memories.

Now as she neared the motel, she saw with regret that the rental car was still parked out front of Collin's room. She'd hoped he'd left without telling her goodbye. Drawing closer, she saw exhaust coming from the back of the SUV. He had the engine running. She hesitated, not wanting to argue with him, hoping he was still congenial and would just leave. After all, he'd be back in a couple days. He hadn't wanted to leave her here. She figured he'd come back to try to convince her to leave with him.

As she started to reach for her motel room key, she realized the door was already ajar. She pushed it open and blinked into the dimness. Collin had her suitcase on the end of one of the double beds. He was just closing it.

"What are you—"

He cut her off before she could ask what he thought he was doing. Anyway, it seemed pretty obvious.

"I packed your suitcase for you," Collin said. "I heard from my associates. We're meeting them this evening on the other side of the border. Which means we have to leave now."

"*We?* Collin, we discussed this. You were going alone. I already told you—"

"I know what you told me, Kate. And I just told you. You're going with me."

"Collin," she said, stepping into the room and closing the door behind her to get out of the cold and away from any prying eyes. She'd gotten the feeling that Shirley only cleaned the motel room next to theirs when they were in one of theirs arguing. All day she'd felt as if she were being watched. "You can't force me to go with you."

He looked at the floor. His hands fisted at his sides. When he looked up, she saw that his face was flushed, and even though it was cool in the motel room, he appeared to be perspiring. "You don't seem to get it. I *need* you."

Was he still talking marriage? "After everything that has happened, I would think—"

"*Nothing's happened,*" he said too loudly for the size of the room. "This man has told you repeatedly that he *isn't* your husband."

She shook her head. "I don't believe him."

He scoffed at that. "I'd hoped that by now you would have come to your senses."

"I'm not delusional," she snapped.

"But you are incredibly gullible," he spat right back. "I'm curious. What were you planning to do? Stay here the rest of your life? Or are you still thinking that you'll take him back to Houston to live in your big house?" He let out a snort. "Even if he would go, he wouldn't fit into your life any more than you fit into his. I got news for you, baby—"

"Don't call me that. I'm not your baby. I'm a grown woman. I know my own mind."

"Do you?" He ground his jaw muscles as if holding back sharp words that promised to bring blood. "His name isn't Jon Harper. You got that much right, anyway. But it's also not Daniel Jackson. It's Justin Brown. He used to be cop. He took down some crime syndicate, and even behind bars, they want him dead. They have a bounty on his head. Someone already tried to kill him. Blew up his car. He's hiding out here. See why he wanted you to get lost and leave him alone?"

She stared at him, telling herself it was a lie. Just something he'd made up to try to convince her to leave with him. "That's not true."

"Oh, it is. I borrowed his coffee mug and sent it to a friend of mine. He ran the man's prints. There is no doubt. He's not your Danny, and all I have to do is drop a dime on him, and those mobster henchmen looking for him will come up here and—"

"You wouldn't do that." Even as she said it, she knew he would. If he was telling the truth…

She turned to pick up a sweater of hers that he had missed stuffing into her suitcase, her back to him, breathing hard as she tried to calm down. Jon wasn't Danny. Collin had found proof. Not that it mattered. She'd known he might not be. But there was something about the man. It was more than a resemblance to Danny. Had she fallen in love with Jon Harper…?

Would she be responsible for getting the man killed because of her feelings for him? Collin would make that call just to spite her if she didn't go with him.

Turning around to face him, she tried to reason with him. "Collin, I had no idea when we drove into this town that—"

"Yes, that we'd stop in some tiny Montana town in the middle of nowhere in the middle of winter," he mocked, "and you'd see your *dead* husband. Then again, are you sure it wouldn't have been some other town, some other man?"

"Don't say that. You don't know how much I hate this. I know I've spoiled your trip."

"You have *tried* to spoil it, that's for sure. This isn't what I wanted, either. I wanted to marry you. I thought we could make a good team. But now that's off the table, isn't it? Not that it matters. You are still going with me up to the border so I can make this meeting with my associates and pick up your wedding dress because I told them you were coming with me. You aren't going to make a fool out of me. After that, I really don't care what you do."

She stared at him. "Your associates will understand and I'll reimburse you for the cost of the dress."

He glared at her, an icy, brittle hardness in those blue eyes that she'd never seen before. "Kate," he said as if talking to an unruly child, "you *are* going with me." Getting her back up, she started to argue that she wasn't, but he cut her off. "Call Danielle." He held out his phone. "Call your daughter."

"*What?*" She looked at him, refusing to take his phone.

"Fine, I'll call her." He punched in a number on his cell phone.

"I don't want you involving my children in this," she

said emphatically. "Collin, are you listening to me?" She started to take a step toward him when she saw that the call had been answered already.

"Put Danielle on the phone," he said into his cell, his gaze on her.

She felt her eyes widen. Danielle didn't have a room-mate at the apartment she'd rented near the campus. Who had he just ordered to put her on the phone? All those thoughts raced around like caged hamsters in the seconds before he said, "Talk to your daughter, Kate." He shoved the phone at her.

Her hand trembled as she took it and put the cell to her ear. "Danielle?"

"Mom, what's going on?" Her youngest daughter sounded terrified.

Kate glared at Collin as she asked her daughter, "Who's with you?"

"Some man. Mom, he has a gun, and he said that if you don't do what you're supposed to, he's going to kill me."

All the air felt as if it had been vacuum-sealed from the room. She couldn't breathe, couldn't speak for a moment. Her murderous gaze was locked with Collin's. She was re-alizing with terror that she had no idea who this man was.

"Danielle," she said, surprised how calm her voice sounded, "don't worry. Just be safe. This should be over very soon. Tell me you're all right. He hasn't tried to—"

"No, Mom. No."

"Okay, just remain calm. Don't do anything to upset him, and I'll talk to you soon." She disconnected and held out the phone. "You hurt my baby, and I'll kill you myself," she said from between gritted teeth as he took his phone.

"No one is going to hurt Danielle, okay?" he said,

sounding like the man she'd agreed to marry. "Nor will I make a call on your…carpenter friend. *If* you cooperate. It's just a trip up to the border. We cross. You be calm, like you told your daughter. You be my fiancée on our engagement trip. You be the woman who's never been to Canada and wants to mark it off her bucket list. I meet my associates, we pick up your dress and we come back across the border."

She stared at him in disbelief. Had he lost his mind? Or was there more to this trip? "You really expect me to believe that's all this is about, meeting some associates and picking up a dress?" she demanded with a shake of her head. "You would kidnap my daughter for that?"

Now that she'd seen this other side of him, she hated to think what they would be bringing back across the border. Something illegal. Look at the extremes he'd gone to, determined to force her to go with him.

"Let's not argue about this," he said. "It's decided."

What had she gotten herself involved in? And now she'd involved her daughter. Not to mention Jon. Worse, until recently she'd been engaged to the devil. Remembering the ring, she reached into her pocket, took out the diamond engagement ring and threw it at him.

Collin ducked, the ring pinging off the wall behind him. "What the hell? Do you have any idea how much that ring set me back?" He turned his back on her to get down on the floor to look for it.

Kate fought the urge to attack him while he was down. But common sense won out. She merely glared at him as he got to his feet, dusting off the ring and then pocketing it.

When he spoke, his voice was rough with emotion. "I don't care what you believe as long as you know that the threats...aren't idle. I didn't want to do it this way, but you've given me no choice."

She was seething but knew she had to keep her head. Now that she knew what Collin was capable of, she had to know just how dangerous he was. "And after I go with you, then what happens?"

"Then I tell my friend to leave your daughter's apartment."

"What about me?" she asked, so furious and scared that her words came out clipped. The fear had her heart thundering in her chest. And yet, she felt strong, she felt in control, even though she knew she was far from it. As long as she could protect her daughter and keep Collin from making that call on Jon, she would do what she had to do. Until she knew they were both safe. Then all bets were off.

But she had to keep her head. She knew she couldn't trust Collin to keep his word. She had to be strong and smart. She told herself she'd been through worse when Danny had left them. She would get through this, too. She would take care of her girls—just as she had always done.

"What happens with you?" Collin said. "I'll drop you off in the first real city in Montana we come to, and you can rent a car and go wherever it is you need to go. As long as you never tell anyone about any of this, you and your daughters will be just fine. So will your...carpenter. How's that?"

She nodded, her gaze still holding his. She didn't believe a word of it.

"Great," he said. "Let's get out of here. Oh, and if you try to pull something stupid—"

"I'm not stupid. I understand. We go to the border. You

do your business. We cross again. Together. And then we're done."

"Suits me," he said and picked up their luggage. "After you." He motioned toward the door.

She opened it and walked out. She could hear him behind her as she stepped to the car, the engine still running. She didn't look down the highway toward Jon's workshop. Looking straight ahead, she opened her car door and froze at the sound of Jon's voice.

"Kate."

She turned to see him limping toward her through the snow. His breath came out in white puffs as he approached the SUV. Out of the corner of her eye, she saw Collin tense, then start toward the man.

Jon held up his hand like a traffic cop. "I just want a word with her," he said and turned to Kate. "Are you sure about this?" he asked, his voice a hoarse whisper.

She met his eyes. Danny's eyes. This man might be someone named Justin Brown, but her breaking heart knew him, loved him. She couldn't bear the thought that she would never see him again. To find him and then lose him... "I have to go. Collin and I are meeting some of his associates who've been skiing north of here in Canada."

"Kate—"

"I'm sorry if I...upset you by coming into your life the way I did. Of course you can't be my husband, Danny. I don't know what I was thinking."

Jon held her gaze for a long moment.

"You heard her, carpenter," Collin said loudly. "We're leaving and not coming back. That's what you said you wanted, right?"

Something changed in Jon's gaze. Just a flicker of anger

followed by what might be regret. "Have a safe trip," he said to her. His gaze shifted to Collin. She could see by the way he stood that he wanted to take the man on. One more word out of Collin, the slightest movement in his direction...

But Collin stepped back, rounding the front of the SUV to go to the back to load her suitcase. She spoke quickly and quietly, hoping Collin wouldn't hear.

"You stay safe, Justin."

Jon heard the name, his eyes widening.

The hatch opened, and Collin threw in the suitcase before slamming it and stepping around to open the driver's-side door. As he slid behind the wheel, he looked at her still standing outside with her door open. "Let's go," he barked.

Kate gave Jon one last look before she climbed into the passenger seat and buckled up. She'd seen the surprise and the worry on his face. He was afraid for her? She was the one trying to save him by warning him.

As Collin shifted into Reverse and yanked the steering wheel around, she couldn't bear to look at Jon's retreating back as he limped toward his workshop. She closed her eyes tight, her heart thudding brokenly in her chest. She yearned to throw open her door and run after him through the snow.

But like she'd told Collin, she wasn't stupid. Her daughter's life was at stake. So was the life of this man now walking away. One wrong move on her part... Worse, whatever business Collin had across the border, it was dirty and dangerous. She hated him for dragging the people she loved into it, but she was in it now up to her neck with no way out.

As he drove them out of Buckhorn, Kate feared she

would never see her daughters again—let alone Buckhorn or Jon Harper. Worse, she was now with a dangerous man. She could smell it on Collin. His desperation warned her just how dangerous he could get.

Even if she did what he wanted, she thought her chances of surviving this engagement trip weren't good.

CHAPTER SEVENTEEN

TOO UPSET TO go back to his workshop, Jon had headed for Earl Ray's house. He couldn't believe that he'd let Kate go with that man. But what could he have done? Kate was a grown woman. Had he been going to warn her about Collin Matthews? Not that it mattered since she was the one warning him.

She'd called him Justin, which meant the report on his fingerprints from the coffee mug had come back. Collin knew who he was. By now he could have let everyone else know. He probably already had ratted him out and was pretending otherwise to force Kate to go with him.

Jon swore. Why hadn't he grabbed her and… And what? Just because he didn't like Matthews, none of this was his business. Maybe the man wasn't headed for the border to do anything illegal. Right.

He hadn't grabbed Kate and kept her from going because she'd asked him not to. He'd seen the pleading in her green eyes. Which meant Collin had something on her. It was the only thing that made sense. Jon's true identify— and what would happen if word got out? He hoped to hell that wasn't what Collin was using to force Kate to go with him. The irony wasn't wasted on him. He'd planned to warn her and she'd ended up warning him.

Because she believed he was her husband, Danny. He swore under his breath as he neared Earl Ray's house. He no longer even knew who he was.

He banged on Earl Ray's door until the older man opened it. "She just left with Matthews," he said as he stepped in. He wasn't sure why he'd come here. Maybe so Earl Ray could tell him that there was nothing he could do.

As he took off his coat and boots, Earl Ray handed him a large manila envelope. "What's this?" Jon asked frowning. "I hope it isn't more bad news about Collin Matthews."

"It's a dossier on you."

He jerked his head up, his nostrils flaring as he looked at the older man who stood in the middle of the room. The expression on Earl Ray's face was one of pity and concern, two things that Jon didn't want to see there. "Where the hell did you get—"

"I put it together myself."

Jon took a step back. "Why would you—"

"Because I had to know."

He didn't need to open the envelope. He knew what was inside. He tried to choose his words wisely. Earl Ray was as close to a best friend as he'd had in years. He told himself he could trust the man. "I've lived here five years. When did you—"

"When you arrived. I had to know what you were running from. I love this town and the people in it. I couldn't have you hurting any of them."

Jon shook his head. "What took you so long? Why show it to me now?"

"I wouldn't have if you hadn't gotten involved with that woman and her fiancé."

"Excuse me? I didn't get involved with her. I did my best to send her on down the road." Earl Ray merely held his gaze. "What's in here?" Jon asked, holding up the envelope.

The old man stepped into the kitchen to tend to the coffee maker that had finished brewing from the smell of it. "Everything."

Jon stared at the man's back, finding that hard to believe. "You weren't a war hero."

"Who says?" Earl Ray demanded with a smile as he turned from the coffeepot with two filled cups. "Sit down."

He sighed as he tossed down the envelope on the table, pulled out a chair and sat. He felt anxious on so many levels. "Why the interest in me?"

"I had to know what you were running from," Earl Ray said. "Not just for the sake of the town as it turns out. But for your own good. I had to know who you were if I was going to protect you."

"*Protect* me?"

"Let's not beat around the bush. You stopped here today to give me a chance to talk you out of this fool thing you're thinking of doing—going after Kate." Earl Ray held up a hand. "Because, you know what will happen if you do. Those men you're running from? If you go after her up to that border, the shit will hit the fan, and when it does, everything will come out. Those men chasing you? They'll know where you are and they'll come for you. It will make it easier for them if you're behind bars."

"It's too late. They're probably on their way. My coffee mug Matthews took? He had my prints run through the system. They already know. Kate just warned me by calling me Justin. I can't save myself, but maybe I can her. She's in trouble and not just because her fiancé is a jack-ass and a probable drug smuggler."

"I agree. But how much more trouble would you be putting her in if you go after her? According to you, you've never laid eyes on the woman until a few days ago. So, what do you care?"

He shook his head. "Whatever made you a war hero, it wasn't because you turned a blind eye and let someone die."

"Maybe not a blind eye, but I was forced to let people die. Sometimes you have to make hard decisions. Kate could be tougher than you think."

"I know he forced her to go with him."

"And how do you know that?"

"Because I tried to stop her." He hated admitting it. "I thought… Hell, I don't know what I was thinking. I thought about telling her what we'd learned about Matthews. Instead she told me that Collins was meeting some of his associates who are on a ski trip up north. You and I both know what's up north, and it isn't a ski hill."

"You think she was trying to tell you where she was going?"

"She wanted me to know that she had already figured out that Collin Matthews was a liar and probably worse. I have no proof that he's headed to the border to commit a crime. But I know he's forcing her to go and she's scared— not for herself but for me. I saw it in her eyes."

His old friend smiled. "You saw all that in her green eyes? And she's a beautiful woman who just happened to see her dead husband in your eyes."

Jon shook his head, refusing to rise to the bait. "It's more than that."

"I suspect it is," Earl Ray said quietly. "Let me ask you this. Let's say you go after her. What are you going to do when you find her? She wouldn't have gotten into that man's car unless he had some leverage on her. It could be you, but I suspect—"

"She has two daughters," he said, remembering her fear. "Mia and Danielle. Mia owns a graphic-design business. Danielle is finishing college at Rice University. It would be just like that bastard to use her daughters against her."

"I'll see what I can do," Earl Ray said. "You don't need to get involved. Especially since you know the cost. Especially since you don't know this woman. We could be wrong about Matthews."

He met Earl Ray's gaze. "Nice try." They weren't wrong, and they both knew it. "Someone has to help her. It's just my luck that she chose me." He'd lived in the shadows for so long, he'd felt incapable of coming out in the light— even if it wasn't dangerous. Now he had no choice. "You know I'm going after her no matter what."

"Of course."

"Then why did you try to talk me out of it?" he demanded.

"Because I had to know how committed you were to this…fool's errand." Earl Ray smiled. "Also I didn't want you going off half-cocked. I wanted to be sure you knew how much you have to lose if you do this. And I wanted your permission to help you."

Jon laughed, shaking his head as he studied the older man. "Thank you." He picked up his coffee and drank it before rising to his feet.

"You have a plan?" Earl Ray asked.

"Collin is meeting some friends at the Canadian border. If it looks and smells like a drug deal, I'm figuring it probably is. No reason to stop him before he's got the goods. Katie should be safe until they cross back into the States and he doesn't need her anymore." He realized he'd said *Katie*. Earl Ray hadn't seemed to notice.

"Which crossing?"

"Not sure. She said they were headed north. That gives him several options due north of here."

"How will you be able to find her?" Earl Ray asked, sounding more curious than worried.

"I put a tracking device on their rental in the middle of last night. Actually two devices, in case he should find one of them," Jon said. His friend laughed.

He checked his phone. "They're headed north no doubt to one of the smaller border crossings. If I had to guess, I'd say they'll cross at Port of Morgan. It ranks as the twelfth least used border crossing between the US and Canada. But there is also Opheim and Turner. They are even smaller, with even less use."

"That doesn't mean they will be less dangerous if things go south." Rising to his feet, Earl Ray walked to his pantry door, opened it to a wall of canned goods. Jon watched him press a panel on the wall. The shelves of cans opened to reveal another wall—this one covered in firearms and ammunition.

Jon let out a low, appreciative whistle. "Expecting Armageddon?"

"I just like to be prepared for anything that might come up." He stopped for a moment as if caught in the past. "I can't go with you."

"No, you can't," Jon said.

"It's not that I'm too old."

He smiled. "No, it's not that. You can't leave Buckhorn. This town needs you. I need you to be here when I come back to return your weapons. Also, I need you to keep this for me." He reached into his coat and pulled out the cashier's check made out of Earl Ray. It was nearly everything he'd saved for the past five years.

Earl Ray met his gaze. "Then you'd better come back."

"WHAT THE HELL was that back there?" Collin demanded not far out of town.

Kate could feel anger coming off him in waves. She pretended to not know what he was asking.

"Tell me you weren't trying to pass a message to Jon right before we left," he snapped and when she didn't say anything, he quickly added, "I should call my friend with Danielle and tell him to—"

"I was just trying to keep the two of you from getting into a fistfight," she said. "I wanted him to know that I was going with you of my own volition."

She waited for her words to soothe him, praying that they did.

"*Skiing?* The man isn't stupid. He has to know there's no skiing to the north of this border."

"But he doesn't know that's where we're going," she said reasonably. "I don't even know where we're going."

She could hear his breathing begin to slow. He shot her a look. She put on her best innocent face and saw him relax a little. Sitting back, she concentrated on the highway ahead as she tried to still her own raucous heart's frantic beat. Jon had gotten the message. She'd seen his eyes narrow, felt him start at just the one word. *Justin*. He had to know that not only she knew—but Collin. Jon had to get out of Buckhorn before the mobsters came after him.

Collin turned on some music, nervously switching from station to station. When he couldn't find one that was static-free, he swore and turned off the radio. She wondered why he'd gotten an older model SUV. With the newer ones, he could have hooked up his phone to listen to music.

Kate felt worry and fear burrow in deeper as she stared at the straight highway stretched out before them with no sign of life for miles. She hadn't even dared look in her side mirror as they'd left town. Instead, she'd stared straight ahead, telling herself she could do this. She had no choice.

Out of the corner of her eye, she watched Collin. He seemed jittery and anxious. Whatever this trip was really about, more was on the line than she'd known. Who were these associates in Canada?

What made her furious with herself was how stupid she'd been. How was it that Collin had fooled her so easily? She'd let him into her life, into her daughters' lives. There was no doubt now that the man he'd turned into in Buckhorn was the real Collin Matthews. That sweet, thoughtful man who'd romanced her and talked her into marrying him didn't exist. Never had. So why had he gone to all the trouble? Had he ever planned to marry her? Or had it all been about this trip and whatever waited across the border?

"Why?" she asked, suddenly needing to know.

He glanced over at her and reached to turn on the radio again. She pushed his hand away from the dial. "Why what?" he snapped.

"Why pretend you were in love with me?"

He glanced from her to the road again. "Who says I was pretending?"

She shook her head. "Did you ever plan to marry me, or was it just all about this trip to Canada?"

He took his time answering. "I bought you a wedding dress. I was planning to marry you," he said without looking at her.

"I'm supposed to believe that?"

He laughed. "Why wouldn't you? You're a beautiful, wealthy woman."

"So, it was the *money*."

Collin chewed at his cheek for a moment. "That was part of it, I'll admit it. But not all of it. I guess maybe I was hoping that when we got to know each other better, I could tell you the truth." He shot a look at her as if trying to gauge how she was taking this. "I would have loved it if we were in this together. I thought you and I could make a hell of a team." His laugh was bitter. "I actually thought that one day you might write *my* story."

She couldn't believe his arrogance. "*Your story?* What exactly is your story, Collin?"

He'd heard the edge to her voice. His face darkened. "I should have known you would never understand, you and your self-righteousness. You and your martyrdom. You think you're the only woman who's ever lost a husband? The only single mom who's struggled to make ends meet?"

"Of course not," she snapped. "I did what I had to do, that's all."

"That's all I do," he said, looking straight ahead as if unable to meet her gaze.

She scoffed. "That's your excuse? Let me guess. Rich

parents who didn't pay any attention to you. Borderline alcoholics. Abuse?"

"It doesn't have to be that dire to feel bad about your life," he snapped. "Sorry if I don't have a hard-luck story to share with you. Certainly not one like yours. I grew up with a silver spoon in my mouth. My parents adored me. Well, my mother did. As I got older, my father…well, he didn't see much of a future for me. When my parents died in a plane crash in their private jet, I inherited everything. Unfortunately, it didn't last long enough—just as my father had predicted. Happy?"

She shook her head. "That's your excuse for whatever this is?" She waved a hand toward the white world outside the SUV's windshield. "What is *this*? Human trafficking? Drugs?"

"Does it really matter at this point?" he asked with a sigh.

"I guess not." She shook her head, disgusted…more with him or herself she couldn't say. "So, you're a criminal."

He scoffed at that. "I'm more like Robin Hood."

"In your dreams," she said.

The muscles in his jaw bunched. She'd made him angry again. She warned herself of the danger and not just for her. "Still, I don't understand why you need me now." She didn't think he was going to answer. She could see him struggling to control his temper.

"You're my cover. A man and his fiancée crossing the border looks better than a single man from Texas up here in the winter making a quick trip to Canada and back." He glanced at her. "You have that hoity-toity look of someone with money, refinement, not to mention that don't-mess-with-me attitude. You're perfect for this. You're above sus-picion."

She couldn't bear to look at him. Turning her head, she stared out at the sculpted white landscape. It seemed to run on forever. "How much farther is it?"

"A few hours. Take a nap. Daydream about your long-lost dead husband. Just remember what's at stake. You're my *fiancée*." He reached into his pocket and shoved the diamond at her. "I paid a pretty penny for that. Put it back on. Play your part, and no one gets hurt."

She took the ring, staring down at it for a long moment before she slipped it back on her finger and closed her fist. "How did I not see what you are really like?"

"Don't be too hard on yourself," Collin said. "I hid it well, but deep down, I think you knew."

"What are you talking about?"

"You sensed it. That's why you held me at arm's length for so long. That's why you probably would never have married me."

She turned to stare at him, hearing the truth in his words. But she'd let it go this far and had only herself to blame. She'd fallen for his sweet talk and his good looks. "I let you into my family. I introduced you to my daughters. I let you into my *bed*."

"But you never really let me into your heart, did you, Kate? It was always Danny. No man could stand up to the *perfect* ghost of your dead husband. Not even the man himself."

The words startled her. She frowned as she said, "You proved that Jon Harper isn't Danny."

"He isn't even Jon Harper," Collin agreed.

"So, why would you say what you did?"

Collin shook his head, clearly regretting his words. "Because, as ridiculous as this all has been, you might be right. I think he really is your husband."

"*What?*" Was he messing with her? "But you said his name was Justin something."

"Justin Brown. Another of his aliases and probably the one that is going to get him killed. But who was he before he became Justin Brown?"

"You aren't making any sense." And yet he had her heart beating like a war drum in her chest. She felt light-headed. If he was saying what she thought he was…

"Earlier when I was at the bar, I got a call from a friend of mine who works at the police department down in Houston. He told me that Jon worked at the same refinery your husband did," Collin explained and glanced at her as if knowing how this news was affecting her. "Quite the coincidence, huh? Apparently in the hospital, he had no memory of who he was before the explosion. But one of the other men in an adjacent bed said he recognized him and that his name was Justin Brown. So, when he left the hospital he was Justin Brown. Or was he?"

She leaned back against the seat and closed her eyes in an attempt to trap the tears. Was it possible that she hadn't fallen in love with a stranger in some small Montana town? Instead, she'd fallen again for the man she'd been in love with for years. But it wasn't until she saw him standing in that woodworking shop that she knew in her heart that against all the odds, she'd found him.

Now she'd lost him again. Worse, finding him could get him killed.

CHAPTER EIGHTEEN

KATE STARED OUT at the bleak landscape. The snow-packed pavement was indistinguishable from the sky overhead or the white fields on each side. She felt a deep need for color, bright, beautiful color, feeling as if she'd gone snow-blind. Earlier she'd seen some black cows, their backs blanketed with snow. She felt claustrophobic, hemmed in by the cold and the snow in this strange part of the world Collin had brought her to for all the wrong reasons.

There hadn't even been any cows for miles. Now nothing broke the total white landscape except an occasional yellow No Passing Zone sign. There was no traffic, no houses, nothing since they'd driven through the town of Loring, which appeared to be nothing more than several empty buildings, a church and a post office with a few houses scattered around but no movement as if everyone was staying in until winter was over.

She wanted to ask Collin how much farther it was to the border. It felt as if they had been driving forever, headed north into colder, snowier country. But she didn't, seeing how nervous he was. He gripped the wheel as if his life depended on it and looked directly ahead. Like him, she feared what might be waiting for them at the border.

As much as she cursed the day she'd met Collin Matthews, she realized with a pang that if she hadn't come up here with him, she would never have seen Jon Harper standing in his woodworking shop. Never have looked into those brown eyes and seen Danny again. The memory filled her with sadness because now she had jeopardized both of their lives.

From a sudden break in the clouds, the sun appeared. In an instant, it turned the white landscape into sparkling ice crystals. The glare was blinding. She fished her sunglasses from her purse, stunned by the brilliance and the beauty. Just seeing the sun after all the days of nothing but falling snow or dull gray skies seemed to lift her spirits and gave her a strange sense of hope.

She reminded herself that this, whatever it was, had only just begun. She glanced at Collin, who'd also put on his sunglasses. He had the radio on again and was humming along with an old rock song on a station he'd managed to pick up. To someone who didn't know him, he looked completely relaxed. He was definitely in control, his look said, of not just his own life—but hers and the people she loved.

Anger simmered, threatening to boil over. She hated his arrogance. He thought he knew her. A former suburban mom who'd only recently traded in her minivan for an SUV. He thought she was easy prey. And he'd been right.

But not anymore. She'd never had more to live for. Danny. It didn't matter that Jon either didn't know who he'd been or hadn't admitted it because he wanted to protect her from his past. He'd made her realize that she could love again with all the intensity she had as a teenage girl. He'd reopened a part of her heart she'd closed off for twenty years. She'd thought that she loved Collin, but he was right, she probably would never have married him. She *had* sensed that something was wrong. Not just because he was pretending to be a man he wasn't. She hadn't felt the kind of love she should have.

Jon Harper had awakened her desire. A fire burned deep in her, a need that only one man could fulfill. That gave her strength. She would see him again. Or die trying.

Collin had underestimated her. Especially this past week when she'd been living in a fog. She knew she'd appeared weak and unsure of herself. Seeing Danny in the woodworker had been such a shock, and when he appeared not to know her…

Well, that was behind her. She had to snap out of it. Too much was at stake. She thought about their suitcases in the back. Had Collin brought a weapon? Would there be a vehicle search at the border? She had no idea. Just as she had no idea what they were picking up. Some kind of drugs, but what? Of course she knew about the opioid epidemic, but little about the actual drugs.

Spotting a cell tower ahead, she pulled out her phone and checked first to see if a person could bring firearms into Canada. Not without registering them. She had her doubts Collin would be doing that—if he had a weapon in his suitcase.

It didn't take long on the browser to find out what drugs were being brought across the Canadian border into the States. A drug called fentanyl was all over the news. A super-strength synthetic opioid more powerful than heroin and one hundred times more powerful than morphine.

"What are you doing?" Collin asked suddenly.

She'd just clicked on an article about a drug bust of fentanyl from Canada into New York of over seventy pounds, with a street value of almost twenty-nine million dollars. "Educating myself," she said.

Seventy pounds seemed like nothing. But then again, how would a person transport that much without it being discovered at the border crossing?

"Educating yourself?" he asked, sounding suspicious.

There was a long list of other products that were banned from being brought into Canada. Did they simply ask you if you'd brought something over? Or did they search your vehicle? She had no idea.

"I just realized that maybe you should give me your phone." He snatched it from her before she could resist. Glancing at the screen, he swore. "What do you think you're doing?" he demanded, pocketing her phone.

"You said you'd hoped I'd be your partner in crime," she said evenly. "I thought I'd better find out exactly what crime we're going to be committing. I'm guessing it isn't marijuana. It's fentanyl. Probably from China, brought into Canada and now headed for the States. How much?" He shook his head. "Come on, I'm curious. We can't have gone through all of this unless there is a big shipment worth a whole lot of money. So, how will you get it back across the border? If it's as big a deal as it says in those articles, then they will be searching every car that crosses." She saw his jaw tighten. "But that's where I come in, isn't it?" She let out a bitter laugh.

"They don't search every car—just the ones that seem suspicious," he said without looking at her. "You just need to stay in character. You hear me, Kate? You're my *fiancée*. We're on an engagement trip because you'd never seen snow and you've never been to Canada. Got it?" He shot her a warning look.

She nodded and dragged her gaze away from what she saw in his blue eyes. Her heart pounded. His reaction told her that she'd guessed correctly. If just seventy pounds were worth almost thirty million, then a lot was at stake. People had been killed for much less.

One good thing, she thought. If he needed her to cross the border with him on the way back with the drugs, then he couldn't harm her until they were safely back across. That gave her little comfort. If caught, she would be considered as guilty as him. She hadn't paid much attention to the length of the prison sentences the men had been given in the New York bust, but she figured it would be years.

Even as she thought it, she knew that was minor compared to what would happen once Collin *didn't* need her. He couldn't let her go. He knew her well enough to know that she wouldn't keep quiet. If it was fentanyl, then it was an extremely addictive drug that had already killed thousands in overdose deaths just last year. She wouldn't be able to live with herself if she let him put that much poison on the street.

He'd have to kill her, but she wouldn't go down without a fight. And if she got the chance, she would take him with her. But how was she going to stop him before he stopped her?

JON DROVE HIS old pickup north along the east side of Fort Peck, a lake with more shoreline than the state of California. He was only a few hours from the border now. He'd checked his phone periodically. Matthews was also headed north, but on the west side of the lake. That gave the man two easy options as far as border crossings: Turner or Morgan.

Turner was one of the few ports that had both the US and the Canadian custom officers sharing the same building. Would Matthews see that as a benefit? Or would he go for Port of Morgan? Both had so few vehicles through each day, would security be tighter? Or more lax? There was still Opheim, Montana, just to the northeast, but it would take more time to reach the way Matthews was going. Plus, at this time of year, the border closed early in the evening.

Matthews still had plenty of time to get across before the borders closed. These small ports were only open from about ten in the morning until about six or eight in the evening in the winter, depending on where he chose to cross. Otherwise, the border was closed overnight.

As he drove, Jon considered his own options. The way he saw it, he had only two. Try to intercept Kate in Canada before Matthews brought whatever drugs he was smuggling across the border. Or wait and take him down with the goods once he crossed back into the States. But could he leave Kate with the man that long, knowing how much danger she was in?

He was taking a chance even coming up here. If he got picked up on either side of the border and the officials ran his fingerprints...

Jon checked his phone. It was as he'd thought. Matthews was headed for the Port of Morgan, north of the town of Loring. If he got that far, he would think he was in the clear. North of there might be the perfect place for an ambush. But not knowing what firepower Collin might have would mean jeopardizing Kate's life.

He couldn't do that. He'd wait and see where Matthews was going once across the border. If Jon was right, Matthews' drug supplier would be meeting him. Given the time of the day, Matthews wouldn't be coming right back across with a payload until morning. That meant Collin and Kate would be spending the night somewhere.

If it was fentanyl like Jon suspected, then Matthews would have to have a way to get it across the border. That usually meant welded storage containers under the vehicle. In which case, the tracking devices would be found. Also, it could mean more than one day in Canada.

If Collin managed to get back across the border with the drugs, then he would be meeting someone stateside to sell them for distribution. Matthews was too clean-cut to be a dealer or even a distributor. No, Matthews was just the mule, Jon thought. Once back in the States, Collin would make the trade: money for the drugs. That was dangerous enough, but once Matthews crossed the border back into the US, he wouldn't need Kate anymore. At that point, she would become a liability he could no longer afford.

Jon swore. He had to find out what Matthews was picking up in Canada, which meant he had to go to Canada. He had the tracking devices on Matthews's vehicle. If he hoped to find him, it would have to be tonight before any alternations were made on the SUV Collin was driving. Which meant his best chance of freeing Kate was tonight.

His phone rang. He'd been expecting a call from Earl Ray, letting him know if Kate's daughters had been found and were safe. But he saw it was Bessie Walker calling. The hair rose on the back of his neck as he took the call.

Even before she spoke, he knew something bad had happened.

"It's Earl Ray," she said, sounding as if she'd been crying. "He's had a heart attack. They took him by ambulance to Lewistown to the hospital. I'm driving there now. He was at the café when he collapsed. He said I had to call you and tell you. Something about a favor he was doing for you? He hadn't gotten it done yet. Does that make any sense to you?"

Earl Ray hadn't been able to find out about Kate's daughters. That was what had been on his mind when he'd collapsed? "How is he?"

"I don't know." Bessie was crying again.

"Call me when you do, and don't worry. Earl Ray is one of the strongest men I know. If anyone can pull through this, it's him." He disconnected, worried about his friend. It was so like Earl Ray to be having a heart attack and worrying about someone else. Jon said a silent prayer for him and one for Kate and her daughters as well.

This put a whole new wrinkle in his plans, though. If Matthews was using one of the daughters or both as insurance to get Kate to do what he wanted, then Jon would be jeopardizing their lives if he took Kate tonight. But if he didn't, this might be his only chance.

As he crossed Fort Peck Dam, once the largest earth-filled dam in the world, he thought about his life and about the beautiful brunette with the green eyes who'd walked into his woodshop and changed everything. If he couldn't save her, then he had nothing to live for. Not that he would be living long once the men hired by the syndicate found out where he was.

But right now, Oklahoma City was a hell of a long way from where he was headed.

COLLIN FOUND HIMSELF watching Kate out of the corner of his eye. He hadn't thought about her cell phone. A mistake, and not his first. She could have just as easily texted the law, he thought as he drove the snow-packed highway north. The border was close now. He'd know soon if he was driving into a trap.

He loved that in this part of Montana, towns were few and far between. That meant that cops were few and far between as well. Unless Kate had notified someone at the border. There could be an armed regiment waiting for them.

He silently berated himself for being so careless, fearing that the woman was going to get him killed. At the same time, he wondered if they still might have a chance with each other. He knew it was beyond hope, but then again, he'd never expected her to go online to research what drugs were being brought across the border. He wondered what else she'd researched. She was smart. That made her dangerous. She would make one hell of a partner in crime, if he could bring her over to his way of thinking.

Ahead he spotted a border-patrol vehicle sitting on a small rise over the highway. As they passed, Collin could see that the officer was on his cell phone. His pulse jumped. Calling the border to let them know he was coming? Just ahead, he could see the lights of the crossing. The building with its chain-link fence and elaborate glass-and-steel structure looked out of place in the middle of nowhere. He slowed, feeling perspiration run down his back and puddle at the base of his spine. He didn't see dozens of armed men, but that didn't mean that they weren't close by. He turned off the radio, telling himself he could do this.

Glancing at Kate, though, he felt another wave of anxiety. She looked too calm, too collected, as if she knew exactly what was going to happen ahead.

He realized he'd taken his foot off the gas pedal. The

SUV slowed to a crawl. He caught sight of a sign saying this was his last chance to turn around before the border.

Stop looking so suspicious, he told himself. If she hadn't called... And why would she, knowing that it would get her daughter killed? Well, then, he had nothing to worry about.

If she had? It was too late to worry about that now.

He reminded himself that he didn't have anything illegal in his possession—not yet, anyway. It was coming back across the border that he had to worry about. He glanced at Kate and felt his heart drop. Unless he was arrested for kidnapping.

An officer in blue looked in his direction from the glass enclosure. He sped up, pulling into a lane next to the building with numerous snow-covered signs detailing what couldn't be taken into Canada. The signs were virtually unreadable because of the snow stuck to them.

As he stopped where another sign indicated, he saw several other officers in the glassed-in office. One of them opened the door and headed for them.

KATE TRIED TO swallow the lump in her throat when she saw the border crossing ahead. A US Customs and Department of Homeland Security officer approached them. He was dressed in a blue uniform with a Kevlar vest, a radio and a weapon at his hip. He approached the vehicle warily. Kate could almost feel Collin's anxiety. If he was worried now, imagine what he would be like when they returned with a load of drugs.

Thinking about her daughter, she leaned forward to say hello to the officer through Collin's now-open window. The man didn't respond other than to ask for their passports. She started to reach for her purse and was surprised when Collin handed them both over. When had he gotten hers out of her purse? Without a word, the officer took the passports inside the building. Neither she nor Collin spoke as they waited.

Collin had left his window down. She shivered, but he didn't raise it. She could see ahead where they would exit the compound to go to the Canadian side. The buildings on both sides resembled car washes with huge glass-and-steel doors that rose on approach.

She could see no other cars, no one else crossing the border this afternoon.

The officer appeared at Collin's side again, holding their passports and looking from one to the other of them. "Ma'am, please remove your sunglasses."

"Kate, he wants you to remove your sunglasses," Collin said tersely.

She realized that it was the second time the officer had asked. She quickly took them off while he checked her face against the photo on her passport.

"How far are you going on the Canadian side?" the officer asked in his no-nonsense tone.

"Swift Current," Collin said. "She wants to do some shopping while we're there. Wedding stuff. We're getting married soon. My fiancée has never been to another country, so since we are on our engagement trip to Montana, anyway..." Collin said and looked over at her. He was smiling, but his look warned her. She could see the nervous tension around his mouth and eyes and knew it would be up to her.

"We're from Texas," Kate said, bending forward to look at the officer. "I'd never seen snow. Now I've seen enough of it, thank you very much."

"How long will you be staying?" the officer asked, his tone full of authority and not the least bit friendly.

"Just a couple of days," Collin said. The officer looked up at them, taking her in and then Collin before he began to question them about items in their possession, going through the list she'd seen online. Collin said they didn't have any of the prohibited items. She noticed the officer looking in the back of SUV before he asked Collin to open the back.

Collin popped the hatch and started to get out, but was ordered to stay in the vehicle as the officer went around to the rear. Kate wanted to turn and watch him but instead snuggled against Collin. He flinched in surprise, then put his arm around her, whispering in her ear, "You're doing fine."

Was the officer looking through their suitcases? After a few minutes, the man returned to the driver's-side window and told Collin he could close the hatch.

Handing back their passports, he gave them a nod and told them to continue straight ahead. Collin put up his window, and they left Montana to drive across the border only to stop on the Canadian side. The large overhead door lifted, and the Canadian officer waved them in. Again they showed their passports and were also questioned, this time with even more suspicion, before being allowed to enter the country.

COLLIN TRIED TO RELAX. It was his first time crossing the border. The sweat that had soaked through his shirt was beginning to dry. He didn't feel as if he was going to jump out of his skin anymore as he saw the sign welcoming them into Saskatchewan. He could almost breathe freely. Coming back across would be worse. With luck they would have the same law officer. Maybe he would remember them, since so few people crossed here.

"You did good back there," he said again, though grudgingly, to Kate, knowing that she had been cooler than he'd been. Having her along and not knowing what she might do had added to his anxiety. But she'd been a trooper. She'd played her role perfectly.

He glanced over at her as he drove down a narrow pothole-filled highway with wheat sheaves on the speed-limit signs assuring him they were now in Saskatchewan, Canada. He still wanted to believe that his dreams of them doing this together weren't that crazy after all.

She said nothing as she looked out at the unchanged white landscape. If anything, there was more snow up here. Earlier there had been a short period of bright sunshine, but now the clouds had moved in again, making everything from the sky to the ground a silvery white in the growing twilight. Soon it would be dark. He was glad they didn't have far to go.

"We made good time," he said, not sure why he was trying to make conversation with her. He felt so relieved, so pleased with the job she'd done. That they had both done. They'd gotten over one hurdle. Kate had come through for him. He was proud of her, and maybe he was feeling guilty involving her.

"You're meeting your *associates* in Swift Current?" There was an edge to her voice. She might have played along back there, but she was still furious with him. He still couldn't trust her, let alone turn his back on her.

"Look, I have no choice in this."

"Everyone has a choice," she said, looking out her side window away from him.

"I'm in trouble financially with my businesses."

"That's why you were going to marry me," she said, turning back to him. "Once we were married, I would have given you whatever money you needed. You didn't have to do this."

He shot her a skeptical look. She could say that now, but he couldn't see himself begging her for money. He did have his pride. To his surprise, though, he told her the truth, something that embarrassed him more than she could know. "This is a different deal. I made kind of a bad investment with a loan shark and then made it worse with a drug deal that went sour. I'm not doing this just for the money. Not completely. I'm being forced to, all right? If I don't make this work, I'm as good as dead."

"If you're looking for sympathy—"

He swore and banged his fist down hard on the steering wheel. The SUV swerved, and he had to grab the wheel to keep them on the narrow, snowy road. "I was just telling you how it is." He ground his teeth, wishing he hadn't bothered, as ahead he had to slow to make the turn toward the first small Canadian town of Val Marie.

"I've been desperate in my life," Kate said, a softness to her tone. There were tears in her eyes when they met his. "I do understand. But I can't forgive you for involving my daughter."

"She's safe. I promise. I just needed leverage. I knew after you found Jon Harper you would never go with me." He saw that he'd been right about that. She didn't deny it. If she had her way, she'd be back in Buckhorn in that woodshop with a man who could very well be her husband. Or a complete stranger. Both preferable to her fiancé, Collin thought bitterly.

"How do you plan to get the fentanyl across the border?" she asked.

He gave her that blank look. "Who said anything about fentanyl?"

"Oh, for cryin' out loud. Don't tell me there isn't a plan. Otherwise—"

"There's a plan, if you must know." He figured there was no reason to keep it from her. She already knew the worst of it. "The car is being adapted with containers on the undercarriage tomorrow."

"Won't they look at the border?"

He shrugged. "Hopefully not. But even if they do, they might not see them. The guy who does this sort of work, I'm told, is very good at hiding any extra storage compartments. But they probably won't look because of you. You aren't the kind of woman who makes cops suspicious."

"Lucky me," she said, glancing in the side mirror at herself as if assessing if that were true or not.

He drove past the first small Canadian town and headed north. "You can't save him," he said after a few miles. "Jon Harper," he added in case she didn't already know. "He's on the run from mobsters. One of them or their friends will eventually find him and kill him. It's why you can never be with him." She said nothing. "It's also why he can't save you."

She was staring straight ahead, giving him nothing but her profile. He was struck by how beautiful she was, how stubborn and determined and loyal. It would take a very special man to have this woman, he realized. Someone much more special than him. The thought angered him and made him think of his father. It turned his stomach that his old man's prediction for his son might come true.

The sudden flashing lights in his rearview mirror startled him. He swore and looked over at Kate. "What did you do?"

"Nothing, I promise," she said, sounding scared. She turned in her seat to look back.

"Don't look back," he ordered. "Maybe I was going over the speed limit. These damned kilometers." Or maybe it was something far worse. Either way, he had no choice. He pulled to the side of the road, two wheels at the edge of the borrow pit, and put down his window. Cold winter air rushed in. The area was isolated, no buildings in sight, with nightfall coming on fast.

Bright headlights filled the car as the light bar on top of the rig flashed. Collin watched a man in uniform exit the vehicle behind them and make his way toward them. He thought about the loaded gun taped under his seat that had come with the rental. He shot a warning look at Kate as he turned to face the officer.

CHAPTER NINETEEN

IT WAS DARK by the time Jon had almost reached the border. He checked his phone. Both signals on Matthew's rental SUV came in clear. He'd crossed the border at Port Morgan, but what surprised Jon was that the vehicle was now headed east. He considered the map on his phone. It appeared that Matthews had turned before Swift Current onto Highway 13 and was now headed in his direction. Where was he going?

The question was answered a moment later when the vehicle turned north again onto Highway 2, headed for Moose Jaw.

His cell phone rang. He'd been waiting for this call. "How's Earl Ray?" he said into the phone, anxious for some good news.

"He wants to talk to you himself," Bessie said and handed over the phone.

"Mia is fine," his friend said without preamble. Earl Ray sounded as weak as his voice. "But it has been several days since she's talked to her sister. Danielle's cell has been going straight to voice mail. Nor has Danielle been in class the past two days."

Jon swore. "She's got to be the one."

"My thought exactly. I have someone going to her apartment. Don't worry. He knows how to handle it. I'll keep in touch. And I have someone watching Mia. Once both young women are safe, I'll let you know."

"Thanks, but how are you?"

"Strong as an ox," Earl Ray said before Bessie took the phone from him.

"He's going to be okay, the doctor said. It was a minor attack. He doesn't want you to worry. I have to go." Before Bessie hung up, he heard Earl Ray in the background. The man was strong. Hopefully, he would be fine. Once both of Kate's daughters were safe, Jon could get Kate. Until then, it was too dangerous.

He drove toward the border. He hadn't called Homeland Security to stop Matthews at the border because he had no evidence that the man was about to break the law. Second, he couldn't put Kate in danger along with her daughters.

He'd been banking on Earl Ray finding Mia and Danielle and making sure they were safe before he did anything. Once he knew, he could get Kate out. Or at least try. He had no idea how many men Matthews was meeting in Canada or what kind of firepower they might have. If he was right about the drugs, then they would all be armed and dangerous.

All he could do, he told himself, was keep going. The Opheim/West Poplar River border crossing was ahead. He knew he would be stopped, his old pickup checked and rechecked along with his passport in the name of Jon Harper. It would take time, time he had—at least for the moment.

He pulled up and put down his window, handing over his passport as if this was old hat. His was the only vehicle in the line this time of the evening. The border would close within the hour.

"Where are you headed?" the blue-suited Homeland Security cop asked.

"Moose Jaw to catch up with some friends, and then maybe over to Regina for a day or two." He had no idea where Matthews would take him. He was covering his bets.

The cop nodded, pulled out a long stick with a mirror at the end and began inspecting the undercarriage of his pickup. "Can you pop the hood, please?"

He did and sat waiting, hoping he looked more bored than worried. He had nothing to hide—except for the weapons taped surreptitiously under his seat.

"You can close your hood," the cop said as he peered behind the pickup's seat. "I see you have some tools in the back?"

"Carpenter," he said without hesitation. "I make furniture."

"Planning on leaving anything in Canada?" No. "Planning on bringing anything back?" No.

"Not planning on anything but food, a motel room and some Canadian whiskey."

"Okay," the cop said, handing back his passport. "Drive carefully."

"Will do," he called out of the window as he drove into Canada.

The next time he checked his phone, the signals on Matthew's SUV had stopped in the middle of nowhere. He waited for them to move. They didn't.

KATE LOOKED OUT at the growing darkness as the officer approached the driver's-side door, her heart in her throat.

Why had Collin been pulled over? He hadn't been speeding. Maybe he'd been red-flagged at the border. Was it possible they'd been waiting for him? That this whole thing had been a setup, and Collin had brought her into his scheme? Were they now both going to jail?

She wanted to yell at the officer that she'd been brought across the border with basically a gun to her head. She opened her mouth, her pulse a thunder in her ears.

"Just wanted to let you know you have a taillight out," the officer said without bending down to look at either of them.

"Thanks," Collin said. "I'll get that fixed."

"Officer," Kate cried, but the rest of her words died on her lips as, with horror, she watched the uniformed man slip Collin a note, which he quickly pocketed. Kate stared in disbelief, telling herself she'd been seeing things. Maybe the cop had written Collin a warning, but she knew there hadn't been time.

Collin put up his window as the Canadian version of highway patrol walked back to his rig, got in and pulled away with a flash of his light bar and was gone. "Something you wanted to say, Kate?"

She heard the edge to his voice as he pulled out the piece of paper the man had given him. Even from where she sat, she could see that it had an address on it.

"That's right, Kate," Collin said, grinning. "Think about what you just saw, if you decide to speak up again," he said as he read the note and, tearing it into tiny pieces, put down his window and tossed it out into the freezing night air. "You really don't know who you can trust."

Kate felt hot tears burn her eyes. She looked away, unable to stand Collin's cocky grin as he started the SUV and pulled back onto the highway.

In the headlights, this part of Canada seemed very similar to what she'd seen of Montana. Except Saskatchewan was flat and barren-looking and much colder. The road signs were different, and so were the license plates on the vehicles that passed, but otherwise the same, she thought. She wondered about the prisons and court systems.

They had been driving for hours. She had no idea where he was taking her. Or, worse, what he was involving her in. She hated what might be ahead. She just wanted it over.

"How much farther?" she asked, her body feeling weary of sitting for so long. "I have to go to the bathroom." She saw what looked like a filling station ahead. Collin glanced over at her as if she were trying to trick him. "It's been hours."

He slowly nodded as if acknowledging it was true and slowed. "You can get out after I fill up with gas, then we can both go inside."

She rolled her eyes, climbing out when he did, but merely standing next to the SUV stretching her legs as he filled the tank. She ignored the warning look he gave her. What did he think she was going to do? Run into the small convenience store and tell the clerk to call the cops? She hadn't forgotten about the patrolman who'd passed Collin the note. Nor about the man with the gun who was with Danielle.

Once he finished filling up the SUV, they both went inside. She headed straight for the ladies' restroom and wasn't surprised when she came out to find him standing outside the door waiting for her.

"You want something to eat or drink?" he asked.

She hadn't realized until he said it that she was starving. He got them both a hot dog and a cola to go. At the register, he fumbled for his wallet before asking quietly if she had any money. She'd hesitated only a moment before she pulled a hundred out of her purse for the gas and the food and drink. The clerk gave her Canadian money for change. She didn't bother concerning herself with the exchange rate under the circumstances.

Once in the SUV again, Collin handed her one of the hot dogs and a cola, and without looking at her said, "I'm afraid I'm going to need you to pay for everything from here on out." She could hear the embarrassment, the anger, the disappointment and resentment in his voice.

Kate had wanted to howl with laughter. She'd basically been kidnapped, forced into crossing an international border and would soon be forced into a criminal act—and her abductor wanted her to foot the bill for all of it?

She kept her expression from showing the roiling emotions bubbling up in her. She couldn't look at him, could hardly form the words. "I figured as much."

Collin sat for a few moments longer before he started the engine and pulled away from the pump. She could feel waves of resentment coming off him. Add that to his anxiety and fear and whatever else made Collin Matthews tick, and he was a man close to the edge. She tried not to breathe too loudly, afraid of how little it might take to set him off.

It wasn't until he'd eaten part of his hot dog and tossed the rest out the window before he spoke. "I know you despise me right now." She said nothing, not wanting to lie, half-afraid it would make matters worse if she did. "I wish things were different. Staying in Buckhorn as long as we did depleted my resources. I thought I'd have enough money for the trip. I was wrong. I'm sorry."

Kate looked over at him then. She'd gulped down her hot dog and now reached for her cola. She was afraid of what might come out of her mouth. "I'm low on cash. You'll have to use my credit card." The card would leave a trail. It wasn't much in the way of a plan, but it was all she could think of.

Then she remembered that he'd been in her purse to get her passport. Had he seen how much cash she had? Also, he hadn't returned her passport. Even if she could get away from him, she wouldn't be able to cross the border without it. She was sure that's the way he'd planned it.

Collin said nothing as he finished his cola, put down his window and tossed the cup out as he drove. He didn't look at her. But when she glanced at him, she saw the set of his jaw and felt a shudder.

THE SIGNALS ON Matthews's SUV had stopped in Moose Jaw. As Jon drove toward the city, he waited for them to move again. They didn't. He stopped at a convenience store for gas and something to eat, drove another hour and then pulled off the road outside of the small Canadian town. Matthews's vehicle still hadn't moved. He slept for a couple of hours, waking at one in the morning.

Jon checked his watch. He had two clear signals where they'd been earlier, still unmoved. From under the seat of his pickup, he untaped two of the weapons Earl Ray had given him, checked to make sure they were loaded and ready.

He wasn't planning on using them. He didn't want to kill anyone. But if he was forced into a corner, he would kill anyone he had to if it meant saving Kate's life. If it came to that, then his cover would be blown. Even in Canada, he wouldn't survive a night in jail.

Once he knew that Kate's daughters were safe, he planned to make his move. Not that it wouldn't be dangerous. Anything he did could jeopardize Kate's life. But he couldn't leave her with Collin any longer than he had to, fearing what could happen to her if he did.

As he drove into Moose Jaw, he thought of Kate. Earl Ray was right about one thing. It was crazy the way he'd gotten involved in this. Just because she'd walked into his woodshop that day and thought he was her dead husband, Daniel Jackson.

Just his luck, he thought. Otherwise he would be in his woodshop right now, working. He often worked late. Instead, he was in Canada, not sure what he was about to get involved in because of a green-eyed brunette with a heartbreaking story about a dead husband.

He was close now, almost on top of the signals. He looked around, surprised to find himself in a residential neighborhood. He'd thought he'd find them in a highway motel.

Kate had said Matthews was meeting associates who were up here on a ski trip. Often there was a little truth in every lie, he'd learned. So did Collin's buddies live here? Or was Matthews meeting someone here?

The signal took him to a house on the edge of a creek. Each lot was large, except for the last one where the signal was coming from. The house was older, as if it had been the original farmhouse on the property and the subdivision had been built up to the west of it. The house also didn't look as well kept-up as the others. A rental? That made sense. Make whatever deal was going down in a nice neighborhood. Both Matthews and Kate were clean-cut enough that the neighbors wouldn't pay them any mind.

He drove around the block, which turned out to be quite large, the creek cutting through the backs of the yards to form a park of sorts.

He checked his watch. 1:37 a.m. The neighborhood was dead quiet. No lights on in any of the houses. A working neighborhood where probably both husbands and wives had jobs to get up for in the morning.

He found a place to park without attracting undo attention. Now the question was how to approach this. He had no idea how many people were in the house or what kind of weapons they would have. He had to assume they would be armed or have a weapon close by, even in the middle of the night.

Matthews had flown to Montana, which meant he could have brought a handgun in his checked baggage on the plane. Or he could have purchased one easily enough once he landed. Jon had to assume that Collin had a weapon or that there had been one waiting for him in the house. If this were a drug deal, then everyone in that house would be carrying—except for Kate.

Because the house wasn't as large as the others in the neighborhood, there wouldn't be many bedrooms. Maybe the deal hadn't gone down yet. His hope was that the associates had rented the house but hadn't arrived yet. Which meant it would only be Kate and Matthews inside.

He knew he could sit here all night speculating on what he was going to find once he reached the house. But there was only one way to find out for sure as he double-checked the weapons. He figured neither was registered, so if he were caught, nothing would trace back to Earl Ray.

With one gun in the top of his boot, another tucked in his back waistband and covered with his coat, he locked the pickup and headed toward the creek. At one time, he'd been a crack shot. He hoped it was like riding a bike.

The night air made his breath come out in frosty puffs as he walked. The snow was deep. He pushed through it, noticing that his limp was getting worse. He was a woodworker now, no longer a cop, no longer chasing down bad guys.

But he knew he could do this because when he was a cop, he was good at it. Only this time the stakes were higher than they'd ever been. He didn't have a badge, was across an international border and was about to blow his cover if he got caught. None of that mattered as long as he got Kate out of this.

He reached the edge of the park and dipped into the trees. By staying near the creek, he would have cover. But at some point he would have to cross the creek. It looked frozen over, blanketed in snow, but that didn't mean the ice was thick enough to hold his weight. Nor did he have any idea how deep the water might be at the middle.

But this side of it provided the best shelter. He moved soundlessly through the soft, fresh snow, not worried about leaving tracks. He could see the back of the house ahead through the trees. He would have to cross the creek at some point and then he would be exposed for twenty yards before he reached the rear of the building. Fortunately the neighbors next to the house had a high fence. He just hoped they didn't have a barking dog.

At the creek's edge, he tested the ice. It was always thinner along the bank. The ice broke under his weight with a loud crack. He felt his boot break through. He took another step—farther out this time, then another. He would hear the ice groaning under his weight. He was almost to the middle when a light came on at the back of the house, and Jon froze.

CHAPTER TWENTY

MATTHEWS RUBBED A hand over his face as he turned on the kitchen light. He couldn't sleep. Aimlessly, he opened the refrigerator and peered around inside. Beer. Leftover pizza and a few condiments. He closed the door and tried the cupboards. Empty except for a large bag of Cheezies. What the hell?

He unrolled the top. Someone had already gotten into them. Not that he minded. He took out a handful. Canada's brand of Cheetos. He could live with that.

His stomach roiled, but he ignored the nauseous feeling, knowing it had nothing to do with what he was putting into his system right now. Nerves. His skin hurt as if his whole body had broken out in a rash. Half the time, he felt as if he would jump out of it.

Too much hinged on this deal going down without any problems. He had to relax. He had to believe that this would work. He'd been assured that the men at this end knew what they were doing and had done it numerous times before without a hitch. He was betting everything on it—including his life.

He had to believe he was in good hands, given the highway patrolman—if that's what the officer really had been—who'd given him the note. So, he shouldn't worry. These people had everything under control.

But even as he thought this, he knew the real hitch was asleep in a bedroom in this very house. Kate. He wanted to trust her, but he knew he couldn't. Earlier, he'd been sure she was about to blow everything when she'd tried to get the officer's attention. Even with leverage, she had too much fire in her.

Which threw him for a loop as he thought of the quiet, easygoing woman he'd targeted. *That* Kate had been docile, easy to manipulate. It had taken more time than he'd expected to work his way into her life, but she'd finally agreed to marry him and take off her old wedding ring. He'd thought then that he had her. And he had, he was sure of it. If the SUV hadn't broken down and they hadn't ended up in Buckhorn... If she hadn't seen that damned carpenter...

But all that aside, he hadn't known this Kate. The one with fire in her eyes, who glared daggers at him. The one who looked as if she could scratch his eyes out. The one who everything about this deal depended on.

Rubbing his neck, he realized that if he'd just taken a different road across Montana everything would be different now. They probably would be planning their wedding—after this quick trip to Canada. She wouldn't have known what was really going down. He would have made sure of that.

Unfortunately, she was too smart, too independent, too much better than him, and she would have realized it even if she'd never laid eyes on that carpenter, if he was being honest with himself. Even if he hadn't had her daughter taken hostage.

Strange how in the middle of the night he often saw things more clearly. Jon Harper—whether or not he was her husband—had made her realize the kind of man she wanted. And that man wasn't Collin. If it hadn't been Jon, then it would have been someone else who opened her eyes.

He felt a bitter twist of his gut at the thought that he hadn't measured up to even some scarred, broke carpenter living in some two-bit town. He'd watched her fall in love with the man within a matter of days. He wasn't even sure that she cared whether the man was her long-lost husband or not.

Balling his hands into fists, he knew he would never forgive Kate for that. How had he thought that maybe everything wasn't lost? Whatever had happened in Buckhorn, it had changed everything. When he looked at her, he saw a different woman. This woman was stronger, indomitable. Dangerous.

It was as if Jon Harper had brought out the real Kate. He thought how ironic that was. Now, though, Collin didn't know what to expect from her, and that made this whole thing even more precarious.

He ate another handful of the Cheezies and closed the bag, stuffing it back into the cupboard. He knew he still wouldn't be able to sleep. He wished he could go for a walk, but no way was he leaving Kate alone. For all he knew, she could be lying in the spare room awake, just waiting for him to do something like that. He hated to think what he might come back to.

As it was, he planned to sleep with one eye open. Opening the refrigerator again, he pulled out a beer and, sitting down at the table, took out his phone. By this time tomorrow, they would be back in the States, his job over. He'd get his cut, and then…

He took a swig of the beer, eyes narrowing. And then what? He thought of Kate in the next room sleeping when he couldn't. At that moment, he hated her even more. How could he let her go when this was over? She'd go to the cops. He had no doubt about that. He'd hoped they would be married after this, so even if she figured out why they'd gone to Canada, she couldn't testify against him.

The thought now made him laugh. She would have seen through him at some point, anyway. Maybe it was better this way. Everything was out in the open. Soon it would be all over. He'd have the money he needed. He could say that he dropped Kate off in a city that had car rentals. The last he saw of her, she was headed back to Buckhorn and Jon Harper.

Everyone would believe him. He'd told her daughter Mia about what was going on, so it wouldn't come as that much of a surprise to her—or anyone in Buckhorn. No one would suspect him when Kate never turned up. In fact, once it came out about Jon Harper's past, he'd be the likely suspect in her disappearance.

And if her body was ever found? He'd make sure it never did happen. But if it did turn up, it would still appear that Jon Harper was the killer. By then, the mob would have taken care of him. The man would finally, truly, be dead. Case closed.

Collin realized there was one fly in the ointment. The younger daughter. Once he'd taken care of Kate, he'd have to order his associate to take care of Danielle. He couldn't afford to leave any loose ends.

He started to relax a little as he finished his beer and got himself another one from the refrigerator. He'd thought of everything. Once he'd taken care of business, he'd place an anonymous call and get the word out in Oklahoma City as to where they could find Justin Brown. That's if Nels hadn't already.

Collin smiled to himself, feeling a little better. Kate had complicated things, but in the end, it was all going to turn out fine. Better than fine. Tomorrow, they would pick up the wedding dress and then the rental SUV would be taken to the shop to make a few minor *alterations* on it.

Once everything was loaded, he and Kate would cross the border back into the good ol' USA. Somewhere before he reached Billings, he'd take care of Kate and her daughter. Once in Billings, he'd take the SUV to another shop who would take care of it. No one would be the wiser. He'd fly home, the majority of his cut stashed away in a foreign bank making him even more money. He'd leave out just enough to gamble with. He wouldn't touch the rest, no matter what. Unless he was on a winning streak.

JON'S PHONE VIBRATED. He stepped back into the trees seeing that the call was from Bessie. About Earl Ray? At this hour? It wouldn't be good news. He hesitated, knowing it would be risky to take the call. He looked toward the house and took a step when it started vibrating again.

He picked up, keeping his voice down. "Is it Earl Ray?"

"I know it's in the middle of the night, but he insisted I call you. You know how he is."

He did and found himself smiling at the reassurance in Bessie's voice that his friend was fine. "He's okay?"

"Won't be able to eat a lot of what I bake, but the doctor said he should recover." He could hear Earl Ray in the background telling her to quit gabbing and give Jon the message. When Bessie started to argue, Earl Ray demanded the phone. "You are supposed to be resting," Bessie said but gave up the cell.

Earl Ray's voice still sounded weak but nonetheless resolute. "He had a man on the youngest one. Don't worry, we have him, and both of Kate's daughters are safe now."

"What if Matthews calls him?"

"I doubt he'll have the need, but if he does, we have it handled," Earl Ray assured him.

"Thank you," Jon said. "You have no idea what this means to me."

"Yeah, I think I do."

"Glad you're okay. I was worried."

"Now all you have to worry about is Katie. And yourself." Earl Ray disconnected, but not before Jon heard Bessie in the background telling him to give her the phone or she was going to call the nurse and get him sedated.

Jon pocketed his cell, relieved. Earl Ray was all right. Bessie was at the hospital with him. It was one less thing he had to worry about. As he started toward the house, he realized that Earl Ray had called Kate *Katie*. Jon had thought that the man hadn't noticed his slip of the tongue earlier today. He smiled to himself. Earl Ray noticed everything.

He could see Collin still in the kitchen, apparently drinking. He moved quickly, covering the expanse of open, snow-covered terrain to come up to the corner of the house. He stood in the dark shadows and waited to make sure he hadn't been seen. The neighbors must not have a dog—at least not one they left outside at night. The girls were safe, but Katie was far from it, unless he could get her out of there.

Now what? He would have loved to take care of Collin. The fact that he was up, drinking by himself, told Jon that the man was alone in the house with Kate. Where were his friends? Maybe they hadn't connected yet. Or maybe this wasn't a drug deal at all. Maybe he really was just meeting some friends.

Then why had Collin put a man on the youngest daughter, Danielle?

Not to mention the fact that Kate hadn't wanted to come along on this trip to Canada. Of that, Jon was sure. Collin had used Danielle to force her. It was a drug deal or something just as illegal. Didn't matter. He was getting Katie out of this.

He moved along the side of the house, staying to the shadows. When he came to the bedroom window, he tried it. Locked. He moved along until he came to a second one. This one was cracked open, even though it was winter. He felt a start. Kate liked fresh air…? Even freezing-cold air…? Why did that jar what felt almost like a memory? It slipped away too quickly to grasp.

Carefully, he lifted the window, waited and, hearing nothing, climbed in.

CHAPTER TWENTY-ONE

KATE WOKE FROM an already restless sleep with a start. She felt a gloved hand clamp over her mouth. Instinctively, she began to fight, only to have her wrists grabbed and pinned to the bed by a second large gloved hand. Her eyes widened in alarm as she tried to see in the darkness, while bucking and wriggling to fight the man off.

"Katie, it's me."

The whispered words next to her ear made her instantly freeze. She blinked as Jon Harper's face came into focus. Her heart surged, tears filled her eyes and she went slack. He released his hold on her wrists first and then slowly removed his hand from her mouth.

She sat up and threw her arms around him, holding him tightly as she gasped for breath, her pulse thundering. He put his arms around her and drew her closer. She breathed in his scent. Her heart was still drumming in her chest and relief had made her limbs weak as she nestled against him, even though his coat felt cold from the outside air. Jon had come for her. This had to be a dream. She couldn't bear the thought that she would wake up and he'd be gone.

Just as suddenly as she'd been awakened, she froze and

drew back. "You can't be here." The words came out in a hoarse whisper. "You don't understand."

He silenced her with a finger on her lips. "Danielle is safe."

She stared at him. "But—"

He shook his head. "So is Mia. We have to get out of here. Now."

She listened and heard what he must have heard. Movement deep in the house. Collin. "He has a gun."

Jon nodded as he moved from the bed to pick up the lamp on the night table. He jerked the plug from the wall, then tore it from the lamp's base. "Get dressed. Stay here." With the cord in his gloved hands, he moved silently to the door and slowly opened it. She desperately wanted to stop him but hurried to dress in the jeans and sweater she'd been wearing yesterday. She found her purse, her mind racing as to what she should grab. When she turned, the doorway was still empty, and she could hear nothing from deeper in the house.

JON MOVED ACROSS the carpet, working his way toward the kitchen and the light emanating from it. He could hear Collin moving around in there. There was the sound of the refrigerator door closing, the pop of a beer being opened and the groan of a chair as the man lowered himself back into it.

He thought about the way Collin had been sitting earlier when he'd seen him through the window. Jon worked his way closer. He could hear the gulp, gulp of the beer, the restlessness as Collin shifted in the chair.

He knew that he and Kate wouldn't be able to leave without being heard. He had to subdue Collin, and he couldn't wait any longer. The lamp cord stretched in his two hands, he peered around the corner. Collin had his back to him in the chair, balancing on the two rear legs of the chair. On the table within reach was a handgun.

Jon could almost feel the nervous energy coming off the man. That made Collin even more dangerous because he was running scared and jumpy as a cat in a roomful of rockers, as his mother used to say. What had to be a memory shocked him for a moment as he tried to picture his mother and couldn't. He shook his head, clearing away any thought other than stopping Collin.

Closing the distance in a few quick steps, Jon looped the cord around the man's neck, twisted it quickly and pulled it tight. The half-empty can fell from Collin's hand to the floor and rolled away, splashing the rest of the beer across the linoleum floor.

Collin was already off-balance. Jon kept him that way as the man gagged and flailed, arms windmilling. At first he tried to reach Jon behind him and, failing that, tried to get his fingers under the cord around his neck as he fought for air. Both Collin and the chair suddenly fell sideways onto the floor, and Jon had to drop to his bad leg to keep his grip on the cord.

Adrenaline pumping, he reminded himself that he didn't want to kill him. It was a relief when Collin quit struggling and passed out from lack of oxygen. Jon checked his pulse. Alive. And out. At least for the moment.

He heard a sound behind him and quickly turned to find Kate standing there. He rose, struggling a little on his bad leg, and limped to her as he stuffed the cord with his DNA on it into his coat pocket. "He's only unconscious. Let's go."

She nodded, looking scared and in shock. He knew the feeling well. They quickly left by the front door, going around the block to where he'd left his pickup.

Once inside the truck and several blocks away, he finally glanced at her and asked, "Are you all right?" He could see that she was shivering uncontrollably. He turned up the heat, knowing that was only part of the problem.

"You came after me." She sounded surprised by that. "Danielle. How?"

"I have a friend who helped." He could feel her gaze on him, feel her need to ask about him, about his past, about how he'd found her and a dozen other questions. They would have to wait. "We can't get across the border until morning."

"Collin took my passport and my phone," she said, sounding scared. "I won't be able to cross the border."

"Don't worry. I'll get you across."

"There's something you should know," she said, sitting forward a little and looking behind them. "We were stopped not far from the border by what I thought was highway patrol. The cop told Collin he had a taillight out and then handed him a note. I was able to see some of what was written on the note. It mentioned a house and a key. I believe it told Collin to go to the house where you found me." She swung her gaze to him, eyes widening. "They're going to find us. Even if we run."

He took in the news, wishing he were surprised. This apparently was a fairly large operation, if cops were involved. "It's all right. We'll go to a hotel with a parking garage for the rest of the night," he told her.

Kate stared out into the winter darkness. It had begun to snow. She looked scared in the glow of the streetlights.

"I don't understand what's going on." She glanced over at him. "How did you find me?"

"I put a tracking device on your rental car." He could feel the intensity of her gaze. While she didn't move, he could feel her drawing back. "You can trust me."

She made a sound close to a sob. "Can I?"

He shot her a look. "You know you can, Katie."

COLLIN WOKE COUGHING. His hands went to his throat. He let out a cry as his eyes came open with the memory. Stumbling to his feet, he glanced around the kitchen before racing into the bedroom where he'd left Kate.

He knew even before he threw open the door that she'd be gone. He swore, tearing into the room to find the window still open where the bastard had climbed in. Jon Harper. He didn't think *Danny* could also be a killer. He should have called the syndicate on him before he left Buckhorn. What had he been thinking?

He hadn't expected the carpenter to come after them—that's what. He'd thought it would be a relief for Jon that they'd left. Why would the man come after them? Because he'd bought into Kate's story about him being her husband?

Or because Jon Harper was the kind of man who had to play hero? Wasn't that exactly what had gotten him into trouble in Oklahoma?

With another curse, he remembered what Kate had said to Jon right before they'd left Buckhorn. She *had* passed a message. How else had the man known where they were going?

Was the woman stupid? Collin had her youngest daughter. All he had to do was make one phone call… His eyes widened in alarm. Unless… He quickly dialed his friend's number. The phone rang and rang. He was starting to panic when Eric answered sounding half-asleep. "Is everything all right there?"

"Fine. What time is it?"

"Never mind. Call me if there are any problems?"

"Right. No problem."

He disconnected, relieved and yet furious that his leverage hadn't kept the woman here. "Kate, you are so screwed. You should never have left with Jon Harper. Now I'm going to have him kill your daughter. It will be your own fault." He reminded himself that that had been his plan, anyway. Not that it mattered. Kate hadn't known that.

His throat hurt like a son of a bitch, that and his growing panic making it even harder to think. He raked a hand through his hair, wondering how long he'd been out. He had no idea what he was going to do now. Worse, what Kate and her knight in shining armor were going to do. Not go to the cops. If Jon Harper had planned to go to the cops, Collin would already be behind bars. Jon Harper had every reason not to want the law involved, even in Canada. After Kate had seen a cop hand him a note, she wouldn't be inclined to head in that direction, either.

So, what did that leave?

Collin told himself that maybe all Jon Harper wanted was to save Kate. If so, then he'd head for the border. With a painful laugh, Collin coughed, remembering that he still had her passport. She wasn't crossing the border. Not unless she planned to tell all. But if she did that, then she would be jeopardizing Jon and her daughter. She wouldn't do that. It seemed she was screwed.

Collin smiled. Maybe things weren't as bad as he'd first thought.

KATE STOOD IN the middle of the hotel's honeymoon suite looking lost.

"It was the only room available," Jon said with a shrug as he locked the door and dragged a chair over to prop against the knob.

"It must have been expensive. How did you—"

He didn't let her finish. He knew exactly what she was asking since she'd seen him slip the desk clerk cash. "I'm not as destitute as I look."

She held his gaze, and he felt something inside him snap. When he'd realized she was in trouble, he'd known that he'd had no choice but to go after her. The odds weren't good that he could save her. But time was running out. He had to make sure she was safe before the hitmen hired by the mob turned up. Even as he'd headed for Canada, he hadn't been sure he was up to saving himself—let alone her. He still wasn't. The odds were against them both— especially if some of the cops up here were involved in the drug business and had friends in low places.

But looking at her standing there, he knew nothing could have kept him from coming after her. This woman had broken down the barriers he'd built around him, going straight for his heart with her stories about an undying love. She'd weathered twenty years alone, living on hope as if it was oxygen. He had no idea how they were going to get out of this, but he would die to save her.

"You must be exhausted," he said quietly.

Kate shook her head and crossed her arms over her chest. "I need to know the truth. Who are you?"

He'd known this was coming. He wished it didn't have to be under these circumstances. He didn't want to give her false hope. "Don't you want to try to get a few hours' sleep? Or how about some food? I understand they have twenty-four-hour room service." Her defiant look said she wanted nothing but answers.

"At least sit down. Please." He softened the last word, seeing the stubborn set of her jaw. He needed to sit down. His leg was aching. He could stand all day at his work-bench, but walking especially in deep snow wore him out quickly because of his injury from the car bombing. The flying pieces of metal had nearly torn off his leg. He'd been told he would need more surgeries, but that hadn't been possible with a bounty on his head.

Kate looked around, found a chair and practically dropped into it. She held her purse on her lap, her knuck-les white from the grip she had on it. He saw how afraid she was. They were practically strangers, and now he'd made her suspicious. She'd seen him choke Collin into unconsciousness—a man she had loved enough to accept his wedding proposal. Clearly, something like that would have changed her impression of him. He suspected she no longer saw him as her saintly husband, Danny. He hauled one of the other fabric-covered chairs closer to her. He thought it might make her relax with his sitting near her. It seemed to have the opposite effect.

They were safe for the moment, but by now Collin would be conscious again. Jon had no idea what the man would do. Contact his friends? He suspected Collin's so-called friends were even further on the wrong side of the law and much more dangerous. Were people out there look-ing for them right now?

"My name isn't Jon Harper."

"I know that," she said too sharply and seemed to catch

herself. "I'm sorry, but Collin already told me that you were a cop by the name of Justin Brown."

He nodded. She'd called him Justin back in Buckhorn right before she'd left with Collin. He thought she'd been trying to warn him that Collin knew. She couldn't know how much he appreciated that—except it hadn't given him a head start so he could run. He'd had to come after her.

"He also told me that Justin Brown might not be your real name, either," she said. "Is that true?"

He met her gaze and held it. "It's true." He watched her swallow. He knew what was coming next.

CHAPTER TWENTY-TWO

COLLIN WENT BACK into the kitchen and checked the time. It would be getting light soon. He began to pace. If he wasn't in so deep, he'd bail and take off. Run. But he knew they would track him down and kill him.

He thought about having another beer but changed his mind. He had to think. Think clearly. Gerald would be coming soon. He cringed at the thought. The man wasn't going to like this. Hell, Collin didn't like this. He would just have to assure the boss that Kate wasn't going to tell anyone. He had her daughter as insurance, and Jon Harper wasn't going to the cops, either.

Collin frowned and stopped pacing to squint down at the floor as he thought about the earlier phone call to Eric. He did still have her daughter, didn't he? He just couldn't understand why Kate would leave knowing what would happen and still she'd gone. That wasn't like her. He thought about his earlier call. Eric had sounded…strange. He'd been half-asleep, he assured himself.

But he couldn't help the niggling feeling that had wormed its way into his skull. He placed the call again, his fingers trembling. "What's going on, Eric?" he demanded.

"Nothing. I'm just trying to get some sleep, but you keep calling."

"You're still at the apartment. You still have Danielle?"

"Of course." Except the answer hadn't come quite quick enough.

"Okay," Collin said slowly, hearing something in his friend's voice this time that he couldn't ignore. "Well, I won't be needing you to babysit her anymore. You should go on home."

Silence, then, "Okay, sure. If you think she doesn't need my protection anymore."

"Exactly. Thanks for watching out for her." Collin disconnected and swore. How the hell had someone found out? The ex-cop had to have more connections than Collin had thought. Somehow, someone had gotten to Eric. Jon Harper had known that Danielle was safe when he'd broken into the house and taken Kate. Otherwise, Kate wouldn't have gone with him.

He swore as he paced the floor, almost too angry and upset to think. He'd lost his leverage, and Jon Harper hadn't just found him, he'd taken Kate. It was one thing to know which direction they had been headed. It was another to find this house. How was that possible? Had Kate seen the address the cop had given him? Even if she had, she couldn't have phoned the carpenter. Collin had her phone.

His head hurt but nothing like his throat. So, how the hell…? It didn't matter. Everything would be fine, he assured himself again. As long as he got back across the border and— He swore.

Money. He wasn't going anywhere without gas money. He hurried back into her bedroom, not surprised to find she hadn't taken her suitcase in her hurry to leave. But she *had* taken her purse. Earlier she'd lied about how much cash she had with her. He'd been counting on that money. He should have taken it from her then.

Now he was going to have to get an advance from Gerald to even leave Canada. The humiliation of it galled him. Not to mention this latest setback. When he caught up with Kate—and he would—he was going to strangle her the way Jon Harper had him. Only he wouldn't stop until she gasped her last breath.

He would find her, too. Somehow. Find her like Jon had found the two of them. The thought brought him back to the question of how Jon Harper *had* found them at this rental house in a quiet neighborhood outside of Moose Jaw. Collin was sure he hadn't been followed and Kate hadn't told.

Which meant… He let out a litany of curses and headed for the garage. Snapping on the light, he looked around for a flashlight. There was one sitting on the workbench. The batteries were half-dead, but there was just enough light that he knew he could find what he was looking for.

Collin located the tracking device and swore before ripping it from the vehicle's frame and crawling back out from under the SUV. *The bastard had put a tracking device on his car?* When? He had to have done it the night before they'd left. Which meant he'd been planning to come after Kate all along.

That didn't make Collin as angry as the fact that once he knew the man had been a cop and maybe worse, he should have checked. He swore again. What kind of criminal was so stupid?

He crushed the device under his boot, not that it did any good now. What an amateur mistake that had been. If he wanted to play in the big league, he had to at least pretend to be shrewder than he was. He hated to think about what Gerald was going to say about all of this.

How *was* he going to explain it to Gerald? He'd have no choice but to tell the truth and hope it didn't get him killed.

"ARE YOU DANIEL JACKSON?" Kate asked, her voice breaking with emotion.

He stretched out his legs. The left one ached. He tried not to flinch, tried not to let her see that he wasn't the strong, capable man she thought he was—let alone the one she wanted him to be. "I don't know who I am." He saw her disbelieving expression.

"Collin said you worked at the refinery in Houston," she challenged.

He nodded. "I did. Apparently I was caught in the explosion. I woke up in a hospital room with a bandage around my head and no memory of what had happened—or who I was. So many people were killed or injured. There was a lot of confusion. I didn't know anything about myself, but I wasn't badly injured like a lot of others, so I was moved to another hospital. It was there that I was told that I was Justin Brown. I had no reason to believe it wasn't true. Justin Brown had no family, so it all added up when no one came looking for me."

"I went to one hospital after another," Kate said, her voice breaking. Hadn't she sensed this was what might have happened to him? But she'd been asking for Daniel Jackson—not Justin Brown. "So you just believed that was who you were?"

"Apparently Justin Brown had only been working at the refinery for a short period of time and staying at some fleabag hotel. When I went there after I was released from the hospital, they let me into Justin Brown's room. I had no photographs, nothing but some clothing and a little money. There was no wedding ring and no wife waiting for me, so I assumed I wasn't married."

"You left your wedding ring by the soap dish in the bathroom that morning," she said. "They found your wallet in the debris. That's why they were so convinced that you were dead." She'd often wondered in her darkest hours if he'd planned to walk away that day and had left the ring behind.

"If you don't know who you are, then how can you believe that you're not Daniel Jackson?"

His sympathetic look seized her heart in a death grip. "Because I can't fathom the thought that I wouldn't have remembered you and my children. I would have known there was someone out there who would be looking for me, missing me, wouldn't I?"

She didn't know what to say even if she could have spoken around the lump in her throat.

"WHAT THE HELL happened to *you*?" Gerald demanded the moment he walked in the door and spotted Collin's neck. He grabbed his collar and jerked it to one side. "Someone *choked* you?"

Collin yanked his shirt closed as he stepped away. "It's nothing."

The man scoffed. "Nothing?" He glanced around. "Where is she?"

"Look, it's no big deal—"

Gerald got into his face. "Tell me what happened." He bit off each word.

"It's the damned woman." Collin sighed and dropped his gaze. "She met this man in Buckhorn—"

"I thought you were engaged?"

"Yeah, well, we were—until she saw this man in Buckhorn who she thought was her husband who died twenty years ago. It's really messed up."

"You could say that. Who is this man?"

"Nobody," he said quickly. "A carpenter who makes kids' toys out of wood for a living." He wasn't about to tell him that Jon Harper was an ex-cop who had a bounty on his head because he'd sent some mobsters to the slammer. Only a fool would trust a man like that.

"You're saying this carpenter, who she thinks is her dead husband, followed you up here to take her back?" That about covered it. "You didn't notice him behind you?"

"There wasn't anyone behind me. I wasn't tailed."

Gerald raised a brow. "Then how did he find you, since you didn't even know exactly where you were going until my guy pulled you over and gave you the address?"

Collin rubbed the back of his neck, but only for a moment before he felt where the cord had cut into his flesh. His throat ached. If he ever found that bastard... He realized Gerald was waiting for an explanation. "He put a tracking device on my rental car."

The man's eyes widened in disbelief. "A *carpenter* put a tracking device on your car? What in the hell aren't you telling me?"

"It turns out that he's also an ex-cop. But none of that matters. I found the device and destroyed it once I realized..." He shook his head. "It's all fine now."

"How can you say that?" Gerald demanded. "At any

moment cops could swarm this place—if they aren't already out there."

"Did you bring the—"

"Of course not!"

"Then, why would the cops arrest us?" Collin reasoned. "I told you, it's cool. She isn't going to do anything. I have someone on her kid. She's not stupid." It was a lie, but Gerald didn't have to know that.

The man merely shook his head and stepped away. Collin felt his breath catch, his stomach roiling suddenly as he realized this deal might not go down now. After everything he'd put into this transaction, it had to happen. He had to convince Gerald. He was flat broke, hounded by creditors, with no chance of paying his debts unless this drug deal went down.

He stepped to the man. "I can handle this."

Gerald turned so quickly, he flinched and took a step back. "*Handle* this? You can't be serious. Something smells rotten. How long have you known this woman?"

"Months. She's a published author with two grown kids, solid and financially set for life. We were getting married once we returned to Texas."

"So, how did this happen?"

He couldn't explain it even to himself. "Bad luck. She saw this man and was convinced he was her dead husband. It was just a fluke, a coincidence." He raked a hand through his hair. "The crazy thing is that Jon might really be her husband."

"*That's* the crazy part?"

Collin fell silent. He didn't know what more to say. There was only one way to prove himself, but that meant the deal had to go through. "I can do this," he said quietly.

He could feel Gerald studying him, assessing the situation and looking as if he was trying really hard not to hurt him.

"I've given it some thought," Collin rushed on. "At the border, if it's the same cop and he asks about my fiancée, I tell him she is staying a few more days at the spa with her friends. With everything she bought, including a wedding dress, there isn't room for her in the car anyway, I tell him and chuckle. Then I add, Maybe I should think about what I'm getting myself into." He was watching Gerald's expression closely. "I will make it work."

"Maybe," Gerald said after a long enough time that Collin was sweating profusely. "But not without the woman and the man you called Jon. Any idea how we might find them?"

"Well…" he said, thinking quickly. Moments before he wouldn't have been surprised if Gerald had pulled a gun and shot him. Now he felt there might be hope. "She can't cross the border. I have her passport and her phone."

"But if she tried to cross, she would tell them about you, wouldn't she?"

"No, I told you. I have one of her daughters. She isn't stupid."

Gerald gave him a look that said he thought Collin was, though. "What's the man driving?"

He described the pickup. "I'm sure it's registered to Jon Harper." He spelled the name for him. "Montana plates." He gave him as much of the plate number as he could remember.

Gerald nodded. "Let me see if I can find them." He looked at his watch. "In the meantime, you have something to pick up." He handed him a piece of paper with the address on it.

"Me?" Collin had hoped Gerald would be bringing the goods to him. Now, it seemed that he was being sent to get them. That way, if anything went wrong, Gerald would simply disappear, and Collin would take the fall.

He tried to breathe through his apprehension as he nodded and turned to leave. Why would Gerald set him up? He'd lose the drugs. The man wouldn't do that. No, everything was fine. The deal was going through. He hadn't blown it. Gerald wasn't going to kill him. At least, not yet. Kate didn't know when he was picking up the wedding dress or where, so neither did Jon Harper. There shouldn't be any problem at the bridal shop. No cops waiting.

But as he drove to the address he'd been given, he also couldn't help feeling as if he was being watched. His skin crawled. He'd asked for this. Begged for it so he could get himself out of trouble. What had he been thinking? If he got caught—worse, if he screwed this up—

He couldn't let himself think about that. He parked in front of the shop, sat for a moment as he tried to calm down. It was early. There was hardly anyone on the street. But that didn't mean they weren't watching from one of the rooftops, just waiting for him to get out of the SUV and pick up the goods.

It wasn't like he had a choice. He couldn't back out now. They'd kill him. It was now or never, he thought as he opened the door and stepped out. A gust of winter air stole his breath. Closing the door, he walked to the front of the shop. The door was still locked, but when he tapped on it, an older woman appeared, unlocked it and ushered him quickly into the dark shop before relocking it behind him.

She led him through racks and racks of wedding dresses

to the back. A huge box sat on the table. "It's all ready," she said.

He stepped to the box and started to lift the lid, but she stopped him. "Best not to disturb the dress. If it is opened at the border, it will just look like a beautiful wedding dress with lots of volume. So be very careful with it."

Nodding, he gently picked up the box. It was incredibly heavy, but he doubted a homeland security officer was going to lift the box out of the SUV or take the dress from the box. The one thing he hadn't seen at the border was drug dogs.

She followed him back through the shop. At the front door, she unlocked it and put up the open sign as if he was just another customer. He walked to the SUV, opened the hatch and carefully put the box in as if it was filled with explosives. As he closed the hatch and went around to the driver's seat, he still couldn't shake the feeling that he was being watched, that any minute cops would be all over him.

He climbed behind the wheel. Still no cops. He started the engine. The street was relatively empty. He let out a laugh. This had been almost too easy. He tried not to look around for Kate or Jon. He'd told Kate about the wedding dress, but she probably thought it was a lie. Even when the bags of drugs were cut from inside the dress, it would still be a beautiful, one-of-a-kind wedding dress. He'd ordered it in her size.

Just the thought of her slim, beautiful body now in Jon's hands... He touched his throat, thinking of her neck and his hands around it. But first he had to get the drugs across the border—without her. Unless Gerald's men were successful and found her—and Jon Harper.

As he drove back to the rental house, he began to get nervous again. What would happen if Jon and Kate couldn't be found?

CHAPTER TWENTY-THREE

WHEN COLLIN REACHED the house, he drove into the garage, shut off the engine and went inside to find Gerald in better spirits. Apparently the man put the word out on the pickup with Montana plates. Jon's truck had been found in the parking garage at a local hotel.

That surprised him. He'd expected Jon to take off with Kate. Maybe not to the border, but at least to run and hide. Not stay in a local hotel. But if Kate told him about the highway patrolman who stopped them, Jon might have realized that running was the wrong thing to try to do.

"You have Kate?" Collin asked, half-afraid of the answer.

"Not yet. My men are waiting for them to leave the hotel," Gerald said.

"What are you going to do with her?"

Gerald studied him for a long nerve-racking moment. "You still need her. Given what you've told me about her feelings for the man, it sounds as if we can use him to get her to do what we want."

Collin nodded. "That's good." Especially since he'd lost Danielle. "She would do anything for him." He hated the bitterness he heard in his voice.

Gerald hadn't missed it, either. "You aren't getting too personally involved, are you?"

"I was planning to marry her," he snapped.

The older man raised an eyebrow. "You seriously thought that was going to happen after this little engagement trip of yours? I think that is pretty naive of you. She doesn't sound stupid. Even if this other man hadn't come into the picture, do you really think she wouldn't have caught on? You just picked up a wedding dress for her that she didn't choose, didn't even get to try on."

"I could have sold that," he said stubbornly. "After all, I talked her into this trip." Gerald said nothing. "She was ready to marry me."

"Until she saw this carpenter she believes is her dead husband."

Collin looked away. "I told you, she might be right about that."

"I suspect so, since he followed her all the way up here to get her away from you."

"He's just that kind of guy," Collin said, thinking how much worse that would make it if his fiancée had fallen in love on their engagement trip with a complete stranger. It wasn't a story he would be telling anyone when this was over. If he lived that long. That was still a chance he couldn't ignore.

Gerald had found Kate. Collin would get her back, and they would cross the border together. That still left a lot of what-ifs. He saw Gerald check his phone.

"Your fiancée is about to get our version of room service."

KATE WOKE FROM a restless, short sleep. For a moment, she didn't know where she was. But then it all came rushing back at her, leaving her emotionally exhausted. She eased out of bed. She wore one of Jon's T-shirts and her panties. She couldn't bear putting on the clothes she'd worn for the past two days.

Pulling the comforter around her, she tiptoed into the adjoining room. Jon lay on the couch, his eyes closed. She stopped to study his face. She couldn't look at him without seeing Danny. Did she just want to see Danny in this man?

Maybe, since it seemed she couldn't trust her instincts after trusting Collin. Had she known something wasn't quite right with him? Was he right about her never getting to the altar with him, even if they hadn't broken down outside of Buckhorn, Montana? Would she have seen through him?

"I'm not asleep," Jon said, startling her as he opened his eyes. He swung his legs off the couch and sat up to look at her. He was still fully clothed as if he'd been biding his time until they left. "Can't sleep?"

She shook her head, swallowing as she met his brown eyes. They were filled with so much concern for her. She'd gotten herself into this mess, and now she'd dragged him into it. And yet, he was worried about *her*.

He moved over to give her room to sit on the couch. They'd talked some before daylight. Jon wasn't much of a talker—just like Danny. It made her heart ache to think of all the wasted years. Danny had been alone in the world because of a mix-up, and so had she. Their daughters hadn't had a father. There was no going back. Worse, she'd now jeopardized his life.

Shivering even with the comforter wrapped around her, she sat down next to him, pulling the thick fabric around her bare legs.

"Do you want me to turn up the heat?" he asked. She shook her head. "I told you last night that your daughters were fine. You can use my phone to call them if you need reassurance."

She looked over at him. It was her undoing. She felt a rush of emotions that threatened to drown her. Tears sprang to her eyes, blurring his face. She opened her mouth to say something, but no words came out.

His expression seemed to crumble as he put an arm around her and pulled her into him. She leaned her head against his shoulder and sobbed out the words, "I'm so sorry. I don't want to get you killed."

He held her tighter. "You won't. I've been living on borrowed time for years now. None of this is your fault."

She shook her head. "This is not what I wanted." She choked on the last of her sobs and pulled back to look at him. "If I'd known that I could be jeopardizing your life—"

"No," he said and did the last thing she was expecting. He kissed her. Suddenly his mouth was on hers, and he was wrapping her in his arms as if he never wanted to let her go.

JON DIDN'T THINK he'd ever known the power of a kiss. Because he hadn't kissed the right woman? Or because he couldn't remember kissing this one? He felt a jolt that rocketed through him, stunning him, leaving him shaken. Hadn't he warned himself about getting too close to this woman? He hadn't planned to kiss her—far from it. But he'd looked into her beautiful green eyes shimmering with unshed tears, and he'd lost it.

For so long, he'd told himself that he was content. That his hermit lifestyle was enough. Until she'd walked into his workshop. Even when he tried not to, he would remember looking up and seeing her silhouetted against the snowstorm outside. He'd caught his breath, feeling a punch to his chest. At the time, he'd told himself that she'd caught him by surprise, startling him. The surge in his pulse, the quickening beat of his heart, all had been nothing more than a reminder that he'd let his guard down, something he couldn't do if he hoped to go on living.

But had he really cared about going on living before she'd walked into his woodshop? Wasn't he merely existing at that point? He couldn't recall the last time he'd actually felt alive. Until Kate.

This woman was the catalyst that had jarred him out of that mere existence and dragged him back into life. Kate and her stories about her beloved husband and her two precious daughters had made him yearn for a life he'd never known, even as he told himself she wasn't talking about him. Even as he told himself it was too late for him even if she was.

She had made him feel, even made him hope, both dangerous for a man like him with a past like his. She'd upended his life even as he'd told himself that the best thing he could do was give the woman a wide berth for both of their sakes. But he hadn't been able to do that once he'd realized that she was in trouble.

Now, he looked into all that green and knew there would be no coming back from this kiss. "Katie." His voice broke as he pulled her to him, deepening the kiss as they clung to each other. What he felt was beyond need. He had to have this woman, knew his life would be worthless without her. The raging heat of that knowledge raced through his veins, stronger than desire, hotter than the passion that caught fire between them.

KATE KISSED HIM knowing that this was the way it was always supposed to be—whether this man was Danny or not. He was the man she wanted desperately as he trailed kisses down her throat and then lifted the hem of the T-shirt as he nuzzled her breasts. Her nipples ached, her center turning molten as if it had been years since she'd made love.

Shoving the fabric aside, his breath hot against her skin until he found the hard point of one breast, then the other. She groaned, arching against his mouth, wanting more, needing more, desperate with that need as she flung off the comforter and Jon took off her T-shirt and threw it aside. She got his shirt off, stripping away the material to press her bare, scalding flesh against his. It took her breath away as he cupped her bottom and pulled her onto his lap.

He kissed her, breathless as he pressed her against him. She shifted to push down his jeans as he tugged her panties down, and then she was sitting on him again. He entered her, his gaze locked with hers. She threw her head back as she rode him. He took one of her nipples between his teeth, rolling her off him, to pin her to the couch. They were both breathing hard as he thrust inside her, taking her higher and higher until she let out a cry, digging her fingers into his strong back.

Jon collapsed onto her for a moment before rolling to the side and pulling her close. "Katie," he breathed against the hollow of her neck.

She closed her eyes, tears leaking out. He'd found his way to her.

The knock at the door made them both jerk around.

They shared a startled questioning look for a moment before they heard the knock again. A male voice on the other
side of the door called, "Room service."

CHAPTER TWENTY-FOUR

COLLIN COULDN'T SIT STILL. He paced the floor, waiting to hear what was happening at the hotel. The worst part was that he had no idea what Gerald had told his men to do. Not kill Kate. They needed Kate. Couldn't really kill Jon—at least not in front of Kate, otherwise they would lose their leverage.

So, why was he so nervous? Because he'd lost his leverage with Kate's daughter. He'd heard it in his Eric's voice. So he was screwed back in Texas as well as in Canada. He feared things could get worse. But once he had enough money he could sneak into Mexico and get lost on some beach until the money ran out.

"Stop pacing," Gerald finally snapped. "You're driving me crazy."

From the look in the man's eyes, that was a dangerous thing to do. "I'm not good at waiting."

"Then take the car down to the body shop." Gerald told him the address. "The walk back should do you good."

"What do I tell them?" he asked.

"Nothing. Just leave them the keys and walk back. It's a couple of miles. You could use the fresh air."

Collin nodded, thinking here he was again, sticking his

neck out while Gerald stayed safe here. The woman at the dress shop would be able to pick him out in a lineup. Same with the mechanic at the body shop. Is that the way Gerald was planning it? Or was Collin just getting paranoid?

He couldn't help but think about Kate as he drove. She and Jon Harper had spent the rest of the night and morning together. Jealousy reared its ugly, green head. Collin didn't want the man touching her. He reminded himself that Jon had been trying to push Kate away. Had that changed? He reminded himself that she was still wearing his engagement ring. Or at least she had been before Jon Harper had whisked her away in the middle of the night.

For all he knew, the two had spent the rest of the night screwing. He ground his teeth at the thought. He hoped that whoever was delivering their "room service" hurt them both.

JON QUICKLY GOT up off the couch and pulled on his clothes, signaling for Kate to go get dressed. She hurriedly picked up her panties and his T-shirt and scurried from the room.

He stepped to the door, tucking his shirt in and zipping up his jeans as he went. He hadn't expected the interruption. The last thing he'd wanted to do was let Kate out of his arms. The knock had sent his pulse hammering because for a while he'd forgotten how much danger they were in.

"Room service," a young male voice called again, this time the voice wavering a little.

"We didn't order room service," Jon called through the door, all his senses on alert. He glanced back at the weapon he'd brought up from the truck. He'd left it on the end table next to the couch.

"It's complimentary for the honeymoon suite," the young man in the hallway said.

Jon glanced into the bedroom. Kate had gotten dressed. She was standing looking at him, looking as worried as he felt. He could see the rise and fall of her breasts, remember them pressed against his chest only moments ago.

"Give it to someone else. We don't need it."

Silence, then, "I'm sorry, but I can't do that. Can I just leave it, please?"

Jon heard that slight waver in the young man's voice. Fear. And not fear that he would lose his job if this honeymoon breakfast wasn't delivered.

Jon motioned Kate back as he dove for his gun on the end table and the door suddenly banged open. As he grabbed the weapon and spun back around, a metal tray filled with dishes crashed into him. Behind the tray was the young hotel personnel, his eyes wide and frightened. Behind him, a hulking man wearing a ski mask charged into the room, gun drawn.

Jon saw the barrel of the man's gun clip the back of the employee's head. The young man went down in the pile of food and broken dishes. Jon had tried to dodge the tray and the hotel employee but failed. Knocked off-balance, he had stumbled back, colliding with the couch to the cacophony of breaking dishes mixing with Kate's scream.

The man in the ski mask shoved his way in, kicking the door closed behind him. Kate had grabbed a buffet lamp from the entrance table, and she swung it, catching enough of the hulking man's head to make it bloom with blood.

Before Jon could get off a shot, the masked man had grabbed Kate and was now using her like a human shield as he pressed the barrel end of his weapon to her temple. The weapon had been equipped with a silencer.

It had all happened in a matter of seconds. The hotel employee lay unmoving, facedown on the floor, a knot forming on the back of his skull. After all the racket, the room fell deathly silent for a few moments before the man motioned for Jon to drop his weapon.

He'd already taken in the situation and knew he wasn't going to get a clean shot—not with the man holding Kate in front of him.

"Do it or I'll kill her," the man said gruffly.

He looked into Kate's wide green eyes, nodded and slowly dropped the gun to the floor, stepping back from it and keeping his hands where the man could see them.

"Now, here is what we're going to do," the man said in a low voice. "You do as I say, and Kate gets to live. Otherwise, I kill you both, and him, too," he said, pointing to the employee on the floor. "If he isn't already dead."

"THE CAR IS READY," Gerald announced as he came into the kitchen where Collin was making himself a sandwich. The refrigerator had been stocked with food apparently, while he'd taken the car down to the garage and walked all the way back. He noticed there was a lot more beer. He would have loved one but didn't want to push it.

He finished making his sandwich. "So, what happened at the hotel?" He'd been dying to know. There could have been a shoot-out. Everyone could be dead. He wasn't sure how he felt about that, but then again, he was suffering from lack of sleep and a general fear that gnawed at his insides day and night.

"Our body-shop man found something interesting on

the car," Gerald continued, ignoring Collin's question. A sharpness to the man's tone caught his attention. "You said you found a tracking device and destroyed it?"

"I did. I can show it to you. It's probably still in the garage where I smashed it." He started to head for the garage, but Gerald waved him back.

"Our man found a second tracking device. Which might explain how Jon Harper found you so easily."

Collin swore. He hadn't even thought to check for a second one. Who put two tracking devices on a vehicle? Jon Harper. The cop. Not the friggin' carpenter.

"I…" He closed his mouth since he had no excuse. He'd messed up again. He didn't want to think about what would happen when he did it a third time.

"As for the hotel…" Gerald was studying him closely.

He took a bite of his sandwich, pretending he hadn't been on needles and pins waiting for word.

"What do you care?" the boss asked, narrowing his eyes at him.

Collin chewed and quickly swallowed. "I just want to know. Crossing the border with Kate will make it easier than without her. She did great on the way into Canada. She—" He broke off, realizing at the same time Gerald obviously did that he didn't want her to be dead anymore than he wanted her to be with Jon Harper.

"You do realize that you're going to have to take care of her when this is all over," Gerald said. "You can't let her live."

"I know." In truth, none of this was going down as he'd envisioned it. Had he actually thought Kate would join him in his misadventures? He sure as hell hadn't planned to have the rental car break down in Buckhorn, Montana, the home of carpenter Jon Harper, ex-cop and possible husband to his fiancée.

Since then, he'd been winging it. But he knew Gerald was right. Kate couldn't be freed anymore than Jon Harper could. Both would go to the authorities straight as a bullet. He gritted his teeth at the thought of how stubborn they both could be. Jon Harper had come to Canada to save a woman he supposedly didn't know from Adam. And Kate…she'd gone with a complete stranger after he'd crawled in her window. The thought made him wince like biting down hard on a rotten tooth.

But could he kill her? He'd done a lot of illegal and immoral things in his life. Murder wasn't one of them. And this was *Kate*. Maybe he didn't love her like a man should love a woman, but he'd wanted her. He'd needed her. Unfortunately, both were still true.

"I'll take care of it," he snapped. "So, are you going to tell me what's going on at the hotel or not?" he asked, tired of Gerald keeping him in the dark.

The front door opened, making them both turn. Collin saw Jon Harper first, then Kate and the man behind her with the gun. Kate's gaze met his. If looks could kill, he'd be a smoldering heap on the floor. *Yeah*, he thought, *I'd be able to kill her.*

CHAPTER TWENTY-FIVE

"TAKE HIM DOWN into the basement and tie him up."

Collin realized that Gerald was talking to him. "Why me?"

"Phil will stay up here with Kate to make sure you don't have any trouble with Mr. Harper," Gerald continued. "Everything you need is in here." He handed him a paper sack from some hardware store.

Collin took the sack and glanced at the closed door the man indicated. He didn't want to do this. He had a thing about damp, dark places. He felt sweat break out and trickle down his spine. "Gerald—"

"Just do it," the man snapped.

The last thing he wanted was to go down there. But Collin knew he had little choice. He could just imagine the men's reaction if he told them about his claustrophobia or his anxiety attacks. After they quit laughing, he'd be lucky if they didn't tie him up in the basement.

He pulled his gun, motioned for Jon to open the door and go down the steep steps first. A single bulb hung from the ceiling at the bottom of the stairway. The dim light exposed an expanse of cold concrete, stacked boxes, several old washing machines in various stages of dying, along with a lot of other junk and debris. The smell rushed up the stairs, gagging him with the musty damp stench of it.

It was exactly the kind of place Collin abhorred. He felt a shudder as he followed Jon down the stairs. At the bottom, he opened the sack and saw a length of cotton rope and several rounds of duct tape.

In the corner, he spotted a straight-backed wooden chair. "Pull that over here," he ordered Jon. For a moment, he thought the man wasn't going to comply. But slowly, the carpenter limped into the corner and drew the chair out into the light. It did Collin good to see that the carpenter wasn't as tough as he had pretended to be. "Sit."

"You know you don't have to tie me up," Jon said in his gravelly, low voice. It felt eerie down here in the circle of light from the overhead bulb. Beyond the dim light, dark-shadowed shapes hunkered in the corners. "You have Kate. I wouldn't do anything to jeopardize her life."

"You already have," Collin snapped.

"I just wanted to get her away from you before you dragged her into something that could get you both killed," Jon said quietly. He sounded so measured. Another reason Kate had fallen for this man. There was something solid about him, honorable, trustworthy. Hell, the man sounded like a damned Eagle Scout. All of that, too, wouldn't be wasted on Kate.

"Shut up." Collin shoved him down onto the chair. Jon almost went over backward but caught himself. His brown eyes darkened. "Just know, if you let anything happen to her, I will hunt you down and kill you. And I think by now you realize that I'm serious."

The way he said it, quietly as if talking about the weather, Collin felt a chill run the length of his spine. He fought the urge to shoot the man and get it over with. Instead, he tucked the gun into the waist of his jeans and ripped off a long piece of duct tape. Grabbing the man's wrists, he forced them together as he began to wrap the tape around them as quickly as possible. He could feel the darkness of the basement as if it was creeping up behind him.

He could also feel Jon's eyes on him. The man's declaration hadn't been a threat. It had been a promise. It was why Collin couldn't have Jon out there hunting him down. He'd make that phone call the first chance he got.

That's if Gerald didn't kill Jon the moment he and Kate left.

Either way, coming after Kate was going to cost Jon his life.

KATE SAW COLLIN'S expression when he rushed back up the stairs. He was pale, sweating and visibly shaking. Had he hurt Jon? Killed him? She took a step toward him but was stopped by the man she'd heard referred to as Gerald. Her heart was pounding. She grabbed Collin's arm. "If you hurt him—"

He jerked free of her hold. "Don't touch me. I'm tired of being threatened."

"He didn't hurt Jon," Gerald quickly assured her. "Isn't that right, Collin?"

He nodded, and she caught his eye. She stared daggers at him, hating him with a passion she hadn't known possible. Collin had gotten her into this, but she'd been the one to drag Jon in. She'd never forgive Collin. But it would kill her if something happened to Jon because of her.

"Make us something to eat," Gerald said. At first she

thought he was talking to her but then realized he was looking at Collin.

"I don't cook," he said angrily, as if fed up with the lack of respect he was getting. "Let *her* do it."

Gerald shook his head. "Scramble us up some eggs. I'm sure you can handle that."

"I didn't see any eggs in the refrigerator," Collin answered.

"Look again. I had groceries delivered, and I definitely ordered eggs," Gerald said. "You'll find everything you need." Collin looked as if he was going to argue, but sighing, said, "Fine. But she's going to help me." He looked toward the kitchen, waiting.

Kate was determined not to move, but then Gerald gave her a nod. It was clear that this man was in charge. Also, she suspected there might be knives in the kitchen. The idea of arming herself had more than a little appeal.

She raised her chin in defiance but turned to go into the kitchen. She could hear Collin's heavy footsteps behind her. When they were both out of earshot, she spun around just inches from him. "What did you do to Jon?" she asked in a hoarse whisper.

Collin looked startled for a moment. "Nothing. I just tied him to a chair. He's fine."

She gave him a withering look. "Nothing is fine about this," she whispered. "Surely you realize that by now." He said nothing. "You think they're going to let you live after this?" She shook her head in disbelief at what this man had gotten her into and himself as well. Couldn't he see how badly this was going to end? "You need to get us out of this."

"I can't," he whispered back. She heard the desperation

in his voice as well as the fear. It appeared he did realize that he was in over his head. Not that it helped, she thought.

"How's breakfast coming in there?" Gerald called from the other room.

"You'll never get out of this alive," she whispered. "And you brought it all on yourself." With that she headed for the refrigerator, turning her back on him.

COLLIN FELT HIS cheeks flush with embarrassment at the truth. Kate was right. He was out of his league. He felt stung by Gerald's contempt for him. Worse, Kate's. He told himself that he would ferry the drugs across the border, meet the distributor, collect the money and show them all. Anyway, there was no getting out of it now, just as he'd told her. He had to make the best of this situation. But for him to succeed, Kate had to be with him when he crossed the border back into the US.

"I really don't know how to cook," he said as she pulled out a carton of eggs, some cheese and a loaf of bread.

"Then get out of my way," she snapped, shoving the loaf of bread at him. "Surely you can make toast." She pointed to a toaster in the corner.

He growled under his breath but took the bread and moved aside to let her do her thing. She was so damned efficient, so in control—even knowing how much danger she was in. He hated her for it because it only served as a reminder of how much stronger she was than him.

Ignoring him, she went to work, beating the eggs in a bowl. From the refrigerator, she took out a red bell pepper and a jalapeño, then dug in a drawer and came up with a paring knife. He watched her out of the corner of his eye as she chopped the peppers into small pieces and threw them into the eggs before grating some cheese in as well.

When the toast popped up, she slid the butter, a butter knife and a small plate down the counter to him. He couldn't believe how calm she was. She had to know that if anyone was getting out of this, it wasn't her. Did she think that Jon Harper was going to save her again? Not likely. He thought of the man down in that cold, dreary basement and wondered when Gerald would order him killed.

JON LOOKED AROUND the basement as he considered what to do. He hadn't expected an attack in the hotel room. But he should have. He hadn't been thinking clearly. He'd assumed Collin would think that he and Kate had taken off on the run. But Collin had her passport. He would have told whoever the brains behind this operation were—the man he'd called Gerald?

Maybe it wouldn't have made a difference if they had run last night, driving across Canada in one direction or another. Kate had said whoever was behind this had help from law enforcement. They would have been located, anyway. He couldn't worry about that now.

Looking around the basement, he spotted an assortment of tools scattered on a worn workbench. He started to slide the chair toward the tools when he felt one of the legs give. It wouldn't take much and he would be on the floor. That wasn't what he wanted. At least not yet.

He carefully rocked the chair until he could get up on his bound feet. Then it was just a matter of working his way slowly to the workbench. Collin hadn't done much of a job with the tape or the rope, as if he was in a hurry to get it over with. He must have realized it was a waste of time binding a man locked in a basement, since Jon was sure they planned to kill him once Kate was out of here.

It didn't take long to find what he was looking for on the workbench. Collin had been acting so strangely, now that he thought about it, hurrying to get him tied up, that he hadn't been paying any attention to the tools or the workbench.

Jon cut quickly through the tape holding his ankles together with the dull box cutter he'd found. Then he went to work on the tape at his wrists. It took only a moment to unwrap the rope connecting him to the chair. He could hear movement upstairs and smell something cooking. He knew he had to move fast. If he were right, Collin and Kate would be leaving soon for the border. Which meant, someone would be coming down those stairs to take care of him.

As he finished freeing himself, he considered his best course of action. He'd never been a hothead, going off half-cocked. Instead, he thought things through, always had.

Free, he couldn't go upstairs and try to take out as many of their abductors as he could. All any of them would have to do was put a gun to Kate's head. No, once he was no longer their prisoner, he would be free to pick the time and place to end this.

He thought of Kate and the jeopardy she was already in. Right now they were using him to keep her in line. Without him, they wouldn't have the insurance they were counting on. But they could still threaten to kill her or hurt her if she didn't comply. He thought of Collin and what he'd seen in the man's face when he'd looked at Kate as she'd entered the house earlier. He'd been relieved to see her alive. Which mean Collin did care about her, although

Jon was too smart to ever trust that the man might be an ally. But he might be used in a crunch.

Jon turned toward the dusty window at the far end of the room. It was small, but he was slim, and he had no choice. If they caught him, it wouldn't be Collin taking care of him this time.

KATE WATCHED THE men out of the corner of her eye as they sat around the table eating. She told herself she couldn't eat a thing but forced herself to get a few bites down. Just before they sat down to eat, she'd excused herself to use the restroom.

Gerald had ordered Collin to make sure she didn't go any farther than the bathroom. Once inside, she'd locked the door and quickly put the paring knife she'd pushed up her sleeve into the top of her boot. Then she'd used the facilities, flushed, washed her hands and come out. Collin gave her a suspicious look, making her realize that he might know her a little too well.

"My breakfast is getting cold," she said as she pushed past him.

Back in the kitchen, Gerald asked if everything was all right. Neither she nor Collin answered. Phil chuckled and then complained that the eggs were too spicy.

"They're perfect," Gerald said. "Delicious. Good job, Kate."

She gave him a nod and ate some of her own. They were spicy. But her insides were already roiling, so it was hard to tell if the eggs added to it.

"Someone is bringing the car over now," Gerald said as they all finished. Kate rose to gather up the dishes. "Help her," he said from behind her at the table. She heard Collin's chair scrape angrily on the floor, and the next thing she knew he was beside her at the sink.

"You can load them in the dishwasher," she said, handing him a plate she'd rinsed. He growled something under his breath that she couldn't make out as she opened the dishwasher for him and pulled out the lower rack.

"Collin, you and Kate will cross the border this afternoon right before it gets dark," Gerald was saying. "I want you to wait until the shift change. I'll call you and tell you when to cross. That means you will have to stop before the border—just not too far from the crossing. Don't cross until you get my call. Once you're safely across, we'll let your friend Jon Harper go."

Kate didn't believe that. She tried to hold her tongue and couldn't. Turning toward the table and the two men sitting there, she said, "You won't let him go."

Gerald seemed surprised that she would argue with him. Beside her, Collin grabbed her arm, but she shook off his hold. Gerald motioned him aside and faced Kate. "I admire the way you handle yourself," he said. "I will let him go. What is he going to do? Call the cops? Incriminate you? Even if he could prove that you're Collin's hostage, the man isn't going to get involved. He has too much to lose if he does. There is a bounty out on him. One phone call, and he'd be dead within hours. So if I wanted him dead and didn't want my own hands dirty, which I don't... What I need to know is if you can do your job?"

She stared back at the man, trying to decide if he was telling the truth or not. Either way, she had little control over the situation. "I'll cross the border with Collin and play my part—but only when I know that Jon is safe."

With a curse, Gerald slammed his fist down on the

counter but quickly got his temper under control. "You don't really have a lot to bargain with," he pointed out. She said nothing. "But in order to have you all-in on this, you have a deal. I will release him and let him know he has to call you. So, you'll be hearing from him by the time you reach the border crossing. I'll call Collin. Jon will call you."

Kate doubted all of it. But it was the best she was going to get. She gave him a nod and turned back to the dishes.

"Collin, go check on Jon, then get ready to leave," Gerald ordered as he walked out of the kitchen. "The car's here. You and Kate are leaving for the border."

COLLIN RINSED HIS hands in the sink, his gaze going to Kate. He couldn't believe that she'd called Gerald a liar to his face. He shook his head as their gazes met. Didn't she realize the kind of men she was dealing with? She looked calm, but he saw her fingers tremble a little as she reached for the dish towel to dry her hands.

He took it from her when she'd finished and dried his own, all the time holding her gaze. What was she up to? Something. What made her so brave? Or was she reckless? He felt a jolt. He knew this woman pretty well. She looked as if she knew something he didn't. As he started to turn away from the sink, he realized what she hadn't handed him to put in the dishwasher.

Collin grabbed her wrist. "Where is it?"

"Where's what?" she demanded and tried to pull free.

"The paring knife you used to cut up the peppers," he snapped.

Gerald stepped back into the kitchen, his gaze on the two of them. "Do you have the paring knife, Kate?" he asked in that patronizing tone of his.

She hesitated but only for a moment as if realizing they would find it on her if she refused to give it up. She didn't need the humiliation of them frisking her. Slowly she nodded, her gaze still locked with Collin's.

"Would you please give it to Collin," Gerald said as if talking to an unruly child.

Kate jerked her wrist free of his grasp and bent down to pull the paring knife from her boot. She held it for a moment, the blade pointed at his chest before she tossed it into the sink. "I need to get my purse and my suitcase," she said and pushed past him and Gerald.

He heard the man laugh. "Nice work, Collin. Now, check on Jon, and let's get you two on the road," Gerald said. "I guess I don't have to tell you to watch her like a hawk. That woman is…" he chuckled appreciatively "…something else, isn't she?"

Collin couldn't agree more as he left the kitchen and headed for the basement door. He figured he wouldn't have to go all the way down the stairs. He should be able to see Jon by just looking through the opening between the ceiling and railing. He entered through the door and snapped on the light. Hadn't he left it on earlier? He stared down the steps, realizing that he wouldn't be able to see Jon from here because a beam was in the way. He'd have no choice but to go all the way down.

But as he started to take a step, he was hit with a sudden prickling on the back of his neck that felt like a premonition. He looked behind him. Through the front window he saw Gerald outside talking on his cell phone. Phil was looking at his own phone in the dining room and not paying any attention to him. And yet Collin had the strongest sensation that if he went all the way down these steps, one of them would slam the door and lock him in the basement.

He quickly turned out the light, closed the door and locked it. "Everything's fine downstairs," he called to Phil as Kate came out of the bedroom rolling her suitcase behind her. He hurried to get his. The sooner they got out of here, the better, he thought. Until he was in the car and on the road, he wouldn't feel safe.

The thought almost made him laugh. As if crossing the border with a shitload of drugs and a woman who hated him was safer.

CHAPTER TWENTY-SIX

JON HAD BEEN about to wriggle out the basement window when he'd heard a voice just outside. He stepped back, caught movement by the large pines at the front of the house. At first he couldn't make out the words.

But then Gerald moved closer. He was talking on his phone. Jon listened, catching enough to feel his blood pressure rise. It was all he could do not to storm upstairs and take his chances. Fortunately good sense kept him hunkered just below the window as he listened until Gerald finished his call and went back inside.

Hurriedly wriggling out the window, Jon dropped down behind the dense pines at the front of the house. He was still shaken by what he'd heard Gerald saying on the phone. His mind raced with what to do about the information. The vehicle that had brought him and Kate to the house was still parked outside. A pine tree blocked it from sight out the front window.

He made his way to it, expecting to find the car locked. Crooks often worried about other crooks robbing them. But there was little inside—except for Jon's duffel, which had been tossed on the passenger-side floorboard where it still lay. Were his phone and guns still inside it?

Quickly picking up the duffel, he ducked down as another vehicle came roaring up the street, followed by another. The first one Jon recognized as the SUV Collin had been driving in Buckhorn. The second was an old pickup that was in the process of being restored.

The driver of the SUV parked it behind the car where Jon was hunkered. He worried for a moment that the man would head for the house. But instead, he left the SUV and walked back to climb into the pickup.

Jon had only a couple of seconds to get moved around to the far side of the car where he was squatting before the pickup roared past. He could feel the hair rise on his neck. He had to hurry. He stared at the SUV, thinking about what he'd heard. How could he let Kate get into that vehicle?

He had no choice. Any other option would get her killed sooner. He figured it would be a while after Kate and Collin left for the border before they would find him missing from the basement. He would do what he had to and hope it was enough.

The first step was retrieving his pickup from the hotel. The weight of the duffle told him that everything was still inside it. He wasn't sure how much time he had before Gerald had law enforcement looking for him. He hadn't gone far when he spotted a mountain bike in one of the neighboring backyards. He vaulted over the fence and minutes later was racing toward downtown Moose Jaw.

KATE COULD FEEL Collin's gaze going from her to the rearview mirror to the highway and back as he drove them out of Moose Jaw, headed for the US border. She wondered why he was so nervous. Because he didn't trust Gerald any more than she did? Nor did she trust Collin.

What would happen at the border? Worse, what did he have planned after they crossed?

Neither had spoken since leaving the house. She'd looked back to see Gerald watching them go as they'd left. His expression was hard to read, but she suspected he was worried that Collin was going to screw this up. Or maybe it was her he was worried about.

"What were you going to do with that stupid little knife?" Collin demanded, without looking at her. There was a hard edge to his voice, a bitterness mixed with fury and fear.

She looked out at the snow-covered passing countryside. Collin hit a bump in the road. Something shifted behind her. She glanced back to see that the rear seats had been folded down to accommodate a large white box.

"It's your wedding dress," Collin said. "I asked you a question. What were you planning to do with that knife?"

"Defend myself," she said, turning to meet his gaze.

"From who?" He swung his gaze toward her. She said nothing and saw the well of anger he was fighting to control. "*You would have stabbed me?*" He sounded disbelieving and hurt along with furious.

It made her laugh. "You can't be serious. I know you're planning to kill me once we cross that border. Do you think I'm an idiot?"

He growled under his breath and gripped the wheel so hard his knuckles turned white.

She knew that was the real source of his anger—not her. She'd witnessed how Gerald had demeaned him in front of her. So she wasn't surprised that Collin would take that anger and frustration out on her if she wasn't careful. "I wasn't thinking of you when I took the knife."

Those last words seemed to take some of the fury out of him. He drove, breathing hard, checking his rearview mirror often. Did he think Gerald had hired someone to follow him to the border?

"This isn't what I wanted," he said after a few minutes. He sounded sad and unbelievably naive.

"What did you think was going to happen?" she asked, regretting the accusation in her tone when she saw him bristle.

"Well, I certainly didn't think you were going to fall in love with someone else."

She looked away, thinking of the kisses, the caresses, the lovemaking and the passion. She'd made love with Jon. She hadn't cared if he was Danny or not. She swallowed the lump in her throat at even the thought that she'd now lost him. Her need for him was even stronger after what they'd shared. She ached inside at the thought that the odds were good that neither of them would get a chance to see each other again—let alone survive this.

"I didn't think you'd brought me to Montana for a drug deal," she said.

"Like I could have told you the truth about the financial trouble I was in. You would have run like hell."

"You don't know that."

He flashed her a look. "Don't kid yourself. You can hardly stand to look at me now."

Kate shook her head, staring at him with disbelief. "You've blackmailed me, kidnapped me and my daughter, involved me in drug smuggling. Of course I'm furious with you." It was more than that, and he knew it. She couldn't stand the sight of him because she knew that once they left that house those men back there weren't going to let Jon go—no matter what they'd said. She held Collin responsible for some of it and herself for the rest.

He drove in silence for the next hour. Kate was fine with that. She preferred the quiet. She needed to think. Maybe the paring knife hadn't been her best plan. It had been her *only* plan. Now she had to decide what to do at the border. If she did what she wanted to, she would be signing Jon Harper's death warrant. But she suspected nothing she did could save him now, anyway.

If she played the role of Collin's fiancée and they managed to get through customs without being arrested, then she knew what would happen. He couldn't let her go. If he did, how could she not go to the authorities? How could she live with herself helping bring that much poison into the country?

She had few options, and ultimately none of them would save her or Jon. Gerald had proven that he had friends in law enforcement. She didn't even know his last name or Phil's, either. What were the chances that they would be arrested? By the time the law got to that house, all sign of them would be gone. She'd be looking over her shoulder the rest of her life because she didn't trust that one of them wouldn't come after her or her girls. She was trapped in this mess because she'd believed Collin and his lies.

"What has he got that I don't?" Collin asked, dragging her from her thoughts. Kate looked over at him, confused for a moment. "Jon Harper," he said. "What did you see in him that very first day? I don't think it was just the likeness to your husband. Whatever it was, you couldn't stay away from him."

She heard the truth in his words. "I don't know," she said honestly. "There was something about him, and once

I looked into his eyes… I think it was the pain that I recognized. It was something we shared."

Collin made a rude noise. "You've looked into my eyes, and you didn't even know that I lied about my age. I'm only thirty-two."

Did he really think that mattered now? she wondered.

"What about my pain? My suffering? You never saw it in my eyes, did you? I'm terrified of cold, dark, damp places," he continued without looking at her. "This one nanny…" He stopped to clear his voice. "She used to lock me in the wine cellar when my parents had left me alone with her. It was just a part of the basement in the house that was small and cramped. She would lock the door and turn out the lights. I could hear her outside the door breathing hard. She would get so angry with me I thought that one day she might leave me there and forget about me and that my parents would never find me."

For a moment, Kate didn't know what to say, let alone what to believe. Was this true? If so, why was he telling her this now? Because he thought they were both going to die? "Did you tell your parents?"

"They didn't believe me. She told them I had an overactive imagination. Sometimes she would leave me there for hours. I would huddle in the corner terrified that the little sounds I heard were mice or something bigger moving around in there with me." He let out a cough of a laugh. "I knew better, but being in that kind of dark, your eyes, your ears, all of your senses play tricks on you."

He'd said he'was born with a silver spoon in his mouth and that his parents were well-off, but she'd suspected there had to be more to the story. Kate didn't want to feel sorry for him. Poor little rich boy.

She thought of her own upbringing. Middle-class family who lived in a modest home, her father worked a steady job with the local utilities company, and her mother stayed home, kept house and raised her. Vacations meant visiting relatives or friends.

When she'd gotten pregnant at sixteen, it had devastated her parents. They'd worried that Danny wouldn't be able to provide for her. But he had—even after the explosion. She'd just never spent the settlement money. Instead, she'd swallowed her pride and moved home for a while because she'd needed her parents' help with the girls since she had to go to work. As soon as she could, she'd moved out on her own with the girls. She'd figured things out for herself. Collin apparently hadn't.

"Her name was Katrina," he said now. "I'll never forget her. I still have nightmares about her."

She looked over at him and felt a chill. "What happened to her?" she asked, trying to keep the fear from her voice.

Collin didn't answer for so long, she knew that her fears had been warranted. "She fell down the basement stairs and broke her neck. They found her by the wine cellar door—and me, just a day after my seventh birthday, locked inside."

Kate heard the pride in his voice and knew. He'd pushed the woman down those steps and then locked himself in the wine cellar to pay back not only the nanny but his parents for not believing him. She couldn't speak. She'd already known how Collin would react when backed into a corner. Once they were across the border, she was a dead woman.

CHAPTER TWENTY-SEVEN

JON HAD WORRIED that something might have happened to his pickup. But there it was parked on the second floor of the parking garage next to the hotel. He looked around, saw no one. There was an SUV parked next to it with British Columbia plates. It took him only a few minutes with the tools behind the seat of his pickup to remove the plates and put them on his truck.

That done, he climbed behind the wheel, started his pickup and drove out of the parking garage. He figured he wouldn't be that far behind Matthews. If he was right, they were headed back to the Port Morgan border crossing. At least he hoped so. He was counting on it as he drove out of town, watching his speed and his rearview mirror.

He told himself that Kate would be safe—until they reached the border. He'd seen a weakness in Matthews and questioned whether he would be able to kill Kate. It wasn't a chance he was willing to take, though. But he was hoping that weakness would give him the edge once he caught up to them.

Jon just had to reach them before they reached the border. Before Gerald made the phone call he'd overheard him talking about on the phone.

COLLIN HAD SUGGESTED she try to sleep. "I would imagine you didn't get much sleep last night at the hotel."

Kate heard the allegation in his voice. She hadn't looked at him, hadn't denied anything, afraid he would see the truth in the heat that came to her cheeks.

But she hadn't been able to sleep. Instead, she'd stared out into the brutal, bright whiteness through her sunglasses even though there was no sun, reminding herself to lower them when they got to the border checkpoint.

She saw the sign as they drove past the town of Val Marie. It wasn't far now to the border. Why hadn't Gerald called? Maybe it was too early. Hadn't he said something about a shift change? Wasn't Collin going to call him?

Collin kept driving. She expected him to pull off onto one of the local roads before they got to the border as Gerald had told him to do. Ahead she could see the flashing lights of the border crossing. She looked over at Collin. He had a death grip on the steering wheel.

"Aren't you supposed to wait until you get the phone call?" she asked, pretty sure she remembered Gerald's explicit instructions. Don't cross the border. Gerald would call when it was time.

Except now Gerald hadn't called. Nor was Collin slowing the SUV. He was ignoring not only her query but also Gerald's instructions. He was going to cross and not wait for the call.

Kate held her breath as they got closer and closer to the flashing lights at the border. Why was he doing this? Just to show them that he couldn't be bullied? It was a little late for that, she thought. This seemed reckless even for him.

"Collin!" She hadn't meant to yell. But it did get his attention.

He shot her a warning look. His face was twisted into a look of abject misery as if he was in pain. "You made love with him. I could tell the moment I saw you." His voice shattered. "I loved you. Maybe not the way Danny loved you, maybe more than he did if he's Jon Harper. Did you ever consider how I felt when you couldn't stay away from that carpenter? Everyone in Buckhorn knew that you two-timed me. Did you make love in his workshop? Right there in front of that woodstove in the sawdust?"

"No. I'm sorry," she said in a whisper. They were going to argue about this *now*?

"Whatever happens now, it's on your head," he said, sending fear careening through her veins, setting off her pulse as he sped up the SUV.

"What are you doing?" she demanded as he raced toward the border crossing directly ahead.

He didn't look at her. "What I have to do."

He was going to kill her. Had to kill her now. Was that what this was about? Getting angry enough at her that he could do it? She could see it on his handsome face. She wondered if the nanny had seen it in that split second before she felt the shove and realized she was headed down those basement stairs.

Looking away, she saw that they were at the border. He slowed, driving past the Canadian side, apparently not required to stop. Ahead on the US side, Collin pulled in, stopping in front of a signal light now glowing red.

COLLIN FELT AS if his brain was on fire. He could hear his blood pulsing in his veins. He tried to calm down only to realize he might be in more trouble than having a cheating fiancée.

On the way across the border yesterday, he hadn't noticed the apparatus they had to pull through that looked like a weigh-station platform. That's because there hadn't been one to the east of it where they'd driven through before.

"What is that?" Kate asked breathlessly.

"I don't know. It looks like it might raise vehicles to look under them." He hated the way his voice broke. Why hadn't Gerald mention this?

"What if they lift up the car?" Kate asked in a hoarse whisper.

"I don't think we'll find out—unless they suspect us." He stared at the red stoplight, waiting for it to turn green, begging for it to turn green.

He was just now realizing what a mistake it had been to ignore Gerald's orders. Maybe the guard who came on in the next shift was planning to wave them right through because he was one of them? By not waiting for the phone call, had he just blown everything? He was thinking what a fool he was, when Kate asked, "What happens if they lift the car?"

"Nothing. Just sit there and wait." He hoped Gerald was right about the guys who added the undercarriage containers being the best in the business because according to the plan, they were filled with enough drugs to make them all rich. Then there was the wedding dress with its small fortune sewn inside. If everything went as planned, this would be the largest shipment yet.

"The light turned green," Kate said, her voice high and squeaky with obvious relief. As he pulled forward a large overhead door opened. He drove in, the door closing behind him.

He didn't look at Kate, couldn't. They weren't out of the woods yet. But once that door opened in front of them and he drove through, they were safe. Unfortunately, the realization of how this was going to end had struck him a few miles back. He had no choice but to kill Kate. It was him or her. He hadn't done all of this to end up buried up here in this frozen country—if you could even bury a body out here in the sagebrush this time of year.

Before that moment, he hadn't even thought about what he would do with her body once he was done. Or even how he would kill her. In truth, he wasn't sure he could, and that made him furious with himself.

Nor had he thought about what ignoring Gerald's orders would mean. If they got through and into the States, then what would it matter? Gerald had treated him like he was stupid. Maybe he was. How else had he ended up in this mess? When had he lost control of everything? He wanted to believe it was when Kate stumbled into Jon Harper's workshop and decided he was her dead husband.

But he knew it was long before that. Now as he watched the Homeland Security cop come out of his glass enclosure, he told himself he didn't care if he got caught. Maybe that would be the best way out. Years of prison? With his fear of small places? No, he'd rather take a bullet.

"Turn off your engine," the cop said. Collin quickly turned off the SUV's engine and put down his window, smiling at the uniformed officer who couldn't seem to crack a smile if his life depended on it.

"Passports," the cop said. It wasn't the same one from before.

Last time, Collin had been ready. This time he had to dig them out. Handing them through the open window, he waited as the officer took them and went back into his cubicle.

He seemed to be gone longer than last time. Collin felt sweat trickle down his back. He shifted in his seat as he stared at the glass and metal door in front of the SUV. He wondered how hard the front of the car would have to hit it to break through.

"What was your business in Canada?" the cop asked when he returned, startling him.

"Just a few things for the wedding," Collin said. "This is our engagement trip. My fiancée wanted to see snow and Canada." He shrugged. "We saw some of both."

"Please put down the window behind your seat," the officer said. Collin did, noticing that it had frosted over because of the temperature outside.

The cop peered in. "What's in the box?"

"My wedding dress," Kate said, speaking up.

The officer continued to peer in for a moment, then returned to Collin's open window. The smile he gave the cop hurt his face. He held his breath, afraid the officer was going to want to look inside the box or maybe even search the car. "We're getting married next week." He sounded happy about that fairy tale, wishing it was true. How different their lives could have been if it was.

As the officer handed their passports back, Kate reached for hers. In front of the cop, Collin had no choice but to let her take it. But he couldn't help smirking over at her. Who was she kidding? She wouldn't be needing that. Not after today, since she wasn't going to be leaving Montana. Not alive, anyway.

"Please wait until I am inside the booth and the door is

open before you restart your engine." With that, the cop walked away.

Collin put up his window, his hand shaking as he restarted the engine as the large door rose slowly. He drove out. He couldn't believe it. They'd gotten through and without Gerald's help. He couldn't help grinning. He could breathe again. His heart was pounding. He'd been so scared that something would go wrong. But it hadn't.

His cell phone rang. He didn't even have to look to know who was calling. He realized he shouldn't have taken matters into his own hands and crossed before he was supposed to. But he had, and he'd made it. No problems. *Screw you, Gerald.* The man would be livid. Right now Collin could have cared less. He let it ring four times before he picked up. By then he could no longer see the border crossing in his rearview mirror. There was no one behind him. No one in front of them.

He was home free with a shitload of drugs worth millions.

JON COULDN'T BELIEVE what he was seeing. He'd been able to catch up to Matthews, who seemed in no hurry to get to the border—given the orders he'd been given. That gave Jon the edge. Matthews was supposed to pull off before the border crossing and wait for a phone call from Gerald.

Knowing what Gerald had planned, he was nervous as it was. He'd been waiting for the moment when he saw the SUV turn off the highway. That's when he'd planned to make his move.

But Matthews hadn't turned off the road to wait for the call.

Instead, he'd seemed to speed up—racing toward the

border. Had Gerald called to change the plan? Jon hadn't considered that. Now he didn't know what to think as he held back, watching from a distance as the SUV pulled in. Even from this far back, he could see the glow of the red light.

What would he do if the border guards found enough evidence to arrest both Matthews and Kate? Had that been Gerald's true plan?

Jon was beginning to panic when the light in the distance turned green and the SUV pulled into the building. He tried to breathe a sigh of relief. But until Matthews got all the way through...

To his surprise, the SUV came out the other side of the building minutes later. Jon shifted into gear, praying he didn't get held up long at the crossing. He'd put in a call to Earl Ray earlier, asking for his help. Earl Ray had promised to do what he could.

Now, as Jon drove toward the border crossing, he found himself holding his breath. So much was riding on his getting across and to Kate before it was too late... He told himself that she couldn't have come into his life to be taken away so quickly. He held on to that hope as he pulled up to the red light and saw both of the officers in the glassed-in area looking at his stolen plates.

CHAPTER TWENTY-EIGHT

COLLIN FELT THE blood rush from his head as he disconnected from the phone call. Speeding up, he dropped over a small hill, pulled off onto the first secondary dirt road he came to, slammed on the brakes and threw the SUV into Park. Swearing, he began to beat the steering wheel with his fist.

"What's happened?" Kate cried, sounding close to tears. "Is it Jon? Is he…okay?"

He stopped swearing and hitting the wheel to stare at her in disbelief before he let out a bitter howl somewhere between pain and laughter. "*Jon?* You think I would get this upset over your precious Jon taking a bullet?" He saw her instant relief and wanted to backhand her. She had no idea how much trouble they were in. How much trouble *he* was in.

"Jon wasn't in the basement when Gerald went down to…release him. Add to that, I didn't make the call before we crossed the border, and he's pissed," Collin said, spitting out each word. "Apparently, there's another vehicle crossing at Opheim. He wanted to coordinate them with us. That's why I was supposed to wait for his call." He swore again as he looked into her wide green eyes. It hadn't been all that long ago that he had lost himself in the depths of those eyes.

"Jon got away?"

"Yes, and no one knows where he is."

Her eyes widened a little more as if now wondering the same thing he was. What would Jon do once free? Collin realized from the look on her face that there was something else she was thinking. If Jon was free and so were her daughters, Collin no longer had any leverage over her. She was dead wrong about the tables turning, he thought. He had a bullet with her name on it. If she jumped out of the car and tried to run, he'd shoot her down in the middle of the road.

Taking a breath, he let it out slowly and tried to calm down. He'd been nervous about crossing the border. But they had breezed through. Who gave a damn about the other vehicle that was crossing at Opheim? He wondered why it mattered that they cross at the same time. Just some stupid plan of Gerald's.

Collin had the drugs. They hadn't been confiscated. He wasn't on his way to prison. He wasn't sure how bad the repercussions would be from double-crossing Gerald, but he realized he wasn't that worried. As long as he made this deal, the man should be delighted that Collin had gotten the drugs through and overlook everything else.

Now all he had to do was meet the distributor. But before that, he was to have gotten rid of Kate. He looked from her to the white empty landscape. This was as good a place as any. He could probably just dump her out here, and she'd die of hypothermia. He wouldn't have to kill her himself.

But he couldn't chance that the stubborn woman would find a way to save herself. Reaching under the seat, he pulled out the loaded handgun he knew was taped there with the silencer on it. "This is all your fault."

He was blaming her? Even in her fear, she wanted to remind him that he was the one who had gotten involved with drug-smuggling criminals. That he was the one who'd lied to her about this trip. Lied to her about how much trouble he was in financially. Basically lied to her about everything.

Eyes narrowed, he was studying her with an intensity that told her this was the end of the line for them. For her.

Kate felt her heart drop as she looked at him and the gun he was holding. Her pulse took off at the sight of the silencer on the weapon. No one would hear the gunshot. As if there was anyone around to hear. This was the way he'd probably always planned it to end. The whole wedding had been a ruse. He'd known she would never go along with becoming his partner in crime.

She met his gaze. This suddenly quiet Collin scared her more than the ranting and raging one. His look sent a chill through her—even more than the gun he now held. There was cold, raw hatred in his eyes. Her blood ran cold at the way he had the weapon trained on her heart.

Her throat had gone dry. "Collin—" Her cell phone rang, making them both start. She recognized the ringtone, but it seemed to take him a moment to realize that it was her phone pealing and not his own. He laid the weapon across his thigh and dug out her phone. He took one look at the screen before his gaze shot up to hers, and he smiled.

"It's Jon calling for you," he said, sounding both incredulous and pleased.

Her heart jumped. "Maybe we should find out what he wants," she said before she realized that Collin wanted Jon to hear the gunshot that killed her.

"Maybe we should," he said. As Collin answered the call, she considered grabbing the gun lying on his thigh.

The sound of Jon's voice stopped her as Collin put the phone on Speaker and handed it to her.

"Jon?"

He repeated what he'd said only moments before, but neither she nor Collin seemed to have understood his words. "You need to get out of the car," Jon said with urgency. "The drugs aren't in the car. They're in another vehicle going to a different border crossing. The car you're driving has a bomb in it. I'm not sure what triggers it. Don't answer your phone in case—"

"Bullshit!" Collin said loudly. Gripping the phone, she started to open her door, but he grabbed her arm. "You aren't going anywhere. He's making this up."

"We don't have time to argue." Jon's voice was calm but determined. "I overheard Gerald on the phone outside the house before I got away. You and Kate are the diversion, so the real load can pass through another crossing without as much attention."

"Why would he lie?" Kate demanded of Collin as she tried to pull free of his hold on her. "Isn't this exactly what you'd expect them to do? Double-cross you? Get rid of us both?"

COLLIN SAW KATE glance behind before reaching for her door handle again. His first thought was that Gerald had sent someone to take care of him. Not that he was buying into anything Jon Harper was trying to sell him.

To his surprise, he saw the carpenter's old pickup bar-reling down the road toward them. How had the man found them again? He swore.

Kate had reached for her door handle, but he was faster. He grabbed her arm in a steel grip as he threw the SUV into gear and took off down the road. He could outrun that old pickup. Because he wasn't letting Jon get his hands on Kate. Not again. He'd kill her before he'd let that happen.

He let go of her arm, fairly sure she wasn't stupid enough to leap out at this speed. The gun that had been on his lap fell to the floorboard. He saw Kate try to reach for it as it fell. He shoved her back.

"There's a bomb in this car," she cried. "You heard what he said."

He shook his head. "That's crazy. It makes no sense." He hated that she had him doubting himself. Gerald was a first-class asshole, but why would he kill the two of them? What would be the point when Collin had promised he would get rid of Kate? Unless Gerald didn't believe that he would. That he could.

Swearing, he tried to concentrate on the narrow, snow-packed road that ran through the rolling foothills. He had no idea where he was going—just that he had to put some distance between them and the pickup. "Jon's lying! He's just trying to get you out of this vehicle. Does he think I'm stupid?"

"What if he's telling the truth? Don't you wonder why Gerald was so insistent that you call before you crossed the border? And why he's so upset now? He said it was about a shift change. Did that ever make sense to you? Collin, Gerald's the one you can't trust."

KATE TRIED TO reason with Collin but knew she was wasting her breath. He had his jaw set. She could tell that he'd rather see the two of them blown to kingdom come than do anything Jon said.

Glancing back, she couldn't see the pickup behind them because of the light snow the SUV's tires were kicking up. Collin had the SUV floored, determined to lose Jon. "Collin, stop!" she cried. "Let this end here."

"Not on your life," he spat. "No way am I going to let him take you."

At this speed, she knew it was dangerous, but he'd left her no choice. She grabbed for the steering wheel. What did she have to lose if there was a bomb in this car set to go off with just a phone call?

"What the hell?" he cried as he tried to hold her off and keep up his speed. The SUV began to fishtail on the snow-packed road as she kept fighting him and jerking at the steering wheel. He was forced to slow down to stay on the road.

She unsnapped her seat belt and attacked him, jerking the wheel so hard that for a moment, she thought the SUV might roll. If there was a bomb in it...

Collin backhanded her, knocking her into her seat. The blow stunned her, and for a moment she couldn't see anything but white as snow began to wash over the windshield. She realized that when he'd swung at her, he'd lost control of the vehicle. He was fighting to get the SUV back on the road and failing.

As they went off the road, the front end of the SUV plowed through the deep snow, burrowing in deeper. A wave of white rushed up over the windshield, seeming to bury them as the SUV came to an abrupt stop.

Kate felt dazed from the blow and the jarring stop, her movements slow and uncoordinated. *Get out of the car,* her brain was screaming. *Get out!* Over the pounding of her heart, she heard the *tick tick tick* of the engine as it began to cool and Collin's heavy breathing. He'd apparently banged his head against the side window. She realized that the airbags hadn't inflated.

As her brain seemed to catch up, she grabbed the door handle again. She had to get out, had to get away. She pulled the handle and pushed the door, but the snow was so high that it didn't want to open. She was trying again, pushing as hard as she could, feeling the snow slowly begin to move away, when Collin picked up the gun from the floorboard and pointed it at her.

"If there is a bomb, then we are going to die together," he said, deadly quiet, and he aimed it at her head.

She threw her body against the door. It fell open, and she fell out into the soft, fresh snow, the door slamming behind her. She heard a pop, and the side window shattered, the glass falling over her like tiny ice cubes. Hurriedly she crawled through the snow toward the back of the SUV. She heard Collin swearing as he tried to get out of the vehicle, the snow blocking him in. She heard her side door open. He was coming after her and when he found her—

His swearing was drowned out by the roar of Jon's pickup engine. He came to a stop where the SUV had left the road, a light snow cloud settling around the truck.

"Kate, get away from the SUV," Jon yelled just a second before, to her horror, she heard Collin firing the gun. *Pop, pop, pop.*

The pickup's side window shattered. She couldn't see

Jon. Heart lodged in her throat, she couldn't even scream as she struggled to drag herself out of the deep snow in the ditch and onto the road. She rushed to the pickup as Jon crawled out the passenger side. He had a gun in his hand as he crouched down beside her.

"Katie. Run up the road over the hill that way," he said, pointing back the way they'd come. She was shaking her head, mouthing *I can't leave you again* over the sound of Collin's gunfire and the tinny pings of the bullets ricocheting off the pickup's body. "Think of Mia and Danielle. Do it for me. Please."

At the sound of more shots from Collin's gun, she felt Jon's shove and took off running up the road. She heard more shots, only louder as Jon returned fire, no doubt providing cover for her. She could see the hill ahead. She didn't think. She didn't question what Jon had told her to do. She trusted him. She just ran, praying he would be right behind her.

COLLIN STOPPED SHOOTING. There was no sign of Jon Harper and that made him nervous as he stayed by the open driver's-side door. He realized he was still standing by the SUV in a couple feet of snow. In the adrenaline-powered excitement, he hadn't felt the cold. But now it settled around him. The deep, snowy quiet, the aching chill that had started with his feet and now moved up his body into his shoulders.

He shivered and waited, ready should there be any movement around the truck. Only minutes had gone by. He looked up the road. He could see Kate. How quickly she'd done as Jon had ordered her. It grated on him since she would have argued with him. Crazy woman. A bomb in the car? She'd believe anything if Jon Harper said it was true.

Still no movement by the pickup. Maybe he'd gotten lucky and wounded him. He considered pushing through the few yards of snow between him and the road to check, but he wasn't sure how much more ammunition he had in the weapon. He'd lost track of how many times he'd fired. He would have to dig another clip out from under the seat.

But he hesitated, realizing that first he had to know the truth. The passenger-side door was still standing open. He reached back to grab the large box with the wedding dress in it. Earlier he'd put the two back seats down to shove the box forward when he loaded their suitcases. When they'd gone off the road, the box had come crashing forward and was now against the back of the two front seats. He lifted a corner of the box. The heaviness of it assured him that it was exactly what he knew it to be. A wedding dress full of drugs. No way was Gerald going to blow that up, so there was no bomb. It had all just been a ruse to get Kate out of the car—and it had worked.

His cell phone began to ring. He pulled it out.

"Don't answer it!" Jon yelled as he suddenly came barreling around the front of the pickup, diving from the edge of road to grab for him. His cell phone dropped into the snow as Jon grabbed his arm and drove him backward away from the SUV. Collin tried to fight him off as the two grappled with Jon driving them both farther back.

Jon was yelling something Collin couldn't hear, when the phone quit ringing—and Collin realized he still had the gun in his hand.

He swung around with just enough room between them to point the barrel at Jon's midsection. He pulled the trigger. The shot made a puff sound with the silencer on it in the closeness between them. He pulled the trigger again. *Click. Click. Click.*

"You fool," the carpenter said, his hand going to his side. Blood seeped from his fingers as he stumbled back.

Collin swung the gun, catching Jon in the face and knocking the man backwards. Caught off guard, Jon stumbled and fell over a rise. Collin watched him roll down into what appeared to be a gully, blood staining the snow in his path. He wanted to go after him and finish him, but he could barely see where he'd landed. He waited for movement.

Behind him, he heard his phone begin to ring again. He turned to look up the road. Kate had stopped at the top of a rise in the road, but he could tell she was already heading back. As if she could save Jon now.

If he'd had ammo in his gun, he would have taken a shot at her. He probably couldn't have hit her—not at this distance with a pistol with a silencer on it—but he damned sure would have tried.

He turned back toward the SUV and the ringing phone. He couldn't wait to tell Gerald that he'd taken care of everything. He had the drugs, he'd gotten them across the border, he'd taken care of Jon Harper and was about to finish things with Kate. He'd get another clip and go after her. Or maybe he wouldn't have to. Maybe she would die of hypothermia before he found her.

What began to sink in was what Jon Harper had been yelling as he'd tried to drag him away from the SUV. The stupid fool really believed there was a bomb in it. Collin might have believed it, but he'd felt the wedding dress box. It had been heavy. Just like when he'd picked it up at the shop.

As he reached his open door of the SUV, he saw his ringing phone lying in the snow down in one of the holes his boots had made. He started to reach for it and stopped, remembering how Jon had been screaming for him not to answer it.

Collin shook his head as he pushed the seat forward and pulled the heavy dress box toward him. It wasn't that easy to lift off the lid. He'd finally had to tear it to look inside. He felt instant relief. Thick sparkly fabric.

His phone quit ringing. He started to close the box when he saw something that shouldn't have been in there. He felt his heart drop as he lifted the edge of the fabric.

Rocks? They'd been piled onto more padded fabric and then covered. When the SUV had gone off the road, though, they'd all shifted, so now two of them were visible. *Rocks?* He was trying to get his mind around what he was seeing when he moved the top fabric and saw what was nestled in the middle of the box. His blood ran cold. An armed explosive device sat huddled in a nest of even more of the expensive-looking fabric. He thought about the woman telling him not to look inside, not to disturb it and to be gentle carrying it.

His phone began to ring again, making him jump. At the same time, a tiny light began to blink on the explosive device. He swore and tried to turn and run, but he'd only taken a step in the deep snow when there was a flash of blinding light, a cracking noise and then nothing.

KATE HAD RUN up the road, the sound of Jon's voice in her ears. *Run! Think of Mia and Danielle.* She'd run like she'd never run before. She'd thought he would be behind her. She'd prayed he would be. But when she'd heard the shots, she couldn't go any farther. Jon wasn't behind her.

She could see the two of them back at the vehicles. Why was Jon still down there? If there really was a bomb...? Maybe there wasn't. Maybe he'd said that only to get her away from Collin, away from the gunfire.

That's when she heard the pop of a shot from Collin's gun. She'd seen Jon stagger and drop into the deep snow. What she did next had nothing to do with reason or common sense. Her body had just started moving back down the road toward him. She would have gone to him had she not been stopped by a blinding flash of light followed by a deafening boom of noise. The explosion had driven her back as the SUV she and Collin had been in moments before turned into a fireball. Debris showered down around the SUV, blackening the snow.

Stunned, her breath stolen from the impact of hot air, she'd stopped and stared at what was left of the SUV. Jon's pickup parked so close suddenly exploded. Even from as far away as she stood, she could feel the heat, smell the caustic smoke that rolled up into the winter-white sky overhead.

She tried to breathe, gasping at the horrific sight. Her gaze swung to where she'd seen Jon fall after the sound of the gunshot. She began to run down the road, her throat on fire from the smoke and her sobs. As she started out across the snowy field, she heard sirens over the crackle of the burning vehicles.

Halfway across the field, she saw movement. Jon was trying to get to his feet from where he'd fallen and rolled down to the edge of a frozen creek. She stumbled through

the snow, nearly falling time and again until she reached
the top of the rise.

She saw him standing there, looking as if it took all
of his strength to do so. She could see the blood that had
soaked through to his coat. He was holding his left side
as he looked up at her. Her gaze met his. What she saw in
his brown eyes made her heart swell as the sound of sirens
grew closer and closer.

Kate felt tears blur her vision as Jon limped up the hill
toward her. She took one step, then another until she was
running to him.

CHAPTER TWENTY-NINE

KATE OPENED HER EYES. They felt gritty. She had to blink a couple of times to focus. When she did, her gaze fell on the hospital bed and the man lying in it. Earlier she'd called her daughters to let them know she was all right and that she would tell them everything when she could. Then she'd hung up and asked to see Jon.

Now getting up from the chair where she'd fallen asleep, she moved to his bedside.

He looked like a stranger lying there. His face had been split open from where Collin had struck him with the gun. The blow had broken his nose. It was now flat-tened and cocked a little to one side. The broken skin had been stitched together from his forehead to his jaw line, an angry slash across his already scarred face.

"He is never going to look like the man you knew," the doctor had told her. She'd assured him it didn't matter. "That's if he comes out of the coma." The paramedics had almost lost him on the flight to the hospital. After that, Jon had gone into a coma. The doctor had warned her that there might be brain damage.

Now as she picked up his hand from where it lay on the white sheet and held it in both of hers, she worried that he was too pale. He'd lost so much blood. But the concussion was what had led to the coma, the doctor had said. His brain had swollen, and if they hadn't relieved the pressure…

She'd read about comas on her cell phone as she'd sat beside his bed. Some patients didn't come out of them. Others came out years later. She knew she would wait. However long it took. She'd waited twenty years for this man. She'd wait another.

Most of what had happened after Homeland Security and the border patrol had arrived was a blur. Jon had taken a few steps and collapsed. She'd held him in her arms until the paramedics carried him to the helicopter that had set down in the road. Before he'd passed out, the only word he'd spoken was *Katie.*

She'd wanted to go with him but hadn't been allowed. She'd been taken to a Homeland Security office, expecting hours of interrogation. But to her surprise, Earl Ray had arrived and whisked her out of there. Together, they'd flown to the hospital. She'd been by Jon's bedside ever since.

It wasn't the large hospital she'd expected. Instead, it was a small private one with only a few rooms. Earl Ray had assured her that a specialized doctor had been flown in to care for Jon. She noticed there were armed guards at the entry to both the hospital and Jon's room.

"Is he under arrest?" she'd asked Earl Ray, sick with what she'd gotten him involved in.

"The officers are here for his protection," the older man had said.

For a while, she'd forgotten about the mobsters who wanted to kill Jon. She'd been too worried that he'd die from saving her. She had no way of knowing if Collin had made that call back in Buckhorn to the authorities, telling them where they could find Justin Brown. Were those criminals searching for Jon even now?

"It won't take much to find him once the story comes out in the newspaper," she told Earl Ray.

He had shaken his head. "That isn't going to happen. At least, Jon's name or yours won't be in the story. You aren't going to see anything about this on the news. It's been taken care of."

While not sure what that meant, she'd seen that it was all the information she was going to get. Her head still hurt from the two explosions, making it hard sometimes to think.

"He saved my life," she'd told Earl Ray. "I realize now that he was even trying to save Collin."

Earl Ray hadn't looked surprised. "It would be just like Jon to save the fool. That's just the way he is."

"I'm here, Jon," she whispered now and lifted his palm to her lips to plant a kiss in its center. "Come back to me. Please, Jon. Come back to me."

She looked up to see Earl Ray enter the room and quickly wiped at her tears as she let go of Jon's hand.

"We need to talk," Earl Ray said.

Kate's feet felt like lead weights as they walked down the hallway to a private room. She could tell by Earl Ray's somber expression that what he had to say was serious. Had there been news about Jon's condition? The doctor said they didn't know when he'd be coming out of his coma—if at all. But she had to believe that he would open those brown eyes at any time and whisper her name. Katie.

"Please, sit down," Earl Ray said as he closed the door to the small room and motioned for her to sit.

She felt as if she couldn't breathe. One look into the man's kind eyes, and her legs felt so weak that she quickly lowered herself onto the couch.

"I'm not sure how much you know about Jon's...situation," Earl Ray said.

She realized he hadn't said *condition* even as she asked, "You mean his medical—"

"No, his past."

Kate nodded. "Collin told me that he was in law enforcement and that there were some killers looking for him because he had busted a bunch of mobsters." Just the mention of Collin sent a shudder through her. She couldn't bear to think about the way he'd died. No one deserved that. If only he had listened to Jon. If only he hadn't done everything he had, including trying to kill Jon when Jon was only trying to save him.

"There has been a bounty out on Jon from before he came to Buckhorn. It's one reason I've had to do the things I have. I've had to go out on a limb and call in a lot of favors. I'd do it again in a heartbeat." He hesitated for a moment. "You need to know what happens next. I'm afraid I have little control over that part. It's one reason I haven't wanted you to talk about what happened to anyone. The official news is that both Collin Matthews died in an unrelated car accident and Jon Harper died in that explosion."

She blinked. "But Jon isn't—"

"No," he said quickly. "He's still alive. Still in a coma. But officially, Jon Harper is dead. His being dead means that no one will be looking for him anymore."

Kate sat back. She didn't know what to say. "You made that happen?"

Earl Ray nodded. "If he pulls through—"

"*When* he pulls through," she corrected. "He's strong. He won't leave me."

The older man's smile was filled with both hope and sadness. "I certainly hope that's true. *When* he pulls through, he can't go by Jon Harper again. That life is over. He can't go back to Buckhorn—at least not as the man he was. You've seen the damage to his face. Plastic surgeons will be reconstructing it, resetting broken bones and covering the scars—all of them, including those from his burns."

"What are you trying to tell me?" she asked, suddenly terrified that she already knew. She began to cry, shaking her head, silently screaming *No!*

"I know how much you love him," Earl Ray said, his voice breaking. "That's why I know you can and will do this to save him—if he doesn't die from his injuries. I know how strong you are. But this means you are going to have to be *very* strong."

"If you're going to tell me that I can't see him ever again—"

"No," Earl Ray said. "That would be too cruel for both of you. But it is going to take time for him to recover if he—*when* he comes out of the coma," he quickly corrected. "There will be months of reconstruction to his face and possibly some physical therapy, depending on what parts of his brain might have been injured. What I'm trying to tell you is that it could be a very long time before he's well enough to even leave the hospital."

"But after that?" she asked, her heart in her throat.

Earl Ray reached for her hand, sending a chill through

her. "When he is completely healed, he will have a new face, a new name, depending on his injuries maybe even some disabilities. He isn't going to be the same man."

"I don't care," Kate said adamantly.

Earl Ray nodded and looked even more serious. "It's not just that. We don't know how he's going to feel when he comes out of the coma. There might be too much damage to his brain. He might not—"

"Remember me?" Her laugh came out a sob. "I've been here before, remember? This time, he will remember me. I'll wait."

He smiled through his own tears as he squeezed her hand. "For both your sakes, I certainly hope so. Now, the hard part. You have to return to Texas and get back to your life as you knew it. We have a cover story for Collin Matthews. He was killed in a car accident on your trip. He'd left you at the motel to run and get a present for you. It was a single-car rollover. He hadn't been wearing his seat belt. His…remains will be cremated. You will take them back to Texas where you will bury them as if the two of you had never changed your minds about getting married. I understand he has no family." She nodded, wondering how she could manage such a lie. "You need to stick to that."

"Wait, no, I can't leave here until Jon regains consciousness."

Earl Ray was shaking his head. "I'm sorry. That's not possible. Any more time here, and you will be jeopardizing Jon's life."

She felt the hard, blunt force of his words. "What is Jon's story?"

"He had left Buckhorn and was attacked on the highway. It was believed to have something to do with his past and a bounty out on him. His life as Justin Brown will come out. In fact, someone will collect the bounty."

All she could do was nod as she thought of Jon lying in that hospital bed and her not being with him when he woke up.

"I pulled some strings," Earl Ray was saying. "I wanted your life in Texas to be as normal as possible. But first, we need to bury Jon Harper in Buckhorn. I don't know if you are aware of this, but everyone back there was betting on you and Jon. You think you can handle his funeral?"

"I can handle anything as long as he lives, and we can be together again," she said quickly.

"I knew I could count on you. He is much loved in Buckhorn. You stole a few hearts in the short time you were there as well."

She wiped at her tears. "You don't know what that means to me."

Earl Ray nodded. "His remains have been shipped back to Buckhorn. The funeral is tomorrow afternoon."

CHAPTER THIRTY

WHEN KATE LEFT BUCKHORN, MONTANA, she'd thought she'd never see the town again. It had broken her heart because it had meant never seeing Jon again. Now returning, she still didn't know if she would ever see him again. Earl Ray had checked. Jon was still in a coma. It was the hardest thing she'd ever done, leaving him at the hospital, but Earl Ray had insisted the only way to save him was to bury him.

Kate knew she had to trust the older man. He'd already done so much for her and Jon and her daughters, by keeping them safe. Still it had been hard to go shopping for new clothing and shoes, to call her daughters and not tell them everything. But for Jon, she would keep the secret. He'd saved her life, hopefully not at the cost of his own.

Earl Ray assured her that he wouldn't leave Jon alone long. He was planning to head back there as soon as the funeral was over—after he dropped her at the airport for her flight to Houston.

"Jon Harper is dead," Earl Ray told her as they drove through the middle of downtown Buckhorn. She nodded, not surprised how little the town had changed. So much had happened to her, and yet everything appeared the same, including all the snow.

"Just remember that the man you knew died trying to escape his past."

"The man I knew died saving my life," she said. "How can I ever forget that? I took so much from him, his name, his life here..." She couldn't bear to think of him still lying in that hospital bed in a coma. What if he never woke up?

"Kate," Earl Ray said. "You brought Jon back to life. He was slowly dying in Buckhorn from regrets, and I suspect you were one of them."

Her worst fear had been that she would return for Jon Harper's funeral and now here she was. She kept thinking of that day when she'd pushed open his workshop door and seen him standing there. She couldn't lose him now. Not after everything they'd been through.

"Are you ready?" Earl Ray asked as he parked in front of the bar where it appeared everyone had gathered. "Jon's funeral will give you a chance to grieve for him openly because he's gone, Katie. That man won't be back."

"I've been grieving for him for years. But now, just the thought that he might not ever wake up or that, even if he does, I might never see him again..." She wiped at her tears. "Are you sure the people of Buckhorn won't tar and feather me for destroying the man they knew?"

He chuckled. "They knew how much you loved him, how much you didn't want to leave him, how much you will always miss Jon."

She nodded, took the handkerchief he handed her and looked out on the beautiful day. It was one of the few clear days so far that winter, Bessie said when she spotted Kate and hurried to her. She said that the funeral was being held at the only space large enough and still open in winter, Dave's Bar.

"The sun coming out is a good sign," Bessie assured her. "It gives us all hope that Jon is in a better place." Kate could only nod, thinking of him back at the hospital. All the townspeople turned out, packing the bar. Even some who had gone to Arizona for the winter had returned.

She need not have worried about how everyone was going to feel about her being there. Even the snowbirds had heard the story of Kate and Jon. The two of them had become legend in town. She thought of him the entire service, unable to hold back her tears. Fortunately, Bessie was there with tissues and a strong arm around her.

Axel Mullen read from the Bible. Vi, Mabel and Clarice sang "Amazing Grace" and "Rock of Ages." After that, anyone who wanted to say something about Jon Harper was offered a chance to speak.

The townspeople came up, one after another. They told stories of Jon's generosity, of his kindness, of his quiet strength. Some of the stories were funny, like those told by Earl Ray, who knew him best. Other stories broke her heart at the small kindnesses Jon had done in the years he'd been here. Jon had been loved in this small, isolated town in the middle of Montana. He would be sorely missed.

She knew she couldn't tell her story, but still she rose and went to the makeshift podium Dave had provided for the funeral. She told about the first time she'd laid eyes on Jon Harper, how much he reminded her of the husband she'd lost. "It was his quiet strength, the love he put into everything he made and the kindness he showed me. I will never forget him."

When it was over, Dave bought everyone a round. They drank to Jon. She wished he could see how much he was loved. Hopefully one day she would get to tell him.

Earl Ray gave her a ride to the Billings airport after Jon's supposed ashes, along with some sawdust from his workshop, had been scattered on the pines near the creek outside town.

The call had come in on the outskirts of the city. Kate could tell by Earl Ray's reaction to the call that it was good news. "Jon came out of the coma," he said. "It's too early to know any more than that." He held up his hand and quickly added, "He's got some major memory loss. The doctor said this isn't his first concussion. So, it was much worse. But the doctor was cautious but optimistic."

"I want to see him," she said, but Earl Ray shook his head.

"It's too dangerous, and you don't want to see him when he can't remember anything, maybe especially you. Trust me, he will heal, and in time…"

She'd nodded, hating to hear that. Time. She'd spent so much time apart from the only man she'd ever truly loved. She desperately wanted him back, not knowing if that would ever happen.

"I'll never forget everything you did for me, Earl Ray," she said when they reached the airport high on the rock rims overlooking the largest city in Montana. "How can I ever thank you?" As they stood outside the small airport in the midday sunshine before the next snowstorm, they seemed almost shy with each other after everything they'd been through. She was going to miss Earl Ray.

"Allowing me to be part of this love story was thanks enough," he said, taking her hand as they stood on the sidewalk outside the terminal. "No matter how it all ends, the two of you have something special. It was like a shooting star, much too quick, I know. But I don't believe it's over.

Like you, I know Jon is strong. If anyone can pull out of this, it will be him because I believe in my heart that you have always been somewhere in his memory. He won't want to let go of you anymore than you do him."

"I have to believe that he'll come back to me." She let out a nervous laugh. "I always have."

"Don't give up hope."

"You know I won't." Kate leaned over to kiss him on the cheek. "Take care of Bessie. She needs you. And whether you know it or not, you need her…"

"There's one more thing," he said as he pulled an envelope from his pocket. "I'm not sure this matters anymore, but still I thought you might want to see it." He raised his gaze to hers. "I hope I've done the right thing. As you know, I was able to get your daughter Danielle free of the man who Collin had holding her as leverage against you. I know I overstepped, but I had some of Danielle's DNA gathered and some of Jon's as well…" He held the envelope out to her.

Kate felt her eyes widen. She stared at the stark whiteness of the envelope reminding her of the winter snow around them before she took it. She already knew, but still her fingers shook as she carefully opened it and pulled out the report inside it. Tears blurred the words. She shook her head and turned to Earl Ray. "Please, I can't read it right now. Tell me."

"You were right. Jon Harper was once Daniel Jackson."

She nodded and, wiping her tears, smiled at Earl Ray. "Thank you." With that she grabbed the handle of her suitcase, turned and walked through the revolving door that would lead her back to Texas.

Once inside the airport terminal, she turned to look back. Earl Ray was gone. So was that moment of sunshine. Snow had begun to fall again.

CHAPTER THIRTY-ONE

JON WOKE FROM what felt like the inside of a coffin. He opened his eyes in confusion and pain, half-believing he had died. He had no idea where he was and little memory of what had happened to him. At first, all he felt was the intense pain. In his head, his face, his side, his entire body.

He started to touch his face but was stopped by a nurse.

"You're in the hospital," she reminded him, not for the first time, he could tell. "You're going to be all right." When he tried to get up, feeling a need to be somewhere important, she said, "I'll get the doctor."

He watched her leave the room before he reached up and felt his face. It seemed to be a patchwork quilt of stitches and bruises and skin. "What happened to me?" he asked as the doctor came in.

"All in good time," the physician said. "Right now, just be glad you're alive. Your brain needs to heal. You need to be patient."

Like the other times, he lay back, feeling weak and hurting as the doctor administered pain medication. He waited to fall back into the black hole he'd only recently climbed out of, knowing at least down there he wouldn't be alone. There was a beautiful brunette with amazing green eyes who came to sit in his room. Sometimes she would tell him stories about a young married couple and two small children. Other times she would hold his hand and smile down at him. He had no idea who she was.

In one recurring dream, she was holding his hand and crying, begging him to come back to her. For some reason, she seemed to think that he'd saved her life.

Each time he woke, she was gone. He would beg someone to tell him what had happened to him. "I need to know," he told the nurses and doctor. "I keep having these crazy dreams."

The doctor would explain about the concussion but little more. "Give your brain time to heal. More might come back with time as your brain fills in the blank spots."

Time. He felt confused, anxious and scared. There were moments when he couldn't remember his name, and he would panic. The doctor kept telling him to be patient.

He was relieved almost to tears when he recognized a familiar face and could even put a name to it. "Earl Ray," he said. "I can't remember—"

"It's all right," the older man said, hurrying to his bedside. "Don't try. It's so good to see you awake. The doctor said you're doing amazing, and in time—"

"In time," he said with disgust. "Why do I feel like there's something that can't wait?" He met Earl Ray's gaze. "I keep having these dreams about a woman with green eyes. I feel like I…know her. Like I have these memories…" He shook his head in frustration. "I know she probably doesn't exist, but I feel like I have to get to her. Does that make any sense?"

Earl Ray chuckled. "Oh, she exists all right, my friend. She's an amazing woman. I'll tell you all about her." He pulled up a chair next to the hospital bed. "Her name is Kate. You call her Katie. She lost her husband twenty years ago, but I'm getting ahead of myself. The best part of the story begins in Buckhorn, Montana, the day Katie's car broke down in the middle of a snowstorm."

CHAPTER THIRTY-TWO

THE TEXAS SUN beat down relentlessly on the patio. Kate watched the automatic sprinklers come on to water the flowers she'd planted around the pool. Everything was in bloom—a riot of colors next to the shimmering turquoise of the water in the pool. A warm breeze stirred the leaves on the oak trees outside the fence that surrounded her house.

After her daughters had left home, she'd often thought about selling the house. Now she was so glad that she hadn't. It was too large for her alone, and yet she loved her yard, especially the wild array of plants and flowers she had growing around the pool.

She'd never thought of herself as having a green thumb, far from it. But since arriving back in Texas, she'd been at loose ends. Winter had left the pool area looking drab. She'd yearned for color after all that winter white in Montana. Sometimes she thought about those days in Buckhorn when it snowed day and night and she'd thought it would never end. She thought about how quiet the snow made the world, how pure and clean it had looked and felt. She thought about the cold stillness and how her breath had come out in frosty puffs.

While she'd never been that cold in her life, she had only good memories of Buckhorn. She thought often of Jon Harper, knowing that he was gone. And as Earl Ray often reminded her when he called, Jon would never be back. She loved getting reports from Buckhorn via Earl Ray. Spring had come, the snow had melted and the snow-birds were returning to open homes and shops. The Closed for the Winter signs were coming down. The fields were greening up, and the air smelled of new growth and pine, he'd told her.

Bessie would be opening her bakery at the edge of town Memorial Day weekend—the official start of tourist sea-son. "You never got to try her fried pies. They are a little piece of heaven," Earl Ray said.

She'd asked him if he was watching his diet after his heart attack.

"I don't have to. Bessie watches it for me," he said with a laugh. "She has me eating fruits and vegetables with every meal."

Kate had smiled. "You sound good." She desperately wanted to ask about Danny but didn't because the news was always the same. He was recovering. The doctors were encouraged by his progress.

She didn't need to ask how Bessie was doing. She could hear it in Earl Ray's voice. The two had gotten closer. She listened as he talked, telling her about people she'd met at the funeral. Sharing the latest gossip. A few names she could put faces to, others not so much. Lindsey, the preg-nant waitress at the café, had had a baby girl. She'd named her Kate. Fred's son Tyrell got in trouble with the law. Nothing new there, according to Earl Ray.

The big news was that Anna Crenshaw's granddaughter, Casey, was returning to town and would be opening up the old hotel on the edge of town. The Crenshaw Hotel had been closed for two years, ever since Anna had died. It had been years since anyone had seen Casey Crenshaw. Everyone was anxious to see if the now grown woman was anything like her grandmother. Rumor was that she was only opening the hotel to put it up for sale. "The place is said to be haunted, has been for years."

Kate had laughed. "Like you believe in ghosts."

"You might be surprised what I've come to believe in," he'd said. "Tell me about you." Kate told him about the latest book she was ghostwriting and about her gardening. She'd discovered that she enjoyed digging in the dirt, but her favorite part was watching what she'd planted bloom.

He always asked about her work and how the girls were doing when he called. The book was done. She was considering another one but hadn't committed yet. Danielle had graduated college and would be teaching elementary school in the fall in a small town in East Texas. Mia's design business was going great guns, and she'd met a man. "Do you like him?" Earl Ray asked.

"He's nice. I think her father would approve."

He never asked how long Kate planned to wait for the love of her life to return to her. He didn't have to. He knew. Until forever.

"Tell Bessie hello for me," she said as their conversation waned. "Tell her I miss her corn bread and ham and bean soup."

"I'll do that. You take care of yourself, Kate."

"You, too, Earl Ray." Pocketing her phone, Kate went back to her gardening.

His name was now Nicholas Ross. He didn't recognize himself when he looked in a mirror. Often when he was shaving, he would stop and stare into the brown eyes looking back at him. They seemed to be the only thing that hadn't changed about him.

For years he'd lived with the scars. But now the ones on the outside were gone, thanks to the surgeons who'd put him back together. He no longer had the limp, either, after surgery on his leg. Even his voice had changed after more surgeries on his throat and face. It had taken months and months, but he was a new person—completely unrecognizable to himself or to anyone else from the man he'd been.

He had to admit, even the scars on the inside seemed to have healed. For all these long, painful months, Earl Ray had been calling him. Each time, he would ask his old friend to tell him about Katie. He loved hearing the stories. Some he thought he could remember. Some of his memory about what had happened had come back. The rest was a muddle of darkness. Except for his nightmares, which were filled with explosions and fire and pain.

But the nightmares had become fewer and farther between. He had been working out every other day, running on the days in between. After months of physicians and surgeries, he felt like a new man. He'd been put back together better than he'd ever been. Now he'd finally been told he was ready.

He hadn't seen Earl Ray for months and was delighted when the man had walked into the room. They hugged, his old friend then holding him at arm's length and nodding his approval.

Nick touched his face. "It's going to take some getting used to."

Earl Ray handed him a large manila envelope. "It's official. You're Nicholas Ross."

"Nick Ross," he said, trying out the name. Then he saw the white business envelope his friend held. "What is that?" he asked, having a bad feeling. All that was on the outside of it was Earl Ray's neatly printed *Nick*.

"Is this what I think it is?" he'd asked, feeling that now-familiar flutter in his chest at even the mention of Kate Jackson.

Earl Ray nodded. "Entirely up to you to decide what you want to do with the information in that envelope." He turned away and changed the subject as Nick took the envelope but didn't open it. "You should have seen your funeral," his old friend said, his back to him. "The entire town turned out for it. Dave even bought a round of drinks." He'd chuckled at that as he tried to breathe. "Axel said such nice things about you. So did a whole bunch of other people."

Nick's gaze rose from the envelope. "The brunette with the green eyes? Was she—"

"Kate was there. She also said some nice things about you."

He smiled. It felt odd, as if he hadn't spent much of his life smiling.

Earl Ray turned to look at him. "All the information on where you can find her is in there."

Nick looked down at the envelope again but didn't open it. "Let's say I find this woman… She won't know me. *I* hardly know me."

Earl Ray laughed. "You'll find a way. Trust me. She found you after all those years. You shouldn't have any trouble finding her—and the two of you finding your way back." His friend hesitated. "Also, there's a DNA report in there—in case you want to know. Entirely up to you. It's your new life."

"I'm not sure where to begin."

"Aren't you?" Earl Ray said.

Nick thought about it as Earl Ray left. He had money that he'd been saving for years. He had been given another chance to start all over again. A new name. A brand-new life at forty-one.

But it was his past that haunted him. A whole hell of a lot had happened to him, most of it he still couldn't remember. Earl Ray had told him not to worry about the man he'd been. That man was dead and buried, his past gone as if it had never happened. Except for the memories of the brunette with the green eyes. Kate. Katie. And now whatever was in this envelope.

He looked down at it, knowing he wasn't all that sure he wanted to face it. If he had been Daniel Jackson, then he'd walked away from his wife and family. How could a man do that?

The doctors had tried to assure him that the refinery explosion had taken all memories of that life from him. He couldn't blame himself. Yet he did. When he thought about Kate, he couldn't imagine walking away from her and two babies. Only a coward would do that. Why would she want that man back?

She wouldn't, he told himself. She just didn't know that. She'd hung on to the memories, romanticizing them, fantasizing about a man named Danny Jackson. No man could live up to that. A man would be crazy to try.

He turned the envelope over in his fingers. Did it matter

what was inside? He wasn't her Danny. He probably never had been, no matter what this document said.

Slowly he lifted the flap on the envelope. His heart was racing. What did he want it to say? That he wasn't Daniel Jackson, never had been? He thought of the way Kate had looked into his eyes in his dreams. She'd been so positive that the truth was right there, according to Earl Ray. Those brown eyes that looked back at him each morning from the mirror?

What if she was wrong? What if whatever was in this envelope proved it? He couldn't bear the thought of breaking her heart. He knew there had been other men who had reminded her of her lost husband. But in those cases she'd always been wrong. He didn't want her to be disappointed again.

The thought made him laugh. He was capable of disappointing her on so many levels if he *was* Daniel Jackson.

He swore and pulled out the sheet, unfolding it with trembling fingers. The words blurred in front of his eyes for a moment. Then the truth surfaced. He stared at the sheet of paper for a long time and smiled. He should have trusted her. Kate had been right. But what did that say about him?

All he had of that time after the explosion were weird memories of waking up in the hospital in Houston with no memory of what had happened or who he was. He'd pieced it together as more patients had been brought in, as nurses scurried around, as families of patients arrived and the story of the explosion came together. He hadn't known his name. It was as if he hadn't lived before that day. No, he didn't know of anyone they could call to let them know where he was.

There were patients who needed medical assistance more than he did. He'd been moved. That's when a fellow patient had said he recognized him as the new guy at the refinery, Justin Brown. He'd been given some clothing and been released from the hospital because they'd needed the bed. He wore a dead man's clothing out of the hospital as he had walked into that new life.

He hadn't known anything about himself. But when he'd looked down at his calloused hands, he'd known he was a laborer in whatever life he had lived. He had no idea of his exact age. He didn't think he was even twenty-one at the time. He hadn't been. After he'd walked out of the hospital, he'd done what he'd assumed he'd always done. He got a job working on a construction site and saved his money. He had no purpose other than to clothe and feed himself, until one day a friend had suggested he apply to the law-enforcement academy.

He hadn't realized it until now, but he'd been lost from the moment he woke up in that first hospital. The explosion had untethered him from people he'd loved and needed. He'd been adrift for the past twenty years.

Tears filled his eyes. Even if he'd never been Daniel Jackson, it was time for him to go home.

As KATE DROVE up the lane to her house, she frowned. There was a pickup parked out front with a boat behind it. She pulled into her drive, the garage door yawning open at the touch of her fingers, but she didn't pull in.

Instead, she was looking in her rearview mirror. The boat was a classic wooden one, long and sleek with red cushions in the cockpit. Her father had always wanted one like it. But that wasn't what had caught her eye.

It was the name stenciled on the back of the boat: *Katie*.

Her heart hammered as she climbed out of her car and squinted in the sun toward the pickup. It was new, didn't even have license plates on it yet.

As a tall man climbed out from behind the wheel, she stared, telling herself he had the wrong house even as her pulse thrummed in her ears. It was the way he moved. No limp. Not Jon. Her heart dropped as he moved toward her.

And yet she could feel the chemistry that arced between them. It wasn't something she wanted to feel because he was the wrong man, she told herself.

He wore jeans, a T-shirt and sneakers along with a baseball cap and sunglasses. "Hi," he called to her. Not Jon's voice. A stranger. A man looking for directions. A man who just happened to have a boat named Katie.

She'd often fantasized how Danny would come back to her. One day she'd open the door, and there he would be. Of course, Earl Ray had warned her that she wouldn't recognize him. But once he told her who he was...

"Can I help you?" she asked as he walked toward her. She still had her keys in her hand, her car door open—just like the garage door.

"I hope so," he said. She waited for him to ask directions. Clearly he was lost, since there was no place nearby to put that boat into the water.

He must have seen how nervous he was making her, because he stopped just a few feet from her. He shook his head as he studied her. "I'm sorry. I'm making a mess of this. I can see that I've scared you. I'm sorry. My name's Nick. Nick Ross. You're more beautiful than even in my dreams."

She stared at him, trying to make sense of the words.

"When Earl Ray told me that the beautiful brunette with the amazing green eyes was real and not just a figment of my delirium, I couldn't wait to see you again. For months I've been trying to get back to you. Oh, Katie." He said it with a softness that made her close her eyes to stem the tears.

She tried to speak around the lump in her throat but couldn't.

"Katie." He was so close now that she felt her name on his lips stir the hair next to her ear. He gently touched her shoulder. "I know I look nothing like the man you knew. Either of them. I'm not sure how they were able to put me back together, but all I could think about was seeing you again. Tell me I'm not too late."

She opened her eyes, reached over and lifted his sunglasses to see his sable brown eyes. "You're right on time," she said, her voice breaking as she threw herself into his arms. He held her tightly as if he never wanted to let her go. Her heart felt as if it might explode.

Finally, she pulled back to look at him. Nick Ross stood before her, his handsome face twisted with anguish. He didn't move, didn't even seem to breathe.

There was no holding back the tears. "Jon." The name came out on a breath.

"It's Nick," he said and smiled. "Think you can get used to that?"

She let the tears fall, even though she was now laughing and smiling. "Nick," she said. "Nick Ross." His warm, brown gaze met hers as she buried her face into his shoulder. It felt as if she'd come home. Finally.

"I was afraid to just come to your door. I know I look so different... I was worried, and then I saw this boat for sale and the name on the back. I knew it was a sign. So, I bought it." His laugh was musical. She wanted to hear it for the rest of her life. "I realized it wasn't just the boat and the name. It was my future."

She pulled back to gaze into those eyes again. "You came back to me."

"As soon as I was able. I couldn't stay away. But Katie, I'm never going to be the man you married," Nick said. "I don't know that man."

"But you are that man, and you're Jon. I fell in love with you both."

He laughed softly. "Any chance you could fall in love with Nick?"

She leaned into him, breathing in his scent. She should have known the moment she saw the name on the boat and the man who walked toward her. She hadn't realized that she'd said the words until he responded.

"That's how I feel. I should have known that I had a wife and daughters when I woke up in the hospital all those years ago. I can't tell you how much guilt I've felt since learning that I was Daniel Jackson. How could I have *not* known?"

"You had a terrible concussion. You didn't even know who *you* were."

"I don't know my daughters. Hell, I barely know you. But I want to get to know you. I want to get to know them. Can you see me for the man I am now? I can't bear the thought that you might always still be looking for Danny."

She shook her head. Her days of looking for Danny were gone. "I fell in love with Jon. Even if the DNA hadn't matched, I would still love you," she said, wiping at her tears of joy. "So, you really bought that boat?"

"How could I not? When I saw the name, I knew that was my future. I want to restore classic wooden boats. Apparently there's money in it." His voice softened. "I feel as if I spent half my life looking for you and not realizing it. Now that I've found you, I'm never going to let you go, Katie."

He pulled her to him and kissed her. It was like a Fourth of July fireworks show. All the chemistry she'd felt between them seemed to explode around them. She melted into his arms, telling herself that dreams do come true. Her husband had come home.

As he drew back from the kiss, he asked, "What will we tell Mia and Danielle?"

"Hopefully, we'll know when the time comes. All that matters is that you're here. That you're back where you belong."

He grinned. "It's nice to be home."

The summer sun lolled overhead as they walked over hand in hand to look at their new boat. The girls were going to love it. And love Nick, too.

No more looking back for either of them. They had the future and rest of their lives together. Kate thought of their daughters, who would have their father to walk them down the aisle at their weddings. She thought of their grandchildren playing on Galveston Beach as she and Danny had when they were young. She thought of all the memories they would make together.

She smiled at her husband as he took her hand again, and they walked up to the house. They were just getting started.

* * * * *

Look for the next novel in the
Buckhorn, Montana series by
New York Times
bestselling author
B.J. Daniels.
Available March 2021
wherever HQN Books are sold.

Pineapples.

Deputy United States Marshal Finnick Reed shoved his SUV into
Park, cut the engine and hit the pavement of the house's driveway.
Unholstering his weapon, he kept low as he approached the lakeside
home from the south. He scanned what he could see of the property, the
soft lapping of water at the shore loud in his ears. The sun had dipped
below the horizon hours ago. Shadows shifted as spears of moonlight
filtered through the ring of trees that surrounded the property. His heart
pounded at the base of his skull. No other vehicles. No lights on inside
the house. Everything was exactly as it should have been. Aside from
the single word he and the only surviving witness of Chicago's most
notorious serial killer had agreed to use in case of emergency that'd been
sent less than twenty minutes ago. *Pineapples.*

She wouldn't have messaged him if she hadn't needed him. She
knew better than to put herself at risk after all these months. Finn closed
in on the front door of the rambler-style house, pressing his shoulder
into the frame before testing the handle.

The door swung open without his help.

Warning prickled at the back of his neck as he stepped over the
threshold. His own shallow breathing cut through the silence, and he
raised his weapon to shoulder level. Heel-toeing through the small
entryway, he kept his boots from echoing off the hardwood, then swung
into the open-concept kitchen and living area. Faint hints of light
penetrated through the bay windows along the opposite wall, casting

shadows through the slats of the dining room chairs onto the floor, and Finn reached over to flip on the overhead light.

No power.

"Where are you, Red?" Camille Goodman, formerly Camille Jensen, had relocated to the sleepy coastal town of Florence, Oregon, with the help of the United States Marshals Service a year ago, almost to the day. As long as her attacker was awaiting trial for the murders of the six women he'd bound, strangled and carved up with his knife back in Chicago, she was Finn's responsibility. And he wasn't going anywhere until he found her. He moved deeper into the house, the slight hint of lavender in the air. Camille. She'd always had a soothing quality about her that he couldn't seem to fight, but her text message brought him to the exact opposite of calm.

She was supposed to be safe here. Protected.

He'd never forgive himself if something happened to her.

He took another step. The crunching of glass filled his ears, the hard edge of something embedding in his boot. Peeling his foot away, he recognized the phone he'd given her to contact him when she'd first been transferred into his custody. Left in the center of the living room. Dropped during a hasty escape?

Shuffling drew his attention down the hall, toward the bedrooms at the back of the house, and Finn swept his arms in that direction and took aim. He followed the sound past a room filled with large flat boxes and frames. Clear. The bathroom door had been shut, and he twisted the knob and pushed inside. Nothing. There was only one more room left in the hall. Camille's bedroom. She had to be there.

Dark spots peppered the hardwood in front of the closed bedroom door, and ice crept up Finn's neck. He slowly reached down to test the texture, but what he thought was blood shifted under his touch. His gut clenched. Red rose petals. Exactly like the ones recovered from each crime scene left behind by the Carver when he'd finished with his victims. "Camille!"

Don't miss
The Witness *by Nichole Severn,*
available February 2021 wherever
Harlequin Intrigue books and ebooks are sold.

Harlequin.com